Advance Praise for
A Billion Reasons Why

"Katie and Luc dance off the pages of this book, making you fall in love with them and New Orleans. A nostalgic trip full of surprises and romance."

—CAROLYNE AARSEN, AUTHOR OF *THE BABY PROMISE*

"A sparkling and lively romance . . . featuring the spunkiest heroine of the year!"

—DENISE HUNTER, AUTHOR OF *CONVENIENT GROOM*

"*A Billion Reasons Why* is a fun, sophisticated romance with Kristin Billerbeck's unique voice and quirky characters. I loved it!"

—COLLEEN COBLE, AUTHOR OF *LONESTAR HOMECOMING*
AND THE MERCY FALLS SERIES

Acclaim for Kristin Billerbeck's previous titles

She's All That

"Christian chick-lit star Billerbeck has moved on from her popular Ashley Stockingdale trilogy with an engaging new novel that features struggling fashion designer Lilly Jacobs and her two best friends, Morgan and Poppy . . . Snappy dialogue and lovable characters make this novel a winner."

—*PUBLISHERS WEEKLY*

"Billerbeck has the chick lit tone nailed, providing the angst without the juvenile whine too common in the genre. Settle in for madcap fun that leaves the reader wanting more."

—*ROMANTIC TIMES*

A Billion Reasons Why

Other novels by Kristin Billerbeck include

What a Girl Wants
She's Out of Control
With This Ring, I'm Confused
She's All That
A Girl's Best Friend
Calm, Cool & Adjusted
Split Ends

A Billion Reasons Why

Kristin Billerbeck

THOMAS NELSON

Since 1798

NASHVILLE   DALLAS   MEXICO CITY   RIO DE JANEIRO

Published in Nashville, Tennessee. Thomas Nelson is a registered trademark of Thomas Nelson, Inc.

Published in association with the literary agency of Alive Communications, Inc. 7680 Goddard Street, Suite 200, Colorado Springs, CO 80920. www.AliveCommunications.com.

Thomas Nelson, Inc., books may be purchased in bulk for educational, business, fund-raising, or sales promotional use. For information, please e-mail SpecialMarkets@ThomasNelson.com.

Publisher's Note: This novel is a work of fiction. Names, characters, places, and incidents are either products of the author's imagination or used fictitiously. All characters are fictional, and any similarity to people living or dead is purely coincidental.

Library of Congress Cataloging-in-Publication Data

Billerbeck, Kristin.
  A billion reasons why / Kristin Billerbeck.
    p. cm.
  ISBN 978-1-59554-791-0 (pbk.)
  I. Title.
  PS3602.I44B55 2011
  813'.6—dc22   2010043882

Printed in the United States of America

11 12 13 14 15 RRD 6 5 4 3 2

TO NANCY TOBACK AND NICOLE CHRISTIAN
FOR MORAL SUPPORT.
AND TO THE BRICKS FOR INSPIRATION.

Prologue

◡

SOMEONE TO WATCH OVER ME

Luc DeForges took the ring from Ian McKenna's trembling hand and raised it to the sunlight that danced through the trees of New Orleans' Garden District. "It's exquisite."

The old man's tight expression relaxed, replaced by pride. "A full carat of diamonds, cushion-cut center set in solid platinum by my grandfather before he left Ireland. You see that workmanship? How he made the center stone appear so much larger than it is by the cuts of the smaller stones? He was a master."

Mr. McKenna's finger shook as he pointed to the ring's bezel. "A gentleman like yourself is sure to recognize quality. You can't buy this kind of craftsmanship anymore." His voice held an edge of desperation.

"I agree with you," Luc said, as he pushed the ring back toward its owner.

Mr. McKenna shook his head. He seemed to be waiting for something more.

Luc tried again. "It appears so much larger, but it's dainty, like Katie. It belongs on a woman like her. The stones are a lighter color than I think of when I picture an emerald."

"Aye." Mr. McKenna's voice sank. "That's because they were hand selected to match my grandmother's eyes. The gems were renowned in Ireland as not merely being green but transparent like worn sea glass. He would have spent the money for darker emeralds if that's what the piece called for."

Luc nodded as the image of Katie's sea-green eyes and red hair flashed through his mind. "I'm certain he would have."

"Notice the detail work in the platinum with the cut emeralds?" Mr. McKenna's eyes watered as he stared hard into Luc's own. "Platinum in an intricate design like this was extremely difficult, usually reserved for royals. He wanted my grandmother to feel cherished above all other brides."

Luc studied the way the metal crossed and intersected in a complicated form of lacy architecture, like a jeweled web. "Any woman in Ireland would have felt that way."

"My mam used to twist the ring around her finger and whisper to Katie that one day, when she found the right man, the ring would belong to her."

"I'll guard it with my life, Mr. McKenna."

Again the older gentleman looked Luc in the eyes. "I

know you will. And I can trust you to make sure Katie gets it on her wedding day?"

Luc held his fist to his heart. "On my honor."

"And you won't tell anyone you have this, you understand?"

"You have my word. Unless you ask for it back, I'll keep it under lock and key."

Mr. McKenna turned toward the sidewalk. "I won't be asking for it back."

Now, all these years later, Luc could still picture the slope of Mr. McKenna's bent back, the way he stepped, broken and wilted, a shadow of the lively man he remembered from his youth. If only he'd known then that he'd be the last person to see Ian McKenna alive, there were so many things he would have done differently.

So many things.

Chapter 1

❧

A Fine Romance

Katie McKenna had dreamed of this moment at least a thousand times. Luc would walk back into her life filled with remorse. He'd be wearing jeans, a worn T-shirt, and humility. He'd be dripping with humility.

That should have been her first clue that such a scenario had no bearing on reality.

"Katie," a voice said.

The sound sent a surge of adrenaline through her frame. She'd forgotten the power and the warmth of his baritone. A quick glance around her classroom assured her that she must be imagining things. Everything was in order: the posters of colorful curriculum, the daily schedule of activities printed on the whiteboard, and, of course, the children. All six of them were mentally disabled, most of them on the severe side of the autism spectrum, but three had added handicaps that required sturdy, head-stabilizing wheelchairs. The bulk of the chairs overwhelmed the room and blocked much of the happy yellow walls and part of the large rainbow mural the kids had helped to paint. The room, with its cluttered order, comforted her and reminded her of all she'd accomplished. There was no need to think about the past. That was a waste of time and energy.

Her eyes stopped on her aides, Carrie and Selena. The two women, so boisterous in personality, were usually animated. But at the moment they stood huddled in the corner behind Austin's wheelchair.

Carrie, the heavyset one in the Ed Hardy T-shirt, motioned at her.

"What?" Katie pulled at her white shirt with the delicate pink flowers embroidered along the hem and surveyed the stains. "I know, I'm a mess. But did you see how wonderfully the kids did on their art projects? It was worth it. Never thought of the oil on the dough staining. Next time I'll wear an apron."

Selena and Carrie looked as though there was something more they wanted.

"Maddie, you're a born artist." Katie smiled at the little girl sitting behind a mound of colorful clay. Then to the aides: "What is the matter with you two?"

Selena, a slight Latina woman, shook her head and pointed toward the door.

Katie rotated toward the front of the classroom and caught her breath. Luc, so tall and gorgeous, completely out of place in his fine European suit and a wristwatch probably worth more than her annual salary, stood in the doorway. He wore a fedora, his trademark since college, but hardly one he needed to stand out in a crowd.

As she stared across the space between them, suddenly the classroom she took such pride in appeared shabby and soiled. When she inhaled, it reeked of sour milk and baby food. Her muddled brain searched for words.

"Luc?" She blinked several times, as if his film-star good looks might evaporate into the annals of her mind. "What are you doing here?"

"Didn't you get my brother's wedding invitation?" he asked coolly, as if they'd only seen each other yesterday.

"I did. I sent my regrets."

"That's what I'm doing here. You can't miss Ryan's wedding. I thought the problem might be money."

She watched as his blue eyes came to rest on her stained shirt. Instinctively she crossed her arms in front of her.

"I came to invite you to go back with me next week, on my plane."

"Ah." She nodded and waited for something intelligible to come out of her mouth. "It's not money."

"Come home with me, Katie." He reached out his arms, and she moved to the countertop and shuffled some papers together.

If he touches me, I don't stand a chance. She knew Luc

well enough to know if he'd made the trip to her classroom, he didn't intend to leave without what he came for.

"I'm afraid that's not possible." She stacked the same papers again.

"Give me one reason."

She faced him. "I could give you a billion reasons."

Luc's chiseled features didn't wear humility well. The cross-shaped scar beneath his cheekbone added to his severity. If he weren't so dreaded handsome, he'd make a good spy in a Bond movie. His looks belied his soft Uptown New Orleans upbringing, the kind filled with celebrations and warm family events with backyard tennis and long days in the swimming pool.

He pushed through the swiveled half door that separated them and strode toward her.

"That gate is there for a reason. The classroom is for teachers and students only."

Luc opened his hand and beckoned to her, and despite herself, she took it. Her heart pounded in her throat, and its roar was so thunderous it blocked her thoughts. He pulled her into a clutch, then pushed her away with all the grace of Astaire. "Will you dance with me?" he asked.

He began to hum a Cole Porter tune clumsily in her ear, and instinctively she followed his lead until everything around them disappeared and they were alone in their personal ballroom. For a moment she dropped her head back and giggled from her stomach; a laugh so genuine and pure, it seemed completely foreign—as if it came from a place within that was no longer a part of her. Then the dance halted suddenly, and his cheek was against hers. She took in the roughness of his face, and the thought flitted through her mind that she could die a happy woman in those arms.

The sound of applause woke her from her reverie.

"You two are amazing!" Carrie said.

The children all murmured their approval, some with screams of delight and others with loud banging.

Luc's hand clutched her own in the small space between them, and she laughed again.

"Not me," Luc said. "I have the grace of a bull. It's Katie. She's like Ginger Rogers. She makes anybody she dances with look good." He appealed to the two aides. "Which is why I'm here. She must go to my brother's wedding with me."

"I didn't even know you danced, Katie," Selena said. "Why don't you ever come dancing with us on Friday nights?"

"What? Katie dances like a dream. She and my brother were partners onstage in college. They were like a mist, the way they moved together. It's like her feet don't touch the ground."

"That was a long time ago." She pulled away from him and showed him her shirt. "I'm a mess. I hope I didn't ruin your suit."

"It would be worth it," Luc growled.

"Katie, where'd you learn to dance like that?" Carrie asked.

"Too many old movies, I suppose." She shrugged.

"You could be on *Dancing with the Stars* with moves like that."

"Except I'm not a star or a dancer, but other than that, I guess—" She giggled again. It kept bubbling out of her, and for one blissful moment she remembered what it felt like to be the old Katie McKenna. Not the current version, staid school-marm and church soloist in Northern California, but the Katie people in New Orleans knew, the one who danced and sang.

Luc interrupted her thoughts. "She's being modest. She learned those moves from Ginger and Fred themselves, just by watching them over and over again. This was before YouTube, so she was dedicated."

Katie shrugged. "I was a weird kid. Only child, you know?" But inside she swelled with pride that Luc remembered her devotion to a craft so woefully out-of-date and useless. "Anyway, I don't have much use for swing dancing or forties torch songs now. Luc, meet Carrie and Selena. Carrie and Selena, Luc."

"I don't have any 'use' for salsa dancing," Selena said. "I do it because it's part of who I am."

"Tell her she has to come with me, ladies. My brother is having a 1940s-themed wedding in New Orleans. He'd be crushed if Katie didn't come, and I'll look like a hopeless clod without her to dance with."

Katie watched the two aides. She saw the way Luc's power-ful presence intoxicated them. Were they really naive enough to believe that Luc DeForges could *ever* appear like a clod, in any circumstance or setting? Luc, with his skilled charm and roguish good looks, made one believe whatever he wanted one to believe. The two women were putty in his hands.

"Katie, you have to go to this wedding!" Selena stepped toward her. "I can't believe you can dance like that and never told us. You'd let this opportunity slip by? For what?" She looked around the room and frowned. "This place?"

The cacophony of pounding and low groans rose audibly, as if in agreement.

"This may be just a classroom to you, but to me, it's the hope and future of these kids. I *used* to dance. I *used* to sing. It paid my way through college. Now I'm a teacher."

"You can't be a teacher *and* a dancer?" Selena pressed. "It's like walking and chewing gum. You can do both. The question is, why don't you?"

"Maybe I should bring more music and dancing into the classroom. Look how the kids are joining in the noise of our voices, not bothered by it. I have to think about ways we could make the most of this."

But she hadn't succeeded in changing the subject; everyone's attention stayed focused on her.

"You should dance for the kids, Katie. You possess all the grace of an artist's muse. Who knows how you might encourage them?"

Katie laughed. "That's laying it on a bit thick, Luc, even for you. I do believe if there was a snake in that basket over there, it would be rising to the charmer's voice at this very minute."

Luc's very presence brought her into another time. Maybe it was the fedora or the classic cut of his suit, but it ran deeper than how he looked. He possessed a sense of virility and take-no-prisoners attitude that couldn't be further from his blue-blood upbringing. He made her, in a word, feel safe . . . but there was nothing safe about Luc and there never had been. She straightened and walked over to her open folder to check her schedule for the day.

Tapping a pencil on the binder, she focused on getting the day back on track. The students were involved in free playtime at the moment. While they were all situated in a circle, they played individually, their own favorite tasks in front of them.

"Carrie, would you get Austin and Maddie ready for lunch?"

"I'll do it," Selena said. "And, Katie . . . you really should go to the wedding."

"I can't go to the wedding because it's right in the middle of summer school."

"You could get a substitute," Carrie said. "What would you be gone for, a week at most? Jenna could probably fill in. She took the summer off this year."

"Thanks for the suggestions, ladies," Katie said through clenched teeth. "But I've already told the groom I can't attend the wedding for professional reasons."

The women laughed. "I'm sorry, what reasons?" Carrie asked, raising a bedpan to imply that anyone could do Katie's job.

It was no use. The two women were thoroughly under Luc's spell, and who could blame them?

"Maybe we should talk privately," Luc said. He clasped her wrist and led her to the glass doors at the front of the classroom. "It's beautiful out here. The way you're nestled in the hills, you'd never know there's a city nearby."

She nodded. "That's Crystal Springs Reservoir on the other side of the freeway. It's protected property, the drinking water for this entire area, so it's stayed pristine."

"I'm not going back to New Orleans without you," he said.

Apparently the small talk had ended.

"My mother would have a fit if I brought one of the women I'd take to a Hollywood event to a family wedding."

Katie felt a twinge of jealousy, then a stab of anger for her own weakness. Of course he dated beautiful women. He was a billionaire. A billionaire who looked like Luc DeForges! Granted, he was actually a multimillionaire, but it had been a long-standing joke between the two of them. Did it matter, once you made your first ten million, how much came after that? He may as well be called a gazillionaire. His finances were too foreign for her to contemplate.

"And who you date is my problem, how?"

"If my date tries to swing dance and kicks one of my mother's friends in the teeth, I'll be disinherited."

"So what, would that make you the fifth richest man in the United States, instead of the fourth?"

"Katie, how many times do I have to explain to you I'm nowhere near those kinds of numbers?" He grinned. "Yet." He touched his finger to her nose lightly. "My fate is much worse than losing status if you don't come. My mother might set me up to ensure I have a proper date. A chorus line of Southern belles. And I guarantee you at least one will have the proverbial glass slipper and think her idea is so utterly unique, I'll succumb to the fantasy."

"Wow! What a terrible life you must lead." She pulled a Keds slide from her foot and emptied sand out of her shoe. A few grains landed on Luc's shiny black loafer. "To think, with courtship skills like that, that any woman wouldn't be swept off her feet—it's unfathomable." She patted his arm. "I wish you luck, Luc. I'm sure your mother will have some very nice choices for you, so go enjoy yourself. Perk up, there're billions more to be made when you get back."

"Sarcasm doesn't suit you, Katie."

He was right, but she didn't trust herself around him. She'd taken leave of her senses too many times in that weakened state. Since moving to California, she'd made it her goal to live life logically and for the Lord. She hadn't fallen victim to her emotions since leaving New Orleans, and she'd invested too much to give into them now.

"I'm sorry," she said. "I only meant that I'm sure there are other nice girls willing to go home and pretend for your mother. I've already done that, only you forgot to tell me we were pretending. Remember?"

He flinched. "Below the belt."

A pencil fell from behind her ear, and she stooped to pick it up, careful not to meet his glance as she rose. "I'm sorry, but I'm busy here. Maybe we could catch up another time? I'd like that and won't be so sidetracked." She looked across the room toward Austin, an angelic but severely autistic child in a wheelchair. He pounded against his tray. "The kids are getting hungry. It's lunchtime." She pointed to the schedule.

Luc scooped a hand under her chin and forced her to look at him. "Where else am I going to find a gorgeous redhead who knows who Glenn Miller is?"

"Don't, Luc. Don't charm me. It's beneath you. Buy one of your bubble-headed blondes a box of dye and send her to iTunes to do research. Problem solved."

He didn't let go. "Ryan wants you to sing at the wedding, Katie. He sent me personally to make sure you'd be there and sing 'Someone to Watch Over Me.' I'm not a man who quits because something's difficult."

"Anyone worth her salt on Bourbon Street can sing that. Excuse me—"

"Katie-bug."

"Luc, I asked you kindly. Don't. I'm not one of your sophisticated girls who knows how to play games. I'm not going to the wedding. That part of my life is over."

"That part of your life? What about that part of you? Where is she?"

She ignored his question. "I cannot be the only woman you know capable of being your date. You're not familiar with anyone else who isn't an actress-slash-waitress?" She cupped his hand in her own and allowed herself to experience the surge of energy. "I have to go." She dropped his hands and pushed back through the half door. "I'm sure you have a meeting to get to. Am I right?"

"It's true," he admitted. "I had business in San Francisco

today, a merger. We bought a small chain of health food stores to expand the brand. But I was planning the trip to see you anyway and ask you personally."

"Uh-huh."

"We'll be doing specialty outlets in smaller locations where real estate prices are too high for a full grocery outlet. Having the natural concept already in these locations makes my job that much easier."

"To take over the free world with organics, you mean?"

That made him smile, and she warmed at the sparkle in his eye. When Luc was in his element, there was nothing like it. His excitement was contagious and spread like a class-room virus, infecting those around him with a false sense of security. She inhaled deeply and reminded herself that the man sold inspiration by the pound. His power over her was universal. It did not make her special.

"Name your price," he said. "I'm here to end this rift between us, whatever it is, and I'll do the time. Tell me what it is you want."

"There is no price, Luc. I don't want anything from you. I'm not going to Ryan's wedding. My life is here."

"Day and night . . . night and day," he crooned and then his voice was beside her ear. "One last swing dance at my brother's wedding. One last song and I'll leave you alone. I promise."

She crossed the room to the sink against the far wall, but she felt him follow. She hated how he could make every nerve in her body come to life, while he seemingly felt nothing in return. She closed her eyes and searched for inner strength.

He didn't want me. Not in a way that mattered. He wanted her when it suited him to have her at his side.

"Even if I were able to get the time off work, Luc, it wouldn't be right to go to your brother's wedding as your date. I'm about to get engaged."

"Engaged?" He stepped away.

She squeezed hand sanitizer onto her hands and rubbed thoroughly.

"I'll give a call to your fiancé and let him know the benefits." He pulled a small leather pad of paper from his coat pocket. "I'll arrange everything. You get a free trip home, I get a Christian date my mother is proud to know, and then your life goes back to normal. Everyone's happy." He took off his fedora as though to plead his case in true gentlemanly fashion. "My mother is still very proud to have led you from your . . ." He choked back a word. "From your previous life and to Jesus."

The announcement of her engagement seemed to have had little effect on Luc, and Katie felt as if her heart shattered all over again. "My previous life was *you*. She was proud to lead me away from her son's life." She leaned on the countertop, trying to remember why she'd come to the kitchen area.

"You know what I meant."

"I wasn't exactly a streetwalker, Luc. I was a late-night bar singer in the Central District, and the only one who ever led my reputation into question was you. So I'm failing to see the mutual benefit here. *Your mother. Your date.* And I get a free trip to a place I worked my tail off to get out of."

She struggled with a giant jar of applesauce, which Luc took from her and opened easily. He passed the jar back to her and let his fingers brush hers.

"My mother would be out of her head to see you. And the entire town could see what they lost when they let their prettiest belle go. Come help me remind them. Don't you want to show them that you're thriving? That you didn't curl up and die after that awful night?"

"I really don't need to prove anything, Luc." She pulled her apron, with its child-size handprints in primary colors, over her head. "I'm not your fallback, and I really don't care if people continue to see me that way. They don't know me."

"Which you? The one who lives a colorless existence and calls it holy? Or the one who danced on air and inspired an entire theater troupe to rediscover swing and raise money for a new stage?" Luc bent down, took her out at the knees, and hoisted her up over his shoulder.

"What are you doing? Do you think you're Tarzan? Put me down." She pounded on his back, and she could hear the chaos he'd created in the classroom. "These kids need structure. What do you think you're doing? I demand you put me down!"

Chapter 2

DON'T GET AROUND MUCH ANYMORE

Luc never broke his stride. He pushed through the school's glass doors as if it was perfectly natural to have a woman flung over his shoulder. Outside, he gently slid her off him and placed her on the sidewalk, or banquette as they called it back home. He grabbed her by the wrist so she couldn't take off for the door. "There. We'll have a little privacy now."

She flipped her head over in front of him, allowing her ponytail to smack him across the face, which seemed as childish as digging her nails into a playground nemesis. "Go ahead. Grab it and drag me back to your cave now, you Neanderthal. Is that how they solve disagreements in corporate America? No wonder this country's going down the tubes."

From her vantage upside down, she noticed Luc's limousine stretched carelessly across the parking lot, blocking the staff's row of compact beaters. At the sight of the driver's impish grin she straightened back up, but not before she heard a set of clicks and caught sight of a man running. "Who was that?"

Luc chuckled. "That was what we call the paparazzi— most aptly named after buzzing mosquitoes, I might add."

"What are they doing here?"

"Right about now? I think they're catching multimillionaire bachelor Luc DeForges being smacked in the face by a feisty redhead's ponytail. Now, *why* I'm being smacked in the face, that will be where their stellar storytelling comes in. Perhaps you caught me cheating on you? Or maybe you're a former roommate of my girlfriend . . . It's anybody's guess."

"Well, go catch him!" She shook his shoulders, then heard more clicks. "Luc! I'm going to be engaged. I can't be seen smacking you in the face with my ponytail!"

"Or shaking me? That looks pretty bad on film too, just so you know."

"Luc, I am a teacher of special needs children. I can't be seen getting violent with a man in front of my school. It could cost me my job!"

"Then you probably shouldn't have done it."

Her mouth dropped open. "You're kidding me, right? This is all part of your elaborate plan to get me to do what you want."

"I told you those stories about me in the tabloids were made-up. The 'bubble-headed blondes,' as you call them. The many 'walks of shame' you supposedly see me taking. Maybe there's another story, that's all I'm saying."

"What you do with your time is no concern of mine."

"It's good for you to see how made-up my image is. It's what sells rags: 'Organic King Is a Dog.' I have to say, though, seeing how boring you've become, I'm hoping they come up with something really spicy so you leave the single life with zeal. Do you think the folks back home will recognize us together? You being upside down and all. I think he got your good side, though."

"Luc! It's not funny! What is Dexter going to say? How do I even explain to him that I didn't invite you here? What's my church going to say?" The more animated she grew, the more sedate he became. She grabbed him again by the shoulders. "Luc!"

"You're so beautiful, Katie. I forgot how those eyes of yours get to a guy."

She dropped her hands to her side. "You're rich and famous. I'm just a schoolteacher. What's my fiancé going to think? I never explained that you were my ex."

"Don't think Poindexter could handle the competition? I'm flattered. That's kind of you, to take his lack of faith in himself into consideration."

Katie felt the blood drain from her face. "Did you just say Poindexter?"

"Poindexter, yeah. He's the one who gave me your address at work. How'd you think I found you?"

"You knew . . . about Dexter?" Her mind churned. Did it

bother Luc that she was about to pledge her life to another? If it did, he showed no sign of it.

"I prefer Poindexter. It fits him."

"It doesn't!" she protested, with slightly too much venom in her voice. She sucked in a deep breath before she continued. "Dex is brilliant. He went to MIT."

"Book learnin'. I figured, but I'm not impressed."

"Fortunately, it doesn't matter what you think."

"Why aren't you engaged already? If he's going to do it, why doesn't he just ask? What's all the talk?"

"If you must know, my ring is back home." Her voice trailed off, and she closed her eyes.

"To get engaged you need your nana's ring? So it seems you *do* need to get back home to New Orleans."

She sighed in defeat.

"It's my business to know about people when I'm entering into a negotiation. Certainly a potential fiancé creates an obstacle to my dating the woman he supposedly loves. I need to factor this into the equation. But it also helps that I know you need to get home, Katie, and I have the opportunity to offer you a free trip." He focused on her stained shirt. "I thought maybe we could help each other out."

"Dex doesn't know about you, Luc. I mean, he knows about you being my boyfriend all through college and of course . . . the rest of it. But he doesn't know you're the billionaire in the tabloids!" She stamped her foot like a toddler. "How could you let this happen?"

"I didn't know they'd follow me here."

"That wasn't part of your brilliant equation?" The edge in her voice was unmistakable.

Luc chuckled. "I never imagined I'd give them the money shot of a woman slung over my shoulder, with a follow-up shot of her slapping me with her lustrous tresses. I imagine that photographer can take a few days off now." He lifted a forefinger. "You're right, this was a great breach of offensive tactics, and I regret the error."

"You can't let that picture be printed." Her throat clamped with emotion. "Luc, I've worked so hard to be this new person. *Please!*"

His rational voice remained unchanged. "There was nothing wrong with your old person."

"That's not what I mean. This is pointless!" She walked back to the doors, and he pressed against them. "I'm not going home with you. I would rather hitchhike across the country or ride the next hurricane in than enter that den of iniquity you call a private jet."

He laughed. "Den of ... never mind. Now that I finally have your attention, Miss McKenna, let's get down to business. As I stated earlier, my brother Ryan is having a forties-themed wedding in approximately two weeks. I can't imagine you'd let him get married without your presence. In fact, I find the option rude and completely out of your character."

"Ryan will understand. I didn't even make it to my own mother's wedding!"

"Where are you, Katie? Where's that girl who can swing dance with the grace of water? The one who can rock a pencil skirt and clunky heels . . . sing a love song so that the listeners think their own hearts are breaking? Where's the Katie that I knew, who could make a man want to go to war just for the sheer pleasure of returning home? Where is *she* now?"

She blinked away her emotions. "Save that garbage for someone who buys your lines and takes the familiar walk of shame from your jet." She turned and strode back toward the building.

"Careful, Katie. It may appear from those pictures as if you're doing your own walk of shame. I wouldn't be so quick to judge if I were you."

"What kind of scorned woman dresses like a *haus frau*?" She spoke the words to the door, but she could feel him behind her and caught his reflection in the window.

"Ah, so you do have some vanity left in you after all." He raised his arm to the sky and caught the limo driver's attention. "Find out who got that shot and offer to pay for it!" His gaze fell back upon her as he gently turned her by the shoulders. "I'll do my best. Hopefully, we know the kid and we can pay him off. Now, back to our negotiations—"

She felt worn and lifeless, like a true rag doll. She'd rather feed the kids eight times over than enter a battle of wills with Luc DeForges. She tugged at the hem of her shirt. "You have no idea what's going to happen in that room if the kids aren't fed on time. Their schedule is crucial. Each day must be like the last with small, announced changes—" She karate chopped her palm for emphasis, and Luc laughed. She felt it to her core.

"Who are you now, Katie?" He looked at her with what might only be described as pity.

"This is who I am!"

"I know you think so." He lifted one brow, as if going in for the kill. "It's a free trip home, Katie. No strings attached. No expectations, and a free forties outfit. Ingrid Bergman or Ginger Rogers, the look is on me. The chance to revisit the old Katie, just to see if she has anything to say to you. Maybe you're right . . ." He stood straighter and stepped away from her. "That part of you is gone, but what have you got to lose? And you wouldn't dare let me announce to my brother I'd failed at something, would you? Besides, if you're planning to move ahead with this wedding, you need your nana's ring."

"My mam can mail it to me."

"We both know she won't. Let's talk price."

"I don't have a price, Luc. I never did. Maybe you're looking for the real Katie in the wrong place." She stared at him, willing him to get how simple the answer really was— all she'd ever wanted from him was his heart. To know she wasn't merely a number in his harem but that she'd been spe-cial . . . loved by him. Even if he hadn't been strong enough to do anything about his feelings, the knowledge would mean something to her.

She stared into his blue eyes and felt her stomach spiral with the connection she felt to him: a physical, life-affirming glow from within that she could never explain, but which formed some kind of bridge between them and seemed inca-pable of perishing.

"I have to go." She walked back into the classroom and saw that Carrie and Selena had everything under control. The kids were being fed, and the room was quiet with the gentle hum of moaning and silverware clanging. She heard Luc trailing her and felt the presence of his warmth near. Whatever the tabloids printed, whatever lifestyle he lived now, Katie knew the man who dwelled within . . . but did he?

She turned to see him staring at the various metal paraphernalia, the wheelchairs, the kids themselves. "The needs here seem endless, Katie. How do you stand it?"

She actually felt sorry for him in that moment. "I love it. I'm doing something to make it better. No one knows what these kids might have to offer the world. They're like little gifts waiting to be unwrapped." She lifted up a pair of plastic shears. "And I have scissors!"

Luc shrugged out of his suit coat. He tossed it over a chair, unbuttoned his sleeves, and shoved them past his elbows. "I'm not leaving until you say yes. We need to feed the kids, we'll feed the kids. What do I do?"

"You're going to help?"

"If that's what it takes."

"Why don't you take Austin then? He eats those sweet potatoes in front of him." She handed Luc a small spoon while Selena and Carrie backed away deferentially, almost reverently. "Let him swallow each bite. He chokes easily. It's a slow process, so if you're in a hurry you might as well go before you start."

Luc opened the small jar of baby food and knelt in front

of the cherubic-looking Austin, who was settled behind a tray attached to his fixed-tilt wheelchair. Austin was seven, but he had the body of an average three-year-old. Severely autistic, he was also allergic to most foods and tended to throw more than he ate. His hands were always stimming; mechanical, repetitive movements that made it hard to get the food into his mouth—not unlike a miniature golf hole that had a revolving door. Though he looked high functioning, he was by far the hardest of the children to feed.

"Hi, Austin," Luc said.

Austin looked at some invisible target in the upper corner of the room.

Luc's first spoonful was met with Austin's clapping hands, and the orange mash exploded into thick droplets that sprayed Luc's slacks and pressed blue shirt. "We missed." Luc scooped up another spoonful.

Selena and Carrie looked at Katie to see if she would take over, but she just crossed her arms and waited.

Luc had slightly better results with the second spoonful, but then everyone's expression changed at the sound of a small giggle.

"He laughed!" Selena said.

"Of course he laughed. Look what he did to my suit. You little bugger!" Luc spoke right into Austin's face, and the boy stared at him. Not through him but actually *at* Luc.

Austin laughed again.

Katie sank to her knees next to Luc. "Talk to him again."

Luc took a rag and wiped Austin's hands to stop their

27

obligatory movement, and the child stilled, mesmerized. *Aware*.

"I wonder if it's your deep voice. Austin's dad doesn't live with him."

The boy giggled again and tried to grab the head of the spoon, which Luc pulled away.

"You think that's funny?" Luc scooped up more sweet potato mash, and Austin batted it away and giggled. "The secret is to aim for his forehead, I think."

Selena and Carrie stopped their cleanup work with the other kids and watched Luc's actions as intently as Katie did.

"Say something else to him, Luc," Carrie said.

"See, women don't understand us boys, Austin. They think if you don't do it their way, you're doing it wrong. But you and me, we know the truth, don't we? We know it's more fun to *wear* our food than eat it, especially when it's orange mush!" Luc stilled the spoon. "Can't you get him a more manly meal?"

Selena giggled. "A manly meal. What would that look like?"

"I don't know. A stew maybe."

"He chokes, Luc," Katie said as she rolled her eyes.

"You're coddling him, that's all. Give a man a little space here. You think they'd never seen a boy eat before," he said to Austin, who still hadn't taken his eyes off Luc.

Austin took the next spoonful of sweet potatoes without a battle and swallowed it without incident. He followed up with another and another until the jar stood empty.

"Score!" Luc cried as he raised his arms into goal position.

"Luc, do you have any idea what you've just done?"

"We ate our lunch. No more of that garbage, all right? I'm going to have the store send something over for the kids to eat. Do you know how many additives and preservatives are in that? We can mash our own sweet potatoes, and that boy won't know what hit him. You add a little brown sugar, and you've got dessert." Luc winked at Austin. "Stick with me, kid."

Austin giggled again. It almost sounded familiar now.

"Will that get me a date to my brother's wedding? Because I'm sort of desperate here." Luc looked straight at her with his brilliant blue eyes, and Austin's fascination didn't seem so out of the ordinary any longer.

Maybe she did have a price after all. "Did you mean what you said about the food?"

"Have I ever lied to you, Katie?"

"I prefer not to answer that question."

"Fair enough. I supply you with decent food for these kids, you'll come?"

"And new high chairs and equipment for the classroom. And one more aide for an entire year." She cut her eyes at him like a film noir actress.

Luc roared with laughter. "I may have created a monster. I do all that, and you'll go?"

She felt breathless, but her answer tumbled out of her mouth regardless. "Yes, I'll go. I guess I do have my price."

"Pleasure doing business with you, Katie." Luc reached over his shoulder and shook her hand.

A wistful sigh escaped her. What might her life have looked like if Luc hadn't developed such a head for business? Not that it mattered. One didn't get consumed by those kinds of emotions and come out better for it on the other side. That only happened on the silver screen with the likes of Fred and Ginger. Love that cost a person everything was too big a risk. Careful, thoughtful companionship made for a healthy relationship, and she'd do well to remind herself of that often until Ryan's wedding came and went.

When she'd left New Orleans, she'd vowed never to let a man have that kind of power over her emotions again, and she'd stuck to her promise. Fiery, passionate emotion made for trouble, pain, and far too much loss—in essence, it didn't last.

This wedding provided the perfect opportunity for closure so that she might commit herself fully to the idea of marriage and practicality. Right after she wore that vintage gown and sang the standards one last time . . . and explained to Dexter why she was photographed flung over a man's shoulder.

Chapter 3

ACCENTUATE THE POSITIVE

Katie danced around her living room with her scrapbook in her arms. As if it was Fred Astaire himself, she allowed the book to take the lead. She flopped on the sofa, opened her calendar, and scribbled inside: *Flowers again today! That's fifteen weeks in a row.* She drew a smiley face beside the words and marked the page with a small heart sticker.

Eileen, her oldest friend and current roommate, turned her face toward Katie from her odd yoga pose with feet pointed to the ceiling. "I don't even have to see it to know what you wrote. I should think if it was so touching, you wouldn't need to remind yourself in print."

"Someday I'll be able to tell our children all about their father's warm touches when we were courting, and I won't need to rely on my feeble memory."

"You'd have to lose your brain altogether not to remember something he did for fifteen weeks in a row." Eileen rolled down onto her back, then flipped over so she leaned on her elbows. "Are you planning on losing your mind?"

"No, I simply like tangible memories. Something I can hold on to."

"What are you writing in your courtship diary about your vacation from your senses?"

"Pardon?"

"I mean, what will you write in there for your kids about how Mommy went to N'awlins with her rich friend in his private jet? Because that's when the kids' interest might be piqued—not in their father's recurring standard flower order. They'll be as bored over that as you are." Eileen sprang into a downward facing dog pose.

"I'm not bored with it! I love it. There's something so life affirming about fresh flowers. I can look into the kitchen pass-through at any time and know that Dexter is thinking of me."

"Katie, no matter how many entries you put in that book, Dexter is not going to be a romantic. I mean, fine, you're going to marry him. He's a good man. I just don't want you to be disappointed. No matter how many junior high school hearts you draw next to his name, Dexter is going to order you what the Internet says is the proper gift for each anniversary. He'll probably have a program created that does it for him."

"What's wrong with that? You and I have a different view of romance, that's all. You say potato, I say po-tah-to."

"No, you say delusional, I say reality check. What does Dexter think about this trip with your ex-boyfriend?"

"Dexter trusts me."

"Like I said, delusional. Any man who trusts his girlfriend with a billionaire—"

"He's a multimillionaire," she corrected.

"A *billionaire* who looks like Luc DeForges—in a private jet alone, is not romantic *or* practical. He's dwelling on another planet. Where was Spock from again?"

"Dex is practical. He knows I need to go home to get my nana's ring so that we can be engaged. He's fine with it, for us. It's a free opportunity and—"

"It's free. Is that the pull for Dexter? Sending you home with a guy who makes your heart go pitter-pat is free?"

"Luc doesn't make my heart go pitter-pat! That was a long time ago. I've grown up."

"This is me you're talking to." Eileen stood up, her lithe little frame looking even slimmer in yoga pants and top, and smoothed a wrinkle from her shirt. She followed Katie into the bedroom and sat on the bed, causing a pile of clothing to topple. "Why haven't you packed yet?"

"Dex is loaning me a suitcase. Mine is held together with duct tape."

"This is ridiculous. Your mam can mail you the ring."

Katie ignored Eileen and calmly refolded her forties-style gray skirt with the tiny wave of ruffles at the back. "Why don't you come along if you're so worried about me?"

"Maybe I will," Eileen said.

"I haven't been home since Paddy died. I don't think an e-mail saying 'Send me my ring' is going to fly."

"Planes go both ways, Katie. Your mam could have come out here more often." She stood. "I've got dinner on. A lemon-grass and shrimp soup. What time will Dex be here?"

Katie glanced at her watch. "Any minute now."

She was glad Eileen liked to cook. Granted, everything she made was some kind of spa cuisine that needed a bulky piece of bread to make it an actual meal, but Katie wasn't complaining. After shoveling foul-smelling baby food into kids all day, the last thing she wanted to do was cook.

"I'm going to get dressed," Eileen said. "You should pass the vacuum, as our mams would say. This place could use it!"

Their apartment was simple, but it had been built in the thirties and had that old-time feel that Katie felt such an affin-ity for. She loved the rounded doorways and original kitchen with its Wedgewood stove. She might have loved that aspect less if she actually cooked. The apartment thumbed its pro-verbial nose at the modern stainless steel styles and cold granite countertops.

But Eileen had obliged because of the price. The rent had originally been out of their income level, but Katie's appreci-ation of every detail convinced the landlord, an older woman who owned the place and lived on the bottom floor, to lower it for them.

Eileen yelled from the next room. "Couldn't Luc just teach some actress to swing dance?"

"I suggested that!" Katie yelled back.

"He could tell them *Glee* needs another dancer. Remember? They did swing dance with Will Schuester and Sue Sylvester." Eileen's voice got closer until she appeared in the room wearing skintight black shorts and a turquoise hoodie. "I just don't see why Luc is back unless he's interested in you." She flipped her jet-black hair outside her collar and tied it up into a loose knot. "It makes no sense. No word from him in how many years?"

"Three," she mumbled. "Ryan's getting married. That's why he contacted me."

"I used to *date* Ryan, remember? I didn't get an invitation."

"That doesn't prove anything, Eileen. Ryan and I were dance partners. That's different from inviting someone he casually dated once or twice."

"Maybe. But you know I wouldn't trust Luc as far as I could throw him." Eileen flexed her biceps. "Granted, I could probably get him across this room, but I still don't trust him."

"If Dexter doesn't have an issue with it, I don't know why you should." Katie folded a red scarf. "I think I'll bring this."

Eileen laughed. "Really?"

"What? You don't like this scarf?"

"I'm not talking about the scarf." Eileen snagged the scarf, crumpled it into a ball, and threw it behind her. It landed in the corner amidst a few dust bunnies. "Told you you should have vacuumed. Katie, you're not safe with Luc."

"If I'm not safe with him, then I shouldn't be marrying Dexter."

"Why tempt fate? Luc's not good for you, Katie. He breaks your heart. Every. Single. Time. He's your Kryptonite, and even Superman is smart enough to know his weakness."

Katie slid onto the bed and grabbed the bedpost. "It's not true. I love Dexter for all the ways he's there for me. He's going to make the perfect husband. I can count on him."

"You could set your watch by Dexter. I know you believe you're past all this emotion and that Luc could never get close enough to hurt you again, but I think you've got too much faith in yourself. Those tears lasted a long time. If you would just admit to me that you still love Luc—at least some part of you loves him—then I'd feel better about your going."

"I love *Dexter*. I'm not just marrying him for practical reasons. I'm marrying him because he complements me so well. I would never cheat on any boyfriend, much less my soon-to-be fiancé. What kind of person do you think I am?"

Eileen placed her hand on the pile of clothes Katie had restored on the bed. "A good one. A sweet and gentle, loving soul who is powerless against the hurricane force that is Luc DeForges. Know your weakness, Katie, that's all I'm asking."

"You've never liked Luc," she accused.

Eileen fell back on the bed and stretched her arms over her head. "I liked him fine before he broke your heart." She spoke to the ceiling. "Granted, I liked his brother better, but I couldn't see you with a guy who danced better than you. It's not right somehow. Ryan was always more like your brother than a boyfriend."

"You didn't like Luc in college. For one thing, you didn't like that he went to Tulane instead of Loyola. You accused me of being a traitor."

"No, you're right. I didn't like him," Eileen admitted. "Why don't you just pick out a new engagement ring with Dex? He'd love to take you shopping and buy you a ring. It's practical. Just make sure I'm out of town when you do it, all right? I don't want to hear him blather on about all the details of its perfection. Besides, your nana's classic antique doesn't seem to fit a Dexter marriage."

"What do you mean? It's my ring, and it fits me. What's more practical than that?" Katie pointed at the brooch on her collar. "I don't like modern things."

"Tacori makes beautiful antique-looking rings. Buy one of them and save yourself some heartache. Yes, I know, the emeralds match your eyes," Eileen said before Katie could protest. She lifted up onto her elbows. "Buy some emeralds that color and put them on the new ring. Dexter will buy you whatever you want. Even *he* can't believe you're marrying him. I've got to go throw the shrimp in the soup." Eileen kicked her legs out and jumped off the bed. "I just don't know how you two can be in love. You're so . . . polite to each other. How will you ever solve serious issues like whether to watch *Monday Night Football* or *The Bachelor*?"

"That's easy. Dexter doesn't like football. So I'm sure we'll solve it by finding something we love doing together."

"Okay, Dexter wants to watch the *Life and Times of the Dung Beetle* in three parts, and you want to watch *The Bachelor*. Now who wins? How do you negotiate?"

"I don't want to watch *The Bachelor*. I'll be married. What's the point?"

"So no married women watch *The Bachelor*? Your desire for tacky television evaporates on your wedding day?"

She didn't answer.

"Katie, the point is, I've seen you go through an entire pint of Ben & Jerry's Phish Food when the wrong bachelorette won on that show. You are denying who you really are. And, girl, face it, you're tacky. You're in the dentist's office. Do you pick up *US News & World Report* or *People*?" Eileen leaned on the doorframe. "Wait, I've got another one. Dexter buys you a Kindle and he stocks it full of biographies on dead presidents and scientific heroes. Do you a) pretend to read them and scan them so you can discuss them at the dinner table or b) say thank you and go score some real books online?"

"Dexter is not that interested in what I read."

The doorbell interrupted them, and they stared at one another, then scrambled—Eileen to the kitchen and Katie to the front door. She drew in a deep breath to clear her head. Dexter had nothing to worry about with Luc, and she'd be sure he understood that. She opened the door briskly and nearly jumped the UPS man before she realized he wasn't Dexter.

"Oh."

"Sorry to disappoint you." He grinned. "Usually people who get a box this big are happy to see me."

Their UPS man was a burly African American with abs you could see through his shirt. Katie had definitely watched too many *Bachelor* episodes, because she always expected him to tear it off in the hallway.

She stared at the box. "Sorry. I was expecting someone else."

"I figured. But you got yourself a nice present here." He held out his electronic clipboard, and she signed for the package. He maneuvered the box, which was large enough to hold a small child, through the doorway and left it beside the entry. "See you next time."

"Yeah, thanks," she said absently, shutting the door.

"That wasn't Dex?" Eileen emerged from the kitchen. "I put the shrimp in. They only need like a minute. I don't want rubbery shrimp."

"Relax, he'll be here. You could set your watch by him, remember?" The doorbell rang again. "See?" She pulled the door open again, and the UPS man stood there again.

"Sorry to bother you. You forgot to print your name beneath your signature."

Eileen ran to the kitchen and came back with scissors. "I turned the soup off." She kicked the door shut with her foot behind the departing deliveryman and, without waiting for an invitation, sliced into the box and peered inside. "I think it's clothes. Who would send you clothes?" She pulled out a lavender crepe paper bundle and ripped it open. A dress tumbled out.

"It's a swing dress." Katie grabbed it and felt the material. "It's an original!" An accompanying tag announced the dress's credentials. It was a navy polka dot sheer dress with a white sailor collar. Katie ran to the mirror that hung over the love seat. "It's gorgeous!" She flattened the dress against her chest and twirled to let the skirt gain flight.

Eileen grabbed the dress from her and shoved it back in the box. "It's from Luc. I'd recognize his carefully choreographed moves anywhere. Send this back."

"It was part of the deal. If I go to the wedding, I get clothes from the era. I negotiated it. It's mine."

"Was this?" Eileen pulled out a *Tattler* magazine. On the cover was Katie's backside slung over Luc's broad shoulder.

On a Post-it he'd scrawled, *I'm sorry about this, but at least I kept your name out of it.*

The headline splayed across the picture read MILLIONAIRE BACHELOR, TARZAN; UNNAMED REDHEAD, JANE. Mortification washed over Katie, and she grabbed the magazine and thumbed through it until she came to the photographs. There was Luc's face all bunched up as her ponytail connected with his nose.

"The pictures are like one of those cartoon drawings where you turn the pages. You know what I mean? Look at me! You can see my face in this one! Anyone who opens this rag is going to know it's me."

"Look at it this way; they'd have to admit to buying a

tabloid first. So are you planning to tell me why Luc has you hoisted midair like a tub of crawfish?"

Katie stared at the image on the cover again. "You can't tell that's me." She grabbed the magazine and scrutinized it from all angles, then she shrugged. "You can't tell it's me!"

"But I know it's you. This is exactly what happens when Luc DeForges is around. What is Dex going to say to this?"

"Where would he see it? Dexter probably doesn't even know that magazine exists." Her mind raced. She knew she had to come clean, but it would just be easier to do so after she got back with her engagement ring.

"You're not going to tell him?" The doorbell rang, and Eileen giggled in her trademark knowing way.

"What is so funny?"

"I was just thinking how you said Luc's mother wanted to have a Cinderella-style lineup." Eileen raised the cover back at her. "Wouldn't it be something if instead of a glass slipper, they were looking for a glass girdle? Spanx?"

Katie raked her fingers through her hair and groaned. "What have I done?"

The doorbell rang again.

Eileen threw the magazine into the box. "There's more." She brought up a gold box the shape of an oversized hatbox.

"Not now. Dex is here. I have to think about how I'm going to tell him about the photos."

"A picture's worth a thousand words. Show him!"

Katie stared at the door, then at the box, and without willpower, she tore into the gold cardboard.

"You always did have to eat dessert first," Eileen said.

Katie tossed the lid off and tore through the tissue paper. Inside shone the coup de grace. The Holy Grail for vintage lovers. She could very nearly hear the heavenly host singing. She had to stop and take a moment. "Luc knows me better than I know myself." She got choked up. "I can't touch it."

"Well, what is it?" The doorbell rang a third time, and they both ignored the sound.

"It's a replica of Ginger Rogers' iconic ostrich feather gown in *Top Hat* where she danced with Fred Astaire."

Eileen placed her fists on her boyish hips. "A replica? He bought you a replica? What's the point of being a gazillionaire if you can't buy the real thing? I mean, Nick Cage bought a real dinosaur skull before he went broke."

"Maybe that's why he went broke. The real dress is light blue, too close to white maybe for a wedding?"

"You better put that away for now until you figure out how you're going to explain the picture to Dexter. And you're going to explain it to him, or I will. The moment you start protecting Luc, it's over."

"No, you're right." Katie snuggled the dress to her collarbone. "Oh, the feel of it. Eileen, feel it!"

"Did they kill something to make that atrocious thing?"

"No, it's ostrich feathers."

"So what's the ostrich wearing now?"

"Ginger fought for this dress. Had lots of tantrums over it, in fact. Look what Luc wrote on the card." She thrust the card toward Eileen. *It's been defeathered and is ready for dancing.* Of course, by defeathered, he meant edited. A feathered dress would always lose some of its feathers. She imagined birds had no better luck. She pressed the card to her chest. "I love Luc."

"You did not just say what I think you did." Eileen crossed her arms. "Because only a crazy person would say such a thing, especially when her fiancé is on the other side of that door, and she has to explain why her heart-shaped bum is on the cover of a tabloid. Katie, Luc's trying to manipulate you, can't you see that? He sends over what *he* wants you to wear." She started to dig through the box, throwing pieces of small, feathered fluff all over the floor.

"What are you doing?"

"I'm looking to see if he sent you lingerie too, with a fake note about what Ginger wore under the dress."

"It was just a figure of speech. I meant that I loved Luc for knowing that Fred Astaire was annoyed by the feathers. It took sixty takes to get the dance right, and the dress shed everywhere. Astaire was a perfectionist, and his temper flared over the extensive takes."

Eileen snatched the dress from her hands. "This is all fascinating, but your fiancé is here." She shoved the dress back into the box and dragged it across the room. "I'll put this in my bedroom until you've had a chance to explain yourself to Dexter over dinner."

Katie waited for Eileen to disappear into the hallway before flinging open the door. Luc filled the doorway, leaning on the doorjamb. But before either of them could say a word, Dexter appeared at his side.

All that Katie could think of was Bette Davis saying, "Fasten your seat belts. It's going to be a bumpy night."

Chapter 4

⌐

At Last

Luc's brows rose as he drank in every aspect of Dexter's appearance: his clothes, his height, his net worth. Katie could practically see Luc's mind churning, the cogs and wheels rotating with all the calculations doubtlessly arriving to his satisfaction. Her insides shook with anger. *How dare he!*

She glanced at her watch. 7:15. Dexter was punctual as usual and still wearing his workday khakis and white button-down. She loved that he was so dependable. In contrast, Luc showed up unannounced, uninvited, and at the worst possible moment for all involved but showing no remorse for his social faux pas.

Dexter walked in and crossed the room to a vase full of

pink roses. "Pink this week," he said, sniffing the buds. "Do you like them?"

"I love them. You're so generous to send the flowers every week. It makes me feel as if I'm starring in my very own movie."

Dexter kissed her near her ear. "You should feel that way. I hope to keep making you feel that way until you could star in *Titanic* as the old woman."

Katie giggled but stopped at the sight of Eileen, standing out of Dexter's line of sight and sticking a finger down her own throat.

"We have to eat," Eileen announced. "My shrimp is already rubbery. Luc? I assume your ill-timed entrance means you're joining us?"

Luc lifted Eileen's hand to his mouth and kissed her fingers. "It's lovely to see you too, Eileen. How long has it been?"

"Not long enough," Eileen replied. "Sit down, I'll go get the pot."

Their table, a cheap Pottery Barn knockoff, boasted three place settings. Katie kept talking while she went to the kitchen to get a fourth.

"Yes, everyone sit down, I'm just going to get another bowl. Luc, you will love Eileen's soup. You should hire her to do demonstrations at your stores. She is such an incredible cook, and everything is healthy so her clients can eat it. She's taken a lot of Mam's recipes and made them low-calorie."

Katie rambled until she returned to the table with a place-mat, bowl, and soup spoon for Luc. "So, Luc, this is Dexter Hastings. My soon-to-be fiancé." She gazed at Dex with pride.

His short-cropped haircut was boyish in style, and his hulking boxy frame made him look like a football player next to Luc's more cut, swimmerlike body. Not that she was comparing them.

"So, Luc," Eileen said as the men shook hands. "You don't think Katie has had enough humiliation for one lifetime at a DeForges family function? You really want to dress her like a pink flamingo for this event? Maybe you can buy her a pair of stilettos and stick her in as a yard decoration when you're finished."

"I don't know if Katie can hold her balance that long, but it's not a bad idea." Luc brushed past Eileen and strode to the table. "I can't wait to have some of this delicious homemade dinner of yours, Eileen. And, Dex, it's a pleasure to meet you. Anyone who sees the beauty in my Katie is a friend of mine." Luc shook out his napkin and laid it on his lap as if he'd been to dinner there the previous night.

"The famous Luc DeForges," Dex said. "So you do exist." He leaned in. "Are you really a billionaire?"

"She speaks of me often, does she?" Luc winked. "Multi-millionaire."

Katie rolled her eyes at Luc's supposedly humble admission.

"Actually, she never spoke of you," Dexter said. "I didn't know you were the rich guy until you said your last name. She just said she dated a guy named Luc back in college. We all make our mistakes." Dexter grinned.

Katie suppressed a smile and sat down at the table. Eileen brought in a pitcher of iced tea and set it between their places.

"You know, I think she did mention you once recently. We were taking out the garbage, and your name came up. 'Gosh, what's that ripe smell? Hey, how's that Luc DeForges doing anyway?'" Eileen set down the pot, and the smell of dirty socks wafted up from the soup. It wasn't one of her better creations to serve company, but then, Luc hadn't been invited.

Luc grinned.

"Katie tells me you're planning to fly her home for our engagement ring. That's very generous of you, I must say. Getting home on a teacher's salary isn't easy," Dex said.

"I would think you'd spring for the ticket, Dex, seeing as how you're saving on the ring and all. Not to mention common courtesy." Eileen wasn't going to let anyone off the hook.

Katie giggled awkwardly. "Let's eat. We don't want that shrimp to get any more rubbery, do we?"

"You need to try the dress on after we eat, Katie. That's why I'm here. I'll need to have it refit before we leave if it isn't right. Not sure we'll have time once we're in Nola—that's New Orleans, Louisiana, Dexter."

"I figured," Dex said. "Thanks for the clarification, just the same."

"There will be rehearsals, garden parties, and of course the wedding itself."

"Katie doesn't sing that kind of torch song anymore, so I'm sure she'll need practice," Dex said. "No broken heart to whine about these days, is there, sweetheart?"

"No." She laced her fingers through Dex's. "I've left the lonely hearts club."

"The fact that you know about dress fittings," Dexter said to Luc. "That the reason you're still single?"

Eileen spit out a mouthful of tea. "Let me pray for dinner." She quickly recited a familiar table blessing, and they all picked up their spoons.

"I hired a dressmaker for Katie." Luc's cheek twitched. "I don't know a thing about women's fashion, but she told me a long time ago that she loved this dress, and I saw it as an opportunity to make her dream come true while she did me a favor. My brother Ryan is a big fan of her singing, and it makes a wedding so much more personal to have someone you know perform."

"We're planning a small wedding," Dexter said. "Just intimate family and friends, so we won't need to put on any kind of show. Just Katie, the Lord, and me. That's all we need, right, baby?"

Luc cleared his throat. "Won't you have 'The Way You Look Tonight' sung?" Luc's gaze drilled into Dex. "That's her favorite song."

"It *used* to be her favorite," Dex said in obvious challenge. They both looked to Katie for clarification.

"We haven't really discussed music yet," Katie said. "We have to get engaged first."

Luc stuck a spoonful of Eileen's soup in his mouth and moaned appreciatively. "Eileen, this is really good. You say it's healthy? No offense, but it didn't smell all that appetizing."

"I didn't have lime. Usually it has a very fresh, citrusy smell. If I'd known the owner of Forages Foods was coming for dinner, I would have asked you to pack a lime. It's a Thai dish. Tom Yum," she said.

"It's delicious and healthy, huh? I might have to get this recipe for the store."

"I'm a personal trainer, Luc. Of course it's healthy. One of my services is to make up menus for my clients and show them how they can lose weight without even trying if they keep fresh ingredients in the refrigerator."

"You have a list of these ingredients?"

"Of course I do, but it's not free. It's part of my service. I still run out occasionally—the lime, for example."

"Did you think I was going to steal the list from you?"

"You've stolen what wasn't yours before. Never can be too sure."

"Mmm. All full." Katie hadn't touched any bread or salad, but she lifted her bowl and brought it to the kitchen. Once at the sink, she leaned on the edge of the old cast-iron basin and breathed in and out slowly. She felt a hand on her back and instinctively knew it was Luc. "Why did you come back?"

"Maybe because I know what your favorite song is. Poindexter can tell you differently. You might even buy into it, but that doesn't make it true."

"A person can change, Luc. My favorite song could change."

"Did it?"

She turned and took the bowl from his hands and placed it in the sink, flicking on the water and letting the stream warm. Steam rose from the faucet. "I'm going home for the wedding. Let's leave it at that, shall we? I'm not the same person I was, and neither are you."

He gave a curt nod. "Will you try the gown on so I at least know it fits? Being different and all, you may have changed your size too."

"Is that a reference to the picture on that magazine?"

Luc stepped forward. "You are more beautiful than the first day I saw you—"

Eileen entered the kitchen with the feathered dress in her hand and pressed it into Luc's chest. "You should hire a date. Surely you can scrape up someone from that dating gene pool of yours—you know the one; has the same IQ as a Barrel of Monkeys game."

Luc whistled. "Everyone seems to know what's best for Katie, but how about if we let her speak for herself?"

"Why don't we?" Eileen crossed her arms.

Luc stood behind the fluff of feathers, and Dexter blinked from the pass-through. Katie felt the weight of their stares in her gut.

Eileen continued, "Why don't we ask Dexter how he feels about Katie going back to this forties-themed wedding. Dex, don't you think it's time she got over her romanticized view of the past and started living in this decade?"

"Katie loves her forties. I don't understand it. I listen to that station of hers, and it all sounds the same to me. But as long as she doesn't make me watch another black-and-white movie, I don't see the harm in her liking those things."

Luc's lip lifted to one side. "Sam Spade? Film noir? *Citizen Kane*? You're not a fan?"

Dex's face filled with mirth and he shook his head. "She made me watch *Casablanca* and *The Philadelphia Story*. Does that count?"

"Made you? She *made you* watch some of the greatest films ever made? Dexter, Katie is introducing you to the sweet life. Would you squander such a gift?" Luc's blue eyes fell on Katie. "When the men were men and the dames were dames."

"Dames?" Dexter leaned over the pass-through. "I was raised by a single mother. She would have killed me if I used that word. I prefer science fiction. Fantasy. We're different, Katie and me. That's what makes us so great together, right?"

He looked to her for confirmation, and she felt shame that he'd used the word *prefer*. Why on earth did it bother her?

"Right. We have an agreement," she explained. "I watch nothing to do with a hobbit, Vulcan, or comic book hero, and in return, Dexter's not forced to sit through a foreign romance, a BBC production, or one of my classic films." She blew a kiss to her fiancé.

"So what do you two have in common, exactly? What do you do together? It's all well and good to have your guy time, right, Dex? But then what?"

Luc plunked his fedora, which he'd removed during dinner, back on his head. Katie wondered if he was trying to send Dexter some kind of underlying message. People assumed Luc wore the hats as part of his eccentric rich bachelor image, but he'd worn them in college, where he was viewed less as an eccentric and more as a weirdo. Like Katie, Luc held an affinity for a simpler time when people's roles weren't as complicated. When swing dancing and big band music ruled the airwaves, and communication didn't include fourteen types of technology, but a simple conversation over coffee and a beignet. Of course, Luc also felt the freedom to heave her over his shoulder like he was working the docks, so maybe she had romanticized prior roles too much.

"You want to try that dress on, don't you, Katie?" Dexter asked her.

Katie nodded so quickly she created her own weather pattern.

Dexter addressed Luc. "That we both want to see her in that gorgeous dress—that's what we have in common. Go put it on, sweetheart. I'm curious what you'll look like as a bird."

Her face burned hot, but she snagged the dress from Luc and scampered down the hallway to her room. She began to belt out "At Last" with enough emotion that it might put Etta James to shame, and she heard Luc laugh from the kitchen. No doubt neither Eileen nor Dex recognized the tune.

Did Eileen really think she should refuse the gown? The thought had never crossed Katie's mind. She hated to admit how her heart leapt when Luc brought up the idea of clunky heels. She clutched the gown as though thieves were lined up along her hallway and snuggled the downy mass of feathers to her heart. They felt like angels' wings against her skin.

Once in her bedroom, she kicked off her Keds and held the gown in front of her reflection. She'd considered having the gown made for her own wedding but nixed the idea rather than explain to Dexter a sudden feather fetish. She exhaled a small whimper. "Oh my goodness, oh my goodness."

Katie had left her great love for period dresses back in New Orleans with her collection, which she'd sold to another struggling student trying to make her way through college the same way. She'd forgotten how the feelings sparked endorphins as though she'd run for miles.

She tossed the dress onto her bed and pulled the door shut. She shimmied out of her jeans and hoodie and kicked them into the corner, where another explosion of dust bunnies erupted.

She fluffed the feathers outward and stepped into the dress. She secured the shoulders, the fit of which was like a cape. She twisted and turned in the mirror and covered her face, peeked through her stretched fingers, then dropped her arms. "At laaaast," she crooned, "my love has come along . . ."

Too paralyzed to zip herself up, she stood mesmerized by her own reflection—she looked like Ginger herself. How she longed to be able to have such beauty when she performed. Back in the day, she'd been reliant upon what the secondhand stores offered.

Someone rapped on the door, and she wiped her eyes and opened it.

"I figured you might need me to zip you up," Eileen said as she moved gazelle-like into the room. She stopped mid-stride.

"Oh, Katie." The two friends stared at one another. "You have never looked more like . . . well, like you."

Katie crumbled into her hands and felt Eileen zip her up. "What's wrong?"

"I miss it. I miss the Barrelhouse Club, I miss singing an old song with passion. Not that I don't like singing in church, I do, but this is what I did out in the world. This is how I connected with barflies and street people and told them about Jesus. They thought I was a star, like their fairy godmother. It's not the same here."

"Don't let this dress cloud your memory. You always wanted to be a teacher. Besides, you need to hurry. Luc is trying to talk sports to Dex out there."

"I still want to teach, Eileen. Nothing makes me prouder than watching the kids hit some milestone. That's not what I mean. It's just that I feel closer to God when I'm singing to the 'least of these.' Does that make any sense?"

Eileen stepped forward and patted her wrist. "Katie, I'm only worried you're muddling all these feelings. If you wanted Luc DeForges, you know I'd support you. Much as I might want to vomit in my own shoes, I'd support you. But if you want to sing and swing dance, you can easily find a club in San Francisco. You don't have to give up your dreams because you're getting married. Dexter wouldn't want you to sacrifice yourself for him."

Katie crossed her arms over her chest and rubbed the feathered cape.

"You've got two guys out there. One has already broken

your heart and disappeared off the radar screen. The other one wants the same things you do: a family, a ministry together, a future. I know your nana's ring means a lot to you, but is it worth losing that guy out there who wants to marry you?"

"Of course not, but this won't cost me Dex. We've agreed that I'll get the ring and he'll ask me to marry him in some surprising and elegant way and present it to me."

"I don't want it to come to blows here. And it will, Katie. You mark my words, it will come to blows. Maybe not in a physical way, but Luc owns you in his own way. You're the hydrant, he's the dog."

"Ewww! You can't come up with a better analogy than that?"

"You're wearing his collar. You have Luc's license around your neck. This dress is his license."

Katie slumped. Everything seemed so simple until she stared at her reflection. Even Eileen had said that Katie looked like herself. Had she abandoned a part of herself for security? "But I love Dexter!" she said out loud.

"Katie?" Luc stuck his head around the doorframe. His Adam's apple plummeted and rose, but he said nothing.

Dexter appeared beside Luc. He crossed his arms like a genie and placed a forefinger to his jaw. "Hmm. I'm not sure what I think."

"It's better with movement." Luc stepped forward and opened his palm to her. "May I?" he asked Dexter.

"Be my guest. I wouldn't know what to do with her dressed like that." Dex laughed.

Katie took Luc's proffered elbow. He circled his arm

around her waist and with the other hand pulled her into him with a spin. Then he pushed her away, and she twirled until she came to the end of his long reach. Luc circled her back and began to sing, "Heaven, I'm in heaven . . ."

Her head fell back, and they began to dance cheek to cheek. The roughness of his evening shadow felt natural against her complexion, and she drank in the familiar scent of him. He dipped her and left her with her back arched and dependant on his arm.

Dexter stood in the doorway. "So that's swing?"

His question broke her dream state, and she pulled her gaze from Luc's. He lifted her to an upright position. She shook her head and untangled herself from Luc's embrace. "That was a waltz," she told Dexter. "Let me teach you." She held her arms up toward his shoulders.

"No, no. Not me. I'm enjoying watching you. I can't see how beautiful you look if I'm right beside you."

"But we'll dance a waltz at our wedding. Come here." She motioned with her forefinger.

"This is swing." Luc took her back and twisted her into a sweetheart, showing Dex the basic steps as if to say how easy it was, then tossing her feet into the air as though she was nothing more than a mop. He lifted her at the waist. "Sidecar!" Luc shouted, and he placed his hands on her hips.

Katie stopped. "I don't think I—" She clasped her hands around Luc's neck and kicked her legs up into an L. She went to one side, then back down again, and he flipped her to the other side, where she lifted up into an L again. Katie squealed with delight in the momentum, and she came back down hard. "I don't think I move that way anymore."

"We're pathetic!" Luc threw his head back. "That is not how you do it, Dex." He twirled her into a basic dip and kept her off her balance. "We have to finish strong."

She pulled herself upright using Luc's neck to straighten up.

"I'll leave the dancing to you two," Dexter said.

She held out her hand, "Come on, Dexter. It's fun, I'll show you."

"I'd better get going," Luc said. "Katie, the gown fits you like a glove. Maybe I should have planned an extra day for us to practice though." He laughed. "Dexter, pleasure to meet you."

Luc shook Dexter's hand and exited the room so quickly, one would think she'd asked for his hand in marriage. Again.

She searched for breath and finally inhaled a gasping current of air. "Won't you at least try? For me, Dexter?"

"You're a good dancer, sweetheart." Dexter pecked her forehead like an old uncle. "But I'm afraid I hung up my dancing shoes at the high school prom."

She tried to kiss him back, more romantically, but his lips were hard and pursed. The movement came off as cold and wooden, with as much passion as a woodpecker has for the tree it's headbutting. She glanced over at Eileen, who had the decency to look away so as not to remind her she was no Scarlett O'Hara. Katie wasn't the sort to incite that kind of passion in men, and one of the finest things she could do with life was to embrace what she was—not pine after things that would never be. It was why she and Dexter were getting married, she reminded herself. He loved her for who she was now, not for some false image she used to inhabit.

"So will you learn one swing dance for our wedding?" she asked him.

"Oh no. We'll have to invite Luc or maybe this brother of his. Ryan, you say? He can dance with you, and the two of you can entertain the crowd. My engineers at work will love it, but if I did it, I'd never hear the end of it."

"At our wedding? You want Luc to dance with me at our wedding?"

"Well, I don't *want* him to dance with you, but if you want to dance like that, I'm afraid I have no choice." He pecked her cheek again. "Katherine, go home and get the ring. Don't overthink this. Our wedding will be perfect."

"Do you like the gown? You never really said."

"It's a bit much for my taste. Drowns out your beauty. You don't need a dress to capture people's attention, you do that all by your lonesome."

She frowned.

"But it's beautiful on you. You'd make a paper sack look good." He pressed another chaste kiss to her forehead.

"Would you stop that? I'm not your niece!"

"What?"

"And I detest the name Katherine!"

"I think you need to eat a little more tonight. You're grumpy. Eileen"—Dexter saluted with two fingers—"excellent dinner, thank you so much for including me. Katie, I left the suitcase in the living room. Do you want me to bring it in here?"

"Yes, please." She sidled up next to Dexter and laid her head on his shoulder. "Does it bother you that Luc is taking me home? You know, in his private plane?"

"If I didn't trust you, I wouldn't be marrying you."

"So it doesn't bother you that Luc-my-old-boyfriend happens to be the billionaire, I mean, multimillionaire Luc DeForges?"

"You never cared for money. If you did, you wouldn't be spending all this effort on a ring that can't be financially worth the travel. As for having his own jet, I suppose that's just a solid business expenditure for a man who travels as much as he does. I've got to go check on my mother tonight, so I have to run. Call me tomorrow." He stepped out of the room and closed the door behind him.

"You were hoping to get blood out of a turnip?"

"Cut it out, Eileen. Is there anyone who would meet your standards for me?"

"After tonight? Pretty much anything male who isn't Dex or Luc. You need a man with a whole name, for one thing." She exhaled. "Dex cares, he's just not good at expressing himself. I assume that's why you carry around that ridiculous scrapbook."

"My father would have been happy I'd found a good man who will care for me and our children!"

Eileen stayed calm but didn't change her tactics. "You

don't have to go home for the ring. Stay here and let Dex buy you one. He may not have seen anything in that dance of yours, but trust me, I felt the electricity. If you were in one of my yoga classes, I'd make you leave for the force field of electromagnetic energy you brought with you."

Katie had to go to New Orleans. It was her last chance to find out why Luc had tossed her from his life like a banana peel off the back of her father's pickup. Love was a decision. A choice. All the leading experts said so, and she'd decided she would love Dexter in a way that honored and respected him. The way she'd loved Luc left her worn out and depleted, like an empty air mattress. Then what use was she? She'd get her ring and closure as well. Then nothing would stand in the way of her life with Dexter.

Chapter 5

FLY ME TO THE MOON

Luc watched intently from the window as Katie approached his plane. He'd wanted to share this part of his life with her for so long, but he treaded carefully. She believed, in some ill-conceived way, that he'd made all his money on the back of her father's failure. It wasn't true, but what was it they said about perception being reality? In regard to Katie, her truth was all that mattered, and he had a big PR fight on his hands where she was concerned. He thumbed through the rag that ran their picture together and smiled to himself. How he'd missed her, that fiery soul that hid behind her schoolmarm exterior. She may have forgotten how God used her passion, but he hadn't. The real Katie was hidden under that bushel of someone else's idea of godliness. He needed to find the kindest, gentlest way to tell her the truth before she married that fellow without a pulse. He only hoped it wasn't too late.

Katie's magnificent eyes drank everything in as she climbed the steps. She slid her hand along the doorframe, as if to appreciate the small details. In many ways she was still like a child, filled with wonder at every new discovery. Luc had made the mistake once of believing Katie's affection for daily living was mere immaturity. Only now did he understand, in his own aloof treatment of the world, that he'd forgotten how to show gratitude. After watching her with Dexter, Luc blamed himself for the practical, lifeless future she'd arranged for herself.

As luxurious as his private plane may have been, the interior came to life as Katie stepped inside of its hull. It was now as it should have been, his surrounding world in color. She made it matter.

He drank her in; her long, luscious legs in a smart white pencil skirt and red polka dot silk blouse. Her shapely legs were highlighted by a pair of sky-high white stilettos, a far cry from the sloppy tennis shoes captured in the tabloid photos. "You wore those to travel?"

He could have smacked himself for the comment the moment it came out his mouth. What he really thought was that he had never seen anything more beautiful than this woman, that he felt honored she would bother to look nice for the trip, and that her effort did not go unnoticed. But it was too late now. It was as if his mouth had separated from his brain and gone completely offtrack.

"I couldn't fit them in my suitcase, and I didn't want to leave them home. They go with the gown. I figure if Ginger could bloody several pairs of shoes for that dance scene, I could fulfill my obligation for one night. Besides, they're for my wedding, and I need to practice in them. Do you like them?" She twisted, and her tender calf muscle swelled toward him.

He choked out a cough. "Your wedding? I thought you weren't even engaged yet."

"Not all of us are billionaires. Some of us have to plan ahead. Aren't they cute with the little Mary Jane bow? Very retro, don't you think?"

"That's right. Not all of us are billionaires. Not even me."

She grinned at his correction. Katie was determined to call him a billionaire. The more he objected, the more pleasure she seemed to take in the label.

"I'm parched." He rubbed his hand across his mouth. "Do you want some water?"

She dismissed his attempt to change the subject. "This way, I'll have them worn in before my wedding and I'll be able to dance blissfully all night, without blisters." Katie twisted her legs a bit more, again illuminating the taut muscles in her calves.

Luc licked his lips, rubbed his chin, and averted his eyes. *How does she do that?* She made him feel as weak as a kitten, and he clenched his fists to combat the emotions. He took the garment bag from her arm. "This is the dress, I assume?"

"That's it. I didn't want to put it in cargo. Just in case something leaks."

"Wise move, but we'd better hope nothing leaks." He laughed. "I'll just hang it back here in the closet. Let me give you a tour." He took her handbag, a slouchy, macramé-looking thing that reminded him of a sea grass chair his momma used to sit in on warm afternoons. Katie made no move to follow him, so he slung the garment bag over his shoulder and studied her fluttery movements. "Are you afraid to fly in a small plane?"

"Wasn't until you asked me." She twisted a strawberry-blond wisp of hair at her neck. "You're far too important to let anything happen to you, so I figure that makes me safe."

"I would never let anything happen to you." He tried to reach for her, but she pivoted and ran her hand along the white leather chair.

"Mmm. Like buttah! I bet if my shoes were made out of this leather, I wouldn't have to break them in."

"You were never one to shy away from adventure. But don't worry—my pilot is navy-trained and sharp as a tack." He began to walk toward the right aisle and hoped she'd follow.

Katie made no move toward the hall. She was still taking in everything within the main cabin.

He waited. "I'll assume the car was there on time. They brought your bags?"

"The driver gave them to the man loading stuff. Down the steps in stowage, I guess." She bent down and glanced out the window, then turned to meet his gaze. "Yep. They got it." Katie straightened her arms and leaned against the table. "I thought you'd be in it."

"Sorry?"

"I thought you'd be in the car when it arrived. It was empty except for the driver."

"I should have been. I wasn't thinking. This weekend I'm here for you. Forages Foods can wait."

She shrugged. "This is a business arrangement. Naive of me to expect you to pick me up, I suppose. You never mentioned that as part of the package."

He stepped toward her and flipped on a switch. Sinatra's voice filled the cabin, and Luc crooned along. "Fly me to the moon . . ." He laughed. "I know, it's a fifties song. That's what you were thinking, wasn't it?"

"I love this song. The date isn't important." Katie put her ear to the speaker. "Good sound system. It's like Frank is here with us."

He hung the gown on a nearby hook and took her into his arms. He'd dreamed of dancing with Katie in his plane, so much, in fact, it was hard for him to differentiate and be in the moment.

She slid the hat from his head. "It's bad luck to wear a hat inside. Not to mention rude." She spun herself away and dropped into the leather bucket seat. He took the seat beside her and peered deeply into the pure, glass-green eyes. She turned and gazed out the window. "Will we be leaving soon?"

"Look me in the eyes, Katie."

She did, and he visibly saw her hard shell dissipate. The pale green of her eyes seemed endless in their depth, as though he could look for a lifetime and never know all of her. He wanted to keep her there, safely beside him, away from anyone who might harm her or, worse yet, dim her light within. He couldn't help but see Poindexter, a man void of real emotion, as a total threat to Katie's spirit. He would suck the life out of her, like a N'awliner sucked the head from a crawdad.

She spoke softly. "It hurts to look at you, Luc."

"Am I that ugly?" He grinned.

"Don't make fun of me. I made a mistake all those years ago because I loved you. I know men are different from women, but somehow I need to know I meant something to you. That night was special, and when I see you with all those women on the tabloids, it feels like my memories are nothing more than elaborate fantasies, that I never really knew you."

His jaw tightened. It killed him to know he'd been the one who hurt her. Now he had to hear that he continued to do so. "You know better than that. Look at me, Katie. At me. Not what the tabloids say, not what the business section says, not what anyone says but your own heart."

Her eyes were wide. "I can't trust my own heart. It sees what it wants to see."

"What does it see?" He placed her hand across his heart.

"Forget I said anything. Dexter wouldn't approve of this conversation, and that's reason enough not to have it."

Dexter. Milquetoast. Dexter wouldn't defend Katie against a manic cat. Luc knew the type, upstanding on the outside, seething with internal anger at their own helplessness on the inside. "No, we *should* talk about that night. The nights that followed. I need for you to understand the truth. Why I—"

She stopped him. "Is someone here with us?"

"The pilot's in the cockpit," he said. Just then, a woman emerged from the back of the plane. "And Linda," he added, but judging by Katie's expression, his explanation lacked full disclosure.

Linda Grubner, his full-time air hostess, prowled into the cabin. Her long limbs crawled with a spider's thoughtfulness and a stalking cat's forethought. Luc looked at her as though for the first time. Normally he looked right past her, but today he noticed that she resembled a nurse on a Spanish soap opera, and he wondered what Katie thought of his hiring her.

Linda possessed sleepy brown eyes and unnaturally engorged lips, but she had a heart of gold and loved her husband with a vengeance—but Katie couldn't know that. Linda smoothed the front of her hips in a sensual way and welcomed his guest.

"You must be Katie. Welcome aboard. I'm Linda, your hostess. Luc has told me so much about you. Katie this, Katie that. Girl, I don't know what you've done to possess Luc so heartily, but if you have any secrets, let me know so I can use them on my husband."

"No, no." Katie shook her head. "You've got it all wrong. Luc and I have been friends for a long time. We simply grew up together."

"Mmm hmm. You are really beautiful. I think I know why Luc is so smitten. Redhead, huh?"

Luc could practically hear Katie's thoughts . . . *And you*

must be the reason for the bed in the back room. He shook his head. Katie wouldn't think such an errant, evil thing. Although the press accused him of being an international playboy, Katie knew him better than that. He hoped.

"Well, Katie, may I get you something to drink?" Linda asked. "I have green tea."

"Green tea?"

"I asked Eileen what I should have on hand for you," Luc explained, "and she told me you liked green tea."

Katie giggled. "I hate green tea. Eileen's life mission is to cleanse everyone from their taste buds."

"Hey now, don't mock being healthy on this plane. People wanting to be healthy paid for it."

"Nothing for me now, Linda. Maybe when we're ready for take off. Thanks. Luc, do you want to show me around now?"

Her calmness alerted Luc—he wondered what she was really thinking. "We can see it later," he said. "I think Rob is about ready to take off."

"Rob's not even on the plane, Luc," Linda said. "Gary wants to know what time I'll be home on Sunday. Any idea yet?"

Luc tried to read Katie's expression, but she revealed nothing. "Maybe about three," he answered absently. "Rob's just doing final checks. He'll be on board soon. To quote our good friend Bette, fasten your seat belt, Katie."

"I'll just wander back first. It's not every day a girl from the Channel gets to walk around on the lush white carpeting of a private plane. You take this all for granted now."

He watched as she tottered down the hallway, the way her pencil skirt hugged her curves seductively. Katie exuded the perfect forties pinup image. She'd placed his fedora on her head, and the shadow over her eyes made Ingrid Bergman's *Casablanca* stint pale in comparison. Their love affair with the past was easily attainable in the here and now, and he reminded himself he'd never backed down from a challenge before. There would never be another woman for him.

He followed her, pointing out the amenities. "The burled wood was an upgrade. Nice, isn't it?" He spoke over her shoulder.

She turned and he looked into those eyes. Those amazing green eyes.

"It's lovely, Luc. I'm so proud of you. I always knew you'd be successful, but I never imagined you'd do this."

"It was a good part luck," he said. "Luck of the Irish Channel."

"It was more than luck. Luck of the Irish never did my Paddy any good." She ran her hand along the wood, and he noted the long, slender fingers. "Paddy's grocery business was a one-man shop. And now look at you. Your private plane is practically bigger than his shop on Magazine Street. He would have been proud of you too."

"You think so, Katie?"

"My father never wished anything but success for anyone. I wish he could have seen what selling vegetables might become. He never would have imagined this."

"Your father had an idea that was ripe before its time. That's all."

"My dad couldn't have conceived of a world where people paid more to eat healthy. It was just something he did because of his love for the land. He'd heard too much about the Potato Famine, and he never wanted to have his family in that situation. Food was the safest option for him, but getting rich was never his goal."

Luc fiddled with the box in his pocket. He could tell her the truth right now. He could hand her what she wanted and let her get off the plane before she ever found out the ring wasn't in New Orleans or in her mother's possession. But that would place her squarely in the arms of Dexter Hastings, a man who wasn't fit to wipe her lace-up forties pumps. The trip would buy him time, and he'd need all of it to make up for what he'd squandered.

He followed her down the narrow hallway of the plane. Five leather seats made up the front half of the plane; the bathroom was in the center, between the two hallways; and in the back was a bedroom. The bed stretched sideways, the width of the entire plane. He'd made the mistake of telling Linda that Katie was his first love, and the cream-colored duvet and brown pillows were sprinkled with red rose petals. A tray at the center of the mattress held two champagne flutes, a bowl of fresh strawberries, and a bottle of apple cider (since he'd also mentioned Katie didn't drink—which might have suggested she wasn't likely to sleep with him on his plane, but apparently Linda's deduction skills didn't go that far). Looking at Katie's wide eyes, he didn't have to be Sam Spade to figure she thought this was part and parcel of a trip on his private plane.

Katie opened the cabinet at the headboard. Upon finding it empty, she slid it shut.

"Looking for something?" he asked, careful to avoid the obvious questions her eyes translated.

"I was just wondering if there was more. You know, to warm me up."

"Did you want there to be?" he said in his most roguish voice, but she rolled her eyes and left the bedroom. He could hardly blame her. *Beyond cheesy.* His fedora style felt less Humphrey Bogart and more sniveling Peter Lorre.

He followed Katie back to the main cabin, where she sank into the white leather seat, kicked off her heels, and rubbed her bare feet on the plush carpet beneath her. "This is heavenly. I bet you have someone else to pass the vacuum in here."

"I pay someone to clean it, yes. Linda does the light pickup."

"And the seduction protocol. Nice touch . . . the rose petals."

Linda opened her mouth to protest, but Luc stopped her. "Linda, could you leave us, please?"

Linda escaped the room with the force of the Savoy Express.

Luc searched for the right words as though his life depended upon his ability to find them. It seemed he stumbled over his words with Katie whenever they mattered, and the thought of telling her the truth ebbed further from his grasp.

"This is nice," she said as she rubbed her hands along

the armrests. "It reminds me of your first clunker BMW. Remember that? You loved that car. You used to wax it all the time, even though it never made a bit of difference. The paint was gone, but I admired your determination."

He had loved that car. He loved the freedom it brought him, the escape from family expectations and the chance to think clearly. Even this plane hadn't brought him the peace of that old clunker.

"We got all the supplies for the school before I left," she said. "Thanks for taking care of that. We're interviewing for the third aide. That's more trouble. We have to have all their credentials in place, 'cause they need to work for the county. It might be easier to hire him or her as a volunteer and let the person be an employee of Forages Foods."

"A deal's a deal," he said.

"We're even, you and me. By the end of this trip, we'll be paid up in full. I will have faced my very public past, so there's no reason to dwell on us any longer. We will be left in the dark annals of history, where we as a couple belong."

"Why this guy, Katie?"

"Dexter's a good man. Solid, committed, and he wants the same things I do. Marriage and a family. He grew up without a father, so he's anxious to overcome that part of his past and be the best father he can."

Luc's stomach recoiled at the thought of someone else fathering Katie's children. His voice blustered harshly. "Solid? Committed? Are you looking for a dog or a husband?"

"I can't have babies with a dog."

Another physical blow to his gut. "How did you meet him?"

"I met him at church. In the singles group."

"Not where . . . how? Did he introduce himself? Did he ask the pastor about you? How did you come to know him?"

She shrugged. "Proximity, I guess. He was there. I was there. We organized so many singles events together, I think the group knew we were a couple before we did."

Luc reached for her hand and compressed her fingers in his grasp. "Katie, about this trip—"

Linda stepped out from the back room. "Sorry to disturb you, but we're ready to take off. I need to pull the door shut."

Katie snatched her hand away and clicked her seat belt. She leaned into her slouchy bag and pulled out a book, which she cracked open, then snapped shut. "I want to watch us take off first. I'll be able to tell my grandchildren about being on the mighty Luc DeForges' private plane."

"Can I get you something to drink now?" Linda asked her.

"Just a water, if you have it."

"Perrier? SmartWater or flavored mineral?"

"Just water, please."

Linda trotted off to the kitchen, and Katie dropped the book into her lap. She opened her mouth but stopped herself. She tried again with the same result.

"I'm still the same man, Katie. The one you see. Not the image. Don't let other people tell you the truth; decide it for yourself."

"The man I knew wouldn't ask me to do this. He wouldn't ask me to show up at a family wedding in front of all the

74

people I lived out my worst nightmare in front of. He wouldn't humiliate me that way."

"Katie, I'm taking you home to make things right. I'd never do anything to cause you harm. Even then I had my reasons . . ."

A scowl crossed her face, but anger gave way to pain as a tear slid down her cheek onto her cherry red Joan Crawford lips. He nearly crushed the velvet box in his pocket.

"Katie, they don't think badly of you for that night. They know I'm to blame."

"I'm not that girl anymore. I know differently now. I'm strong enough to stand up in front of all of them, to sing my heart out and dance to as much Glenn Miller as I can stomach. They didn't define me. They only made me a stronger version of myself."

He squeezed her hand again. "Stop battling me, Katie. Trust me. Just a little."

Linda emerged from the kitchen, a SmartWater in one hand and a glass in the other. "Can I get you anything to eat before we take off? Crackers? Brie? Sliced apples? I'll be serving lunch at eleven thirty unless you request it earlier."

Katie lifted her water, unscrewed the cap, and took a long swig. "No glass. I'm Irish. We like it out of the bottle."

Luc laughed, and Linda stood stick-straight. "That's all, Linda."

Katie stared at him. Her mesmerizing green eyes captivated him beyond reason, as though they had a direct line to scramble his brain. Those eyes spoke volumes, more than most women translated in fifteen minutes of speech. She blinked slowly, her lips slightly parted, and he wondered if he was ready for whatever she had to say.

The best defense is a good offense.

"You're wrong about my family," he said. "My mother cared deeply for you."

"She loved me as long as I knew my place, and I do. I hope you've told her I'm engaged elsewhere, so your family knows my sights are no longer set on the wonderful and mighty Luc DeForges. Your mother can make some other worthy girl queen of the castle. It's a position I no longer covet."

"Katie." He dropped his chin, pained that she could believe such things about him. But what had he done to prove his love for her? She didn't know the truth. She couldn't know the truth, or it would only put her father's death more into question. He clutched the box in his pocket again and wondered how he could protect her from the truth and still manage to explain why he possessed her grandmother's wedding ring.

He hadn't thought this through. He'd never give that engagement ring to Poindexter. He hadn't held on to it for eight years to give it to Katie for a loveless practical marriage. He'd had his suspicions about her engagement, but meeting Dexter Hastings only confirmed his thoughts. Katie had given up on love, and Luc had no one to blame but himself.

~

Chapter 6

Easy Living

A wall of hot, thick, moist air assaulted Katie as she stepped off the plane. Her forehead sprang moisture before she'd reached the second step. She'd forgotten the sluggish weight of the summer weather in New Orleans. How a simple exercise like breathing required more effort. She had, in fact, lost her gills. She slid her heels back on before she stepped onto the tarmac. Raising her arms above her, she embraced the steamy heat. She closed her eyes and stepped back into the memories, when she smelled the sweet jasmine and raced to suck on cherry popsicles before they won the battle and melted, draping her in a sticky mess.

"You okay?" She felt Luc's hand in the center of her back.

"I'm home," she yelled over the noise of the tarmac. "It's been eight years!" Her mind filled with thoughts of food. There were delicacies that could only be found in New Orleans, and when her feet hit the ground, dreams of oyster po' boys and blue plate mayonnaise made her lick her lips. "Can we eat now?"

"You're home in style." Luc waved a hand toward a waiting limousine. "A triumphal entry. Did you notice how quiet my jet was compared to all the rest?"

"Luc, sweetie, you have the biggest trophy and the best."

"I only meant—"

She slipped into the car. "My mother will say I'm putting on airs."

"That she will. Wait until she gets a load of the feathers."

"Where do the pilot and Linda stay while you're gone?"

Luc touched her face. "You always did make sure everyone was taken care of, didn't you?"

"I'm not a doormat any longer, if that's what you mean."

The driver appeared at the door, slammed it shut, and came around to the driver's seat. He was a fat black man with an affable smile and a silver front tooth. "Where y'at?"

"I'm good, Leon, how are you?"

"Oh, you know, I's all right. Who dat ya got wit ya?"

"This is Katie, but she's no tourist, Leon. She's from the Irish Channel. It's been eight years since she's been home."

"No kiddin'?" Leon whistled. "Eight years. You ain't gon believe the changes. What street? You gon yo momma's?"

"My momma moved," Katie said. "To the Upper Garden District."

78

"Too bad. Master DeForges, you'll have to take her by the new Irish Channel. She won't believe her eyes. All them new shops and restaurants."

"Katie's dad owned my first shop. That's how I got my start."

"The one on Magazine Street? No kidding. Well, ain't that something. Where you live now?"

"California," she answered. "Northern California."

"That's a right shame."

"It's not home, that's for certain."

Naturally, the Irish Channel would be up and coming once her mother moved away. If there was a way to lose money, her family had always been gifted with the ability. If Luc was gifted with an ability to turn vegetables into gold, her mother was gifted with the ability to melt precious metals into useless minerals. Fortunately, her mother cared little for the finer things in life, so Katie imagined it didn't make much difference to her one way or another—as long as there was a bounty of food on the table.

The drive from the airport brought her to the harsh reality of seeing Mam, and Katie's pulse increased with each passing block. Luc slid closer to her in the limo, as if he sensed her rising anxiety. It was as though she felt the cloud lowering over her, the fog muddying her mind and her goals getting lost.

Luc took her hand and held it on the black leather seat. "It will be fine. I'm with you."

"You're going with me?"

"Don't you want me to? It's been a long time since you saw your mother. Have you even met her new husband?"

Katie shook her head, and he tightened his grasp around her fingers. She ventured a look at his face and immediately averted her eyes. She pulled her hand out from under his.

"It's all right to ask for help, Katie. Your mother never was the easiest woman to get along with. She just wants you to be happy."

They looked at one another and laughed.

"No, she doesn't!" they said in unison. Her mam wanted to tell her *how* to be happy, tell *everyone* how to be happy.

"Do you think she'll give me the ring?"

He glanced out the window before answering. "If she has it, I do. What could that ring mean to her now? It belonged to your father's mother, not hers. It's not worth a lot. It isn't as if the stone's the size of a golf ball."

She paused. "How would you know that?"

"Know what?"

"That the ring isn't valuable. How do you know that? My grandmother died before I ever met you or Ryan."

"I just assumed that your grandfather came from Ireland to work the docks. He didn't come with much, right? I'm sorry, maybe I assumed too much. I didn't mean—"

"No, you're right. He didn't. The ring isn't valuable, in fact. I mean, it's priceless to *me*, but in terms of . . ." She was blabbering. Eileen had told her to keep it brief, not to engage Luc any more than she had to, which is why she'd stuck her nose in a book for the entire flight. "Never mind."

"Don't you think your mother will want to meet Poindexter before you're engaged?"

"Dexter. His name is Dexter. Could you give me the benefit of calling him by name? And no, I don't think my mother will want to meet him." She fought the urge to say more.

"Your mother isn't going to meet Dexter until your wedding day? That seems strange, Katie. Even for you. I know this place brings up a lot of emotion for you, but it's in your blood. Can't ignore it forever."

"I've done a pretty good job for eight years."

"That you have." Luc sat back in his seat. "What did Dexter think of the magazine cover?"

"Gosh, would you look how this place has changed? I hardly recognize it," she said, gazing out the window. "So many new buildings—"

"Meaning, you didn't show the magazine to him?"

She turned toward him, her face red with shame. "Not yet, but I will. See, Luc, you get that I'm the type of girl who ends up with my bum on the cover of a national magazine and why I would be doing something like smacking my ponytail across somebody's face. But I'm not that girl anymore, so explaining that scenario to Dexter isn't as easy as it sounds. He knows me as the lead singer in the church band and the hardworking teacher who takes her job home with her at night. He doesn't remember an awkward, gangly girl who posed as a lounge singer to make her way through college."

"What do you mean, awkward? When were you awkward exactly? You were stunning then, and you're stunning now.

And I thought the pictures were very telling. Dexter should know he's getting an Irish temper, don't you think? Full disclosure and all that?"

"I don't have an Irish temper with Dexter. He's a calming influence, like the sea. You are the only one who brings out my temper, which is ultimately why it was a good thing you dumped me."

"I didn't dump you, Katie. When I watched you in the sound booth, Ryan told me you were way out of my league and not to bother. I never got that out of the back of my mind, I guess."

She forced a laugh. "So that's why you turned down my proposal? I was out of your league? Really, Luc? That's so convenient, and I'll bet it works great in the Southland. Here, let me try it. You were too good for me"—she draped the back of her hand on her forehead and took on a Southern accent—"so I dumped your sorry self."

"You *should* try that. Want me to dial Poindexter for you? He'd buy that line easily enough. He obviously believes in his own magnificence. But just for the record, things did not go down that way between you and me. Your memory is flawed."

She could feel Luc's voice, low and rich, in her chest. Somehow she'd never managed to shed the sense of security that resonance gave her.

"Luc, you've had eight years to fix whatever happened between us. You want me to believe it's a coincidence that you have to ensure I sing at your brother's wedding? Tell me this isn't just your ego and your competitive nature kicking in. Once you were convinced I'd choose you over Dexter, you'd fly off into the sunset and do whatever it is billionaires do with their time. Nibble on gold bars? Silverplate your toilets?"

"Are you through yet?" Luc asked in a tone that told her no one questioned him any longer. "I suppose it's useless for me to keep saying multimillionaire?"

"It makes no difference to the rest of us, Luc, but if it helps you sleep at night, go ahead, correct me. I'm more curious about your selective memory on dumping me. Tell me, what is it a billionaire such as yourself calls it when a young woman such as myself asks a man she loves to marry her because he said he wanted to get married, and such a young woman believes he may be too frightened to ask, so she, not being a wilting violet . . . and seeing as how she already has the engagement ring—what would you call it if she asked, and he said no?"

"Simple, really. I'd ask why."

"Rejection, thy name is Luc. Or is there a fancy French word for it? A Creole word? Acadian? Something you say up in the Garden District that works better than *dumped*? Please do inform me, so's I ain't so ignorant."

"Ooowee, she got yo numba," Leon said from the front seat. "She from the Channel, all right."

With that, Luc punched a button, and the window between them closed. "As I was saying, I did not dump you. I wanted you to finish grieving your father before we made any big decisions. I'm a planner, Katie. I was trying to do what was best for the two of us, and you were just moving full steam ahead rather than face your father's bankruptcy, then his death."

"It doesn't matter now." She tilted her chin toward the sun. "As you said, it was for the best. Oh, Luc!" She pointed out the window. "There's one of your stores! What does that feel like? To see something you built right out on the street like that?"

"I didn't say it was for the best, I said—"

She cut him off. "I promised Eileen we wouldn't talk about this without a chaperone. She said I need a witness or my brain gets all scrambled. I want the truth, but I need to take my time digesting it, like a good jambalaya—and maybe have the aid of a good friend, like Tums."

"Your brain was well enough to devour that book so that you didn't have to engage in conversation on the plane."

"Eileen says that you need to respect my boundaries. She told me that it's all right for me to set limits on what we discuss."

"Fine, Katie. I'm respecting your boundaries, not to mention all this New Age crap Eileen's spouting. Let's change the subject. Do we have time to stop by your father's store? I'd like you to see what I've done to it."

She twisted her knees around and faced him again. "Luc, you could have bought any business in the city. Why my father's?"

"Are you willing to hear the answer, or will the truth cross your boundaries?" Luc pressed the button again, and the window between the driver and the backseat lowered. "Leon, don't take us on St. Charles."

"Yes, sir."

Luc raised the privacy window again.

"Thank you."

"You have to face it sometime."

"But not yet, thank you. I'll bet Leon's never seen you so indecisive."

"Redheads scramble my brain." Luc took her hands into his. "Some part of you still trusts me, Katie. Some part of you questions what's written about me, because you know the truth. If you didn't, you wouldn't ask me about your father's store at all. You'd believe I bought it only because I saw dollar signs where a feeble old man was running out of energy to sell his vegetables." He pressed her hands to his chest. "You can feel the truth. Why can't you own it?"

She raised her eyes to him and felt his warm breath and the heat from his neck. When she looked into his eyes, the questions evaporated. "My family lost everything." She pushed off his chest and sat up straight. "How did that happen if you paid a fair price for the business? Paddy died before there were any answers, and you certainly didn't offer any. What was I supposed to think? What were any of us left to think?"

"I thought you'd give me the benefit of the doubt. Because I loved you, Katie. Because I still love you."

His words stopped her cold. "Eileen was right. You're scrambling the facts again, and I know less than I started with. I should never have come here with you. You're right, that I do want to believe you, but the fact is, I have no reason to trust you. Do I?"

"I suppose you don't."

"I'm not the same ignorant girl who followed you around like a puppy dog. I don't fall for your sweet words that drip like honey from your mouth anymore. That may work on your Hollywood starlets, but it won't work on me. Not anymore."

The way he looked at her, with those deep and meaningful gazes, she knew she was no match for him or his wiles. Why did she want to believe in him so heartily? She pictured Dex's bouquet in the kitchen pass-through—every Monday, come rain or shine. The little hearts and smiley faces that marked her scrapbook with all the thoughtful things he did for her. *Stability*. Luc's love went in and out with the tide. He'd perfected luring women. All the tabloids said so. He scooped them as easily up as an Arabi boy trapped crawfish.

As the car drew them farther into the city, she turned and faced the window again. Remnants of Hurricane Katrina loomed everywhere. Mostly in vast improvements, not the devastation. Granted, they weren't in the Lower Ninth Ward, but the city appeared cleaner. N'awliners had taken pride in their city, and when she was threatened, showed what they were made of. The changes reminded her of what her heart once looked like after Hurricane Luc DeForges.

She heard a click, and Nat King Cole's smooth voice emanated from the sound system. "I Love You for Sentimental Reasons." It was their song, the easy, smooth jazz stylings, the simple melody with a voice and feeling so pure, the words so haunting. It erased so much and took her back to those early moments when Luc introduced her to the jazz music scene, when one could easily pretend that the 1940s were alive and well and a poor college student, so inclined, could make a pretty penny singing the standards for visiting tourists. As though in a trance, she laid her head back on the seat and listened to the words. *I hope you do believe me. I've given you my heart.*

Luc sang the last part along with Nat, and when Katie opened her eyes, she saw him as though for the first time: worldly, knowledgeable, gorgeous, and *oh, so very danger-ous.* Her mother had warned her what boys from the Upper Ninth used girls like her for, but she was putty in his hands. Luc's mother may have introduced her to Jesus, but Luc introduced her to the Swing Era, and it was hard to say which one had changed her life more. If her faith were stronger, Luc would be no threat to her. Or to her life with Dexter. So why did she feel Luc's very presence beside her?

The limo pulled up to the house. She clutched the door's armrest. "Luc?"

"You knew her address," he said. "It's impossible to avoid St. Charles altogether, Katie. At some point—"

"But why here?"

Luc pulled her hand from the door and held it tightly. "She always wanted to be Uptown. Don't read too much into it."

"This can't be a block from where Paddy was killed. How could she? Does she pass it every day without so much as a glance?"

"Your mam might wonder how you could leave home without looking back."

Katie yanked at the door handle and let herself out before Leon could come around. She stepped onto the banquette and stared up at Mam's new house.

No shotgun houses here, with clumsy air-conditioning units poking out from the windows of buildings that showed their wear and tear. Uptown's houses stood tall and romantic with their ornate spindles and fancy porches, with upper terraces under the old shade trees.

"She started a new life here, so let's assume the best. Perhaps it was to honor your father."

"I don't think I can go in there." She knew everything about her stance screamed of desperation, but she didn't care. "Luc, I need to find a hotel. I can't stay here."

"Come to my mother's. She'll be happy to have you."

"Your mother won't have any room with the wedding on Saturday. Just take me to the French Quarter for the night."

"I'm not taking you to the French Quarter by yourself. You'll stay with us. If the rooms are filled, you'll stay in my room. I'll sleep in the pool house on the sofa."

"No." She straightened. "I don't need to be rescued. I'll do this." She strode toward the streetcar's tracks. "I'll do this alone."

He kicked his long legs out of the car and stood. "No," he stated plainly. "You won't. Leon, keep Katie's things in the trunk. She'll be coming with me to my mother's house."

Leon smiled as though he was used to Luc pulling that trick.

"I'm not staying at your mother's. Leon, I'll need to go to a hotel after this."

"Leon, I pay your salary. Katie's coming with me."

Katie heaved a sigh and climbed the front steps to her mother's new home, which wasn't actually all that new. She'd lived there for six years, been married to a new man for five. The house was a Queen Anne Victorian, divided into two townhouses. No doubt it was the only way her mother could afford to live Uptown, even with the insurance settlement after her father's death. Katie peered through the beveled glass window that lined the doorway.

"It's already been salmonized," she said, referring to the way her mother painted all interiors with a bright orange/pink color that made Katie feel as though she was living inside a fish. "It's another shrimp boil in the house."

Luc looked inside. "It's not that bad. It's Southern, and she likes it."

"You can take her out of the Irish Channel, but you can't take the Irish Channel out of my mother."

Katie rang the doorbell and tapped her foot on the painted front porch.

Luc shielded his eyes and peeked in the window again. "Is she expecting you?"

"I told her I was coming."

"Maybe she got the day wrong."

"She's really not in there?" She peered in the window again. All of the knickknacks and tchotches of her past lined the clean white mantel. She couldn't help but smile at the sight. The house had rich cherrywood floors, an ornate white banister, and gold bars lining each step, but her mother's touch was everywhere. If Irene McKenna Slater could make an Uptown house look early-American garage sale, she could do it to perfection. "I don't think she's here."

"Why don't we leave a note? Leon can bring us back this evening after supper."

She gazed at the long black vehicle, Leon's tubby body leaning against it with his feet crossed at the ankles. "I'll just wait. Why don't you have Leon get my things?"

Luc took her by the elbow. "I don't think so. First off, I'm not leaving you here alone. You'd call for a cab and check into a hotel. You really think I don't remember your tactics at all?"

"My *tactics*?"

"For getting your way. You're not exactly subtle, Katie. Not for a Southern woman."

Katie gave up and allowed herself to be led back down the stairs. She heard a door open and swung around to see the neighbor's door ajar and an elegant young woman in the doorframe. She looked like a New York socialite; white cuffed trousers and a multicolored tunic that clung loosely to her body with several necklaces hanging to her waist. The woman's arm slithered up the doorframe.

"Are you looking for the Slaters?" the young blonde asked.

"I am," she said. "I'm Katie McKenna, Irene's daughter."

"Oh yes, she said you were coming." The woman perused her, as if casually trying to ascertain the make of china on the bottom of a plate. "From California, right?"

"That's right." At least Mam remembered she was coming.

"Your momma's getting her hair done, and Rusty's at work. She always gets her hair done on Tuesdays—must not have expected you until later." The neighbor tipped her chin toward the limousine. "That's some car you got there. Hope you didn't waste your money counting on your momma seeing it."

Katie focused on the lantern hanging over Mam's door and swallowed her disappointment. "He works? Rusty, I mean. I haven't met him yet." She moved up the staircase toward the young woman. It seemed strange that a perfect stranger knew more about her own mother than she did, but did anyone truly know Irene Slater? Or did she slip in and out of personas as it suited the situation? She wondered what her mother was like now that she was someone else's wife.

"He's a shrimper. A commercial fisherman. You haven't met him? I thought they'd been married awhile." The woman leaned with her back against the doorframe and crossed her arms.

Something about her familiarity startled Katie. Her mam wasn't exactly the sharing sort.

"Season's closed now. Maybe he's catching grouper or catfish now, I don't really know. But he left early this morning, so I assume he's working. People keep weird hours in this city. We don't ask any questions."

Katie shrugged. "No, sure. I get ya. We'll be back later."

"I'm Helena. Y'all want to come in and wait?" Helena swung the door wide open, its beveled glass sending rainbows of light shards toward them. "You can come in for tea or coffee and wait here. I can rustle something up."

"Gosh, that's so sweet, but I'd like to freshen up and maybe unpack." She also had the urge to get away from this strange woman who seemed to be a creepy character from a Hitchcock film.

"You're not staying with your momma?"

No doubt that sounded strange, but Katie cared little how it sounded. "Oh, I'll be back." She sprinted down the stairs and flashed her eyes at Luc.

He grinned. "Nice to meet you, Helena!" He waved and pressed Katie's back until they were seated in the car once more. He closed the door and laughed. "Was it me, or did we just wander into a Tennessee Williams play?"

"Let's go see the streetcar. I may as well get this over with. It beats spending the afternoon with Blanche Dubois."

Chapter 7

If I Had You

Luc trailed behind Katie. She hesitated with each step and kept looking back for reassurance. He'd nod, and she'd move forward again. For once, she'd appreciated that Luc didn't listen. His silent support behind her drove her on to do what she had to do.

Where was Poindexter now, when Katie needed a strong hand at her side? Dexter probably had no idea Katie's dad had called her "the Empire of his eye," in homage to her favorite apple. If he even knew the difference between an Empire and any other kind. And he'd never know how she'd come by the nickname Katie-bug.

Luc knew Dex's type: competent at his job but not

management material—maybe on a few committees at church, a smile plastered on his face, but not an ounce of genuine joy in his soul. Righteous and heartless. No doubt the man had let Katie off the leash to show himself as the bigger man, unafraid and overly confident. No man who truly loved Katie would ignore such a threat or trust another man's honor before the vow was made.

Or maybe Luc just knew his own intentions.

They walked slowly, solemnly. Unlike the jazzy celebration of a typical New Orleans funeral, this walk brought no joy or release from mourning. As they approached St. Charles Avenue, Luc felt Katie's steps slowing further. She turned her face to him, and he reached for her. "I'm right here, Katie. Let's do this. Your dad's not here. He's rejoicing with the host of heavenly angels, maybe feeding them fresh grapes. This walk is for you, not him."

Katie nodded and took his proffered hand. "Was my father sad that day? I mean, did he—"

"Paddy wasn't himself. He was distraught but not in the way the insurance company tried to portray. He wasn't desolate. He just wasn't himself, not jovial, and he was worried about what was next. He knew the business sale would cover the debts. He had no reason to do what they implied. You and I both know Paddy valued life too much to take his own."

"The insurance company just didn't want to pay. That's why they started that vicious rumor. All those years my dad hyped insurance, and that's how they repaid him; dragging his name through bayou mud."

"No one ever believed it, Katie. Your father wasn't capable of such an act. He was upset, but he couldn't have hurt you that way if he tried."

"Some people did believe it, and worse, some said it. They told my mother his soul wouldn't go to heaven, that he'd committed a mortal sin."

"People can be cold sometimes. You know the truth. Your father loved you so much. He would never choose to be away from you, Katie. Never."

She halted and let her head drop to his shoulder. He pressed her head against his chest and wrapped his arms around her. They stood on busy St. Charles Avenue, cars rushing by, the rattling of the streetcar in the center median, and he felt her tense frame relax in his embrace. Her body trembled underneath him, and he circled his arms around her tiny waist. Her eyes swam behind a wall of tears as her gaze focused on the grass-covered central median and the tracks.

Between them and the tracks, more cars bustled by on their way uptown, or perhaps to Audubon Park. Life went on around them, oblivious to the heart-wrenching struggle going on inside the woman he loved. Eventually another streetcar came into view in the historic green, and Katie's body stiffened against him. He tightened his grasp upon her until the car passed and her stance released.

"My father loved this city, everything about it. I wonder if he laughed in heaven, maybe found it comical that his demise came from the St. Charles streetcar, that he'd been eliminated by the tourists he thought of as a blight on his beloved city."

"Maybe he did." Luc thought of the crooked posture of Mr. McKenna that fateful day and how sidetracked the old man appeared after giving up his last family valuable. He wished he understood why Paddy had left the ring with him. And why on that fateful day? If only he'd gone with him and made sure that he'd gotten home. Katie's life would have been different.

The man's Irish pride wouldn't allow him to run the business after Luc purchased the store. Luc learned a lifelong lesson from that; never thumb your nose at opportunity, and don't ever let pride blind you to the right course of action. His riches had brought him nothing that Mr. McKenna didn't have in his small vegetable shop. Money brought respect from all the wrong people.

"Katie, you've had enough. Let's go. Do you want to go and find your mother? No doubt she's getting her hair done in one of those fancy new salons on Magazine Street."

"I can wait." Katie started walking toward the house again, and he noticed how easily she maneuvered the uneven, cracked sidewalk in her heels. As she swayed rhythmically in front of him, he marveled at what a dancer's body she still possessed. As if she was born to swing and move with the grace of a wildcat. He remembered the first time he ever saw her, on the stage at the Barrelhouse. She seemed to have been transported from the forties in a heavenly, redheaded Betty Grable package.

Suddenly Katie turned on her heel in front of him. "Do you think her husband is a boy toy?"

"Do I what?"

"My mother's husband. He works, so he's got to be young enough to work, right? Do you think he's young enough that it's scandalous?"

"I think you would have heard by now if he was. What's he look like in the Christmas card?"

Katie shrugged. "My mom doesn't send them anymore. At least not to me. She said she didn't want me to have any preconceived ideas."

"Sounds like 'boy toy' is a preconceived idea. She should know her daughter better. The truth is better than your imagination."

"They got married in Vegas, and she sent a picture then. He just looked like a working stiff, tanned, leathery skin. I never thought it was a possibility, so I didn't look too closely." She started walking again. Then she turned and smiled. "I did it, Luc. I saw where my dad died."

"You did. I'm proud of you." He paused on the street and felt in his pocket for the velvet box. "Katie, before we get back to your mother's house. About your father. That day."

He wanted to tell her that her father had looked after her, that he'd taken care of things, but he stopped mid-thought. He didn't want her to think Mr. McKenna had given him the ring so that he might end his life. That wasn't the case. Luc knew it wasn't, and yet he'd kept the ring a secret rather than let the insurance company think they had evidence concerning Mr. McKenna's demise.

He only had five days to tell Katie the truth, or as much

of it as she could digest, but his mouth wouldn't relinquish the words. Naturally, he had his own selfish reasons for wanting to hold on to the ring. Maybe he'd been selfish all along to keep it, to avoid the love he felt for her rather than hurt her with facts her father had kept from her. He felt torn, ripped up inside, and time was closing in. Poindexter loomed with his offer, while his own inaction sent Katie into the arms of another man.

"Luc, what is it?"

"Nothing. I'm glad we came here. It's done, right?"

"Next up, fear of commitment," she said.

"Katie, I need to tell you something—"

Katie's cell phone rang, and her body tightened again. She pulled away and left him in that way she did—where she went away, though her body never moved. She fumbled through her floppy purse until she pulled out the phone and cut off the persistent rendition of "In the Mood."

"It's two already?" she asked before answering. "Hello . . . Yes, we're here at my mom's house, but she's not here . . . No, no problems with the flight." She paused. "No, I haven't gotten the ring yet, but I haven't seen my mother either . . . Yeah, he's right here. You want to talk to him?"

Katie handed him the phone, which he could hardly refuse without looking like a wuss.

"Hello?" He couldn't imagine what Poindexter had to say to him.

"Yes, this is Dexter Hastings speaking."

"I figured. What can I do for you? You need someone to kiss her good night for you?"

"Funny. Listen, I know Katie had to go home to get that ring, but I would appreciate it if you didn't let her spend too much time around her mother. I don't think the woman is a good influence on her."

Luc turned away from Katie. "It's her mother," he said quietly. "Katie survived childhood, I think she'll make it through the next few days."

"Be that as it may, Katie and I have gone through a proper, biblical premarital class, which spoke of leaving one's family to cleave to your new family. I see no reason why she should start up a new relationship with her mother now that all that water is under the bridge. So . . . do I have your word?"

"My word for what?"

"That you'll keep Katie from her mother's undue influence?"

"Dexter, Katie's a grown woman. She does what she wants." Luc looked right at Katie when he said the words. "Have you met our little Katie?"

"Katie is going to be my wife, and I would like her to be free of this baggage when she comes to marriage. That's hardly too much to ask from a longtime friend such as yourself."

"I think it is, actually. Chin up, Dex. Things are never so bad they can't get worse."

"Shakespeare?"

"Bogart." He snapped the phone shut and handed it back to Katie. "What is wrong with that guy?"

"Did you hang up on him?"

"Shakespeare? Give me a break. Katie, you can't marry that guy. He thinks dealing with your mother is a violation of your marriage contract. I can't wait for him to meet her and see who is actually in charge here. There's something not right about him."

"Well, that's the pot calling the kettle a certain color." Her phone rang again, and she walked ahead of him and answered it. She kept staring back at him as she spoke.

How could his beloved Katie, whose heart beat wildly on her sleeve, give up so much to enter into a marriage void of real love? And it was void, like Dexter himself. Luc's own motives suddenly felt very selfish. As if Katie was a pump that needed to be primed. His treatment of her had affected her in ways he couldn't possibly imagine, and he got to watch the whole nightmare play out in front of him. Not until now, when he witnessed what she was willing to give up for marriage and a family of her own, did he understand the repercussions of what he'd done.

"Don't marry him!" he shouted ahead to her. "You want to get married, we'll get married, but you can't offer up your hand for that. Are you kidding me?"

She shushed him with a wave of her hand and finally said good-bye and closed her phone. "As irresistible as that heartwarming gesture was, I think I'm going to stick with my fiancé." She laughed. "I'm not desperate to get married." She forced his eyes to hers. "I'm not settling, Luc. I'm marrying Dexter because he wants the same things I do. Because Dexter would never let me make a fool of myself in front of his family. Or reject me in front of all of our acquaintances. Maybe he's not all moonlight and roses, but maybe I had enough of that. Maybe I learned that pretty words amount to a lot of nothing in the long run."

His jaw twitched. "I was a kid, Katie. A jerk, all right? Are you ever going to forgive me?"

He stood on the cracked sidewalk and watched her gentle, feminine stride as the distance between them increased. He'd let eight years pass without telling her the truth. Only an idiot would have allowed a girl like Katie, with her perfect reddish-blond hair and absorbing green eyes that saw into one's soul, to languish for eight years. Whether it was love of money or just an avoidance of reality by staying busy, he'd raised his own grave. Was it any wonder she stood ready with the rake to push his bones to the back of the vault?

"I forgive you, Luc." Her smiling eyes spoke the words, so that he felt them. "I forgave you a long time ago. Is that what you wanted to talk with me about?"

He stood, transfixed by her eyes, filled with warmth and a connection he'd never known before. He touched her face and let his hand trail her cheek. "You can't marry Dexter."

"Luc, there are a billion reasons why I'm going to do just that."

Chapter 8

~

It's Been So Long

Katie felt Luc's presence behind her; like a sixth sense, her body registered his closeness. She wished to high heaven that would stop. It was unnerving. Maybe it was only their shared love of the forties time frame that bound them together. After this week, she'd leave that in her past too. And if that didn't work, she'd trample his fedora under her stiletto. This time she'd give the photographer her full name, spelling included.

The hanging moss draped from the eerie, life-filled oaks that might have told stories for centuries. She slowed down, savoring her walk past the galleries with their porch swings behind wrought iron gates, breathing deeply the moist air with its intoxicating scent of magnolias. Each step reminded her what made the city of New Orleans greener, richer, and deeper than any destination she'd hope to travel to. The energy of the place filled her with warmth and soothing memories of good food, laughter around the table, and—love. She felt enveloped by the atmosphere and the emotion of being wrapped up in someone's arms.

"It's like the city has a pulse, isn't it?" Luc asked, as if reading her mind.

"A steady one," she agreed.

"With the occasional palpitation." He swept his gaze to the ground and back to her. "Katie—"

"You know what I love about my job. What do you love about hawking vitamins?"

He cocked a brow. "That's what you think I do?" He strode in front of her. She quickened her step and followed.

"Vitamins, herbs, green algae drinks that no human with taste buds can swallow, homemade soups that taste like someone softened the cat food with vegetable broth. Oh, and baked goods minus the gluten and any sense of moisture. Do I have everything now?"

He looked behind him. "I see the real Katie has returned. Obviously, overcoming the St. Charles' streetcar caused a spark. My soup is good. Have you ever tried it?" He pointed to a fountain filled with green water as they passed a house. "It may look like that, but it tastes fantastic."

She laughed. "Luc, I love your stores, and everything is delicious. But I'm a teacher and Eileen's a yoga instructor. She makes everything herself. Haven't you ever heard you're supposed to shop the outside of a market for the freshest, cheapest ingredients?"

"I've heard it. Done everything I can to overcome that advice, including requiring customers to take a more round-about tour of the store, not dash in and out of aisles."

"I was just testing to see if I could still get to you. It appears I can."

"Congratulations."

"Least I could do. I like to keep that ego of yours in check, especially after making my tabloid debut. Maybe I'll get my own reality show now. Mam would be so proud." As they passed the houses in her mam's neighborhood, it dawned on her how little had changed inside of her. She could take out a stick right now and run it along the fence with a clacking sound, and listen to Luc's ideas and dreams as though she was nineteen again and her whole life was in front of her.

Mam's house came into view, and they both halted. "Before your mam sees us . . . have you told Dexter? About us, I mean?"

"What choice did I have, Luc? I can't marry a man without his knowing about my past. It wouldn't be honest—especially since half of New Orleans knows and he'd find out eventually."

"I'm sorry, Katie. You meant more to me than that. What happened was my fault, and I take—"

"Save it. It doesn't matter now. We were weak, and I guess we both paid the price."

"I don't want to pay the price for the rest of my life, Katie. You're the only woman I ever lov—"

She put her fingertips over his mouth. "Don't say it. Don't ever say it to me again. If you can't say it in front of Dexter, don't say it to me."

Her phone rang again, Etta James resonating on the street. Eileen.

Luc threw his hands in the air. "Doesn't that guy have a job?"

Katie walked away from him for privacy. "Hello."

"Katie, how are things going? What was the plane like?"

"Good. Good. Jolly ride here. Yes, Luc is right here."

"Call me the minute you ditch him, okay?"

"We're in the Garden District—near where my father . . . you know. Luc was kind enough to make the trip with me."

"I'm worried about you. I couldn't teach my class this morning, thinking of what Luc might try on the plane. Did he try anything? Because if he tried anything, so help me—"

Katie looked back at Luc. "Things are fine."

"Did he try to kiss you?" Eileen grumbled more. "I knew I shouldn't have let you go alone. The lech."

"Nothing of that nature, no." She twisted away from Luc's ear.

"Just remember. Whatever he's said to you? He's probably told three women the same thing this week."

Katie looked back at Luc and truly wondered. Could a man be that good at faking devotion? She turned away again. "You'd be proud of me. I know my future, and I'm going to leave the forties where they belong after this week. My nana wouldn't want me living in the past. It's no good romanticizing an era that's long gone. There are no heroes. No one is coming to rescue me."

"You don't need rescuing. You are a modern woman, capable of taking care of yourself. So it's a little weird you listen to music from a bygone era and worship dead crooners. At least you didn't bring voodoo with you. Listen, I'm trying to get my classes covered so I can come. My momma says Pokey isn't doing well, and I don't want to miss his last days. It's bad enough I abandoned him with my mother."

Pokey, named after the Pokey Little Puppy, was the runt of a litter of puppies left outside her father's store when the girls were in college. Katie and Eileen had taken the puppy home to the dorm but soon got caught with their contraband, so Pokey had to live with Eileen's mom.

"What's the matter with him?" Katie walked ahead of Luc to get a little privacy, but she turned toward the street rather than approach the final walk to Mam's house. Leon had been quietly trailing them in the limo, and Katie wondered if Luc would get in and leave her there on the street, but they both stayed in position, as if Katie was a pace car in the world's slowest race.

"Duh, he's old. Momma says he groans all day and walking looks painful, so I'm coming home. I thought I might as well come while you're there. Kill two birds with one stone and all that."

"Can you afford to come on such short notice?"

"Yeah. I'm going to bill Luc for all the time I've spent pulling you out of your misery. I mean, he owes me more than airfare in Ben & Jerry's alone."

"Eileen, you are not going to take advantage."

"Are you kidding me? You will not feel sorry for him. I just have to find someone to take over my five a.m. boot camp and I'm covered."

"It can't be true that there's another person willing to get up at that time to hurt other people for money."

"I change people's lives," Eileen said in her drill sergeant voice. "There is nothing like a workout at the crack of dawn. It detoxes the mind, wakes up the brain, and gets one recharged for life. Who *wouldn't* want to take my place is the question."

"People who would rather have Cocoa Pebbles with coffee for breakfast at around, say, nine a.m.?"

"Don't you dare eat garbage while you're out there. And tell your mam no fried anything!"

"I'm kidding. I have Café du Monde here. Why on earth would I bother with cereal when I can have beignets?"

"Seriously, Katie, that food takes years off your life. Are you bugging me to avoid discussing your feelings for Luc? The plane ride didn't rekindle anything, right? You're not going to do anything stupid while you're gone?"

"I'm fine. I'll be home on Sunday with the ring—and maybe a few extra pounds."

Eileen sighed. "Call me back after you see your mother and as soon as you ditch Archie Leach. Did you notice my Cary Grant reference? That was just for you."

"Speak of the devil," Katie said. "Mam's sitting on her rocking chair in her own wrought iron gallery under the balcony. If I could give you a visual, she'd be the creaky old man in the Pirates of the Caribbean ride. Eileen, you should see her place. No more shotgun house that you could send a bullet through in one fell swoop. She's in the Garden District, in a real house with a wrought iron balcony and spindle fencing. She has a real New Orleans garden. She's practically a lady of leisure."

She felt torn by how much better Mam's life had apparently become after Paddy's death. She was a living, breathing advertisement for the benefits of life insurance.

"Just get the ring and come home. That city gets under your skin, Katie, and that dream world of yours with the big bands and men in fedoras and suits. I'm worried you're going to sing one jazz standard and I'm out a roommate. It's dangerous out there. Especially for you. Don't forget it."

Katie nodded, though Eileen couldn't see her. "I know. Pray for me. God brought me home for something."

"You're not feeling anything for him. Right?" Eileen pressed.

Katie ventured a glance at Luc, then cupped her hand around the cell phone. "Right." She didn't know which bothered her more—that she'd lied, or that she was still too weak to overcome Luc's pull.

Eileen wasn't finished. "You don't *have* to go to the wedding, you know. Get the ring and come home. You don't need to do Luc any favors."

"No, I know."

"What if you sing that song and everything that you once had for him comes back to life? Then by next week he's moved on. Just bail on Luc, like he did on you. You owe him nothing, Katie. Get the ring and come home."

Katie's head throbbed. She didn't know what to think. She looked at Luc and she believed him, saw the best in him. She looked at the space between them, thought of the time that had elapsed, and Eileen made complete sense. "I'll call you in an hour. We're at Mam's now."

"Katie, that man is a menace. This is why you're marrying Dexter, remember? He's safe. His love isn't a roller coaster."

"I know. You're right." Love was patient. Love was kind. Love wasn't a g-force ride. She said good-bye to Eileen and put her phone away.

Luc caught up with her and pointed. "Did you see your mam on the gallery?"

"I'm still trying to digest it. She looks happy, like the lady of the manor, doesn't she?"

He grasped her hand and pulled her toward him. "Before we go in—" He put his cheek beside hers and whispered in her ear. "I do love you, Katie-bug, and I'll say it to you in front of Poindexter and anyone else who's willing to listen. Is that what you need?"

She pulled his fedora down over his eyes. "I need you to let me out of your grasp."

He released her hand.

"Not that one. This one," she said, motioning between them. "Luc, what we had once was incredible. It was beautiful.

It showed me how deeply I could love someone. But you have your life and I have mine, and for both of our sakes it's time to leave this fantasy where it belongs. In the past."

She tried to will any residual emotions from her core, to judge him impartially, as if he were any other guy on the street, but she found that impossible. No matter how hard she tried, she couldn't help but see something deeper than his outward good looks, which seemed no more than a fancy wrapping. How many guys longed for the world to be a simpler place where a man wore a fedora and made a woman feel completely safe and protected, even after he'd broken her heart?

She forced herself to swallow the truth. She didn't see inside his soul; that was something her childhood fantasies created. He was just a man. A man like King Midas, who turned everything to solid gold, including the beating flesh of her heart. He left things in pieces behind him, a trail of lost beliefs and places only God could fill. She blinked several times, but nothing she'd done gave her immunity. Silently they approached her mother's house as a united front.

She watched as recognition came across Mam's face and the swing on the gallery stilled. Mam stood and ran down the steps toward her. "Katie!" Then darkness crossed her expression. "What's *he* doing here?"

Age seemed to have no effect on Mam. The black hair was still as jet black as the day Katie left. Her hazel eyes were still bright and full of mischief. Mam had the X factor, whatever that was, and she radiated warmth, but she also saw life through a certain lens. Getting along with Mam meant peering through the same glass.

"Mam, Luc flew me home. Remember?"

"Hmm. Well, you're here now. Nice to see you, Luc. Good-bye." Mam took her by both hands. "I can't believe you're finally home. My baby girl." Mam squeezed her cheeks and kissed her on the lips. "No excuse for not coming home sooner."

"I'm home now."

Mam lowered her voice. "Why isn't he leaving?"

Luc nodded his good-bye, tipping his hat. Something had passed between him and her momma, and Katie couldn't imagine what it might have been. The fact that Luc hadn't married her was ancient history. Maybe it had something to do with Luc creating a billion-dollar industry out of Paddy's business. Maybe any allegiance to Luc felt disloyal. Mam may not have thought too highly of Luc, but she'd never been rude to him, or to anyone, that Katie could remember.

Mam's Southern manners won out. "I suppose you want some tea," she said.

"That'd be nice, thank you," Luc said.

Mam huffed. "You always was too good for the likes of normal folk, Luc DeForges. Just like your momma. You go on now. I'll get you some tea because it's hot out here, but then you be on your way."

"Mam!" Being rude to Luc was one thing, but going after a momma, that was pure low.

"He's got no business being here, Katie Marie. You belong

to another man now. It's not right, and I won't have any more gossip in this town about my daughter."

"It doesn't matter what people say now."

"Katie, you do as I say."

Luc tipped his hat. "I'd best be on my way. Thanks for the offer of that tea, Mrs. McKenna."

As Katie looked down on the street, Leon and the limo were there, as if Luc's every movement was choreographed and Leon knew the steps.

Mam watched Luc grab Katie's suitcase from the trunk and set it on the porch. Then he hightailed it back to the car. Any good Southern boy worth his salt knew better than to mess with an angry momma.

"You forget about Luc DeForges," Mam said. "He'll pick himself up and dust himself off, don't you worry."

"I'll meet you tomorrow at the club," Luc yelled from the limo. "I rented it out at noon so you could practice your song with the band. Do you want me to send a car? And, Mrs. McKenna, I'm sorry to have offended you."

"Slater," she called back. "It's Slater now! You don't have to yell our business across the whole neighborhood, you hear?" Mam turned toward Katie. "You'd think his momma raised him better than that up there in that big house."

Mam opened her arms again, and Katie fell into them willingly. Her mother still smelled divine, just as Katie remembered: the scent of gardenias, citrus, and a potpourri of kitchen spices. Mam smelled of spring, nourishment, and happiness. How was it her momma could singlehandedly calm her down and send one of the richest men in the country scurrying for higher ground at the same time?

Katie didn't let go for a long time. She just embraced her mother with the grip of a gator. Mam scowled at the back of the limo as Luc drove off.

"Your new beau doesn't have a problem with you dancin' with the likes of that bum?" Irene McKenna's voice had the nasal quality and lilt of Brooklyn, but she was from the Irish Channel and lived there her whole life until moving Uptown after Paddy died. She still *warshed* the clothes, though she no longer had to save *quatas* for the Laundromat.

Katie had to be careful not to fall back into the habit of "tawking" as she had when she entered Loyola University and first became aware of her Irish Channel accent.

"I'm sorry, sweetie, that wasn't a proper way to welcome you home. Let me look at you." Mam pulled away and took her by the hands. "Oh, Katie, you're more gorgeous than ever. God sure did bless you, love. Your Paddy's mother was a true beauty, even when she was in her eighties. Fresh as a daisy and a twinkle in her eye. I never liked having a mother-in-law prettier than me. This guy, Dex . . . his momma ugly?"

"No, Mam."

"But uglier than you, right?"

"Well, older than I am. I never thought about—"

"No worries for you. You inherited your nana's looks in spades. It's like I'm seeing a ghost. A beautiful, ethereal ghost. Only I think you're even prettier than Paddy's mam. It's all that zinc oxide I made you wear as a child. You'd be prettier still if you lived here and not in that dank California air. A Southern girl needs to care for her dewy skin. That's why we stay put. How many Southern drawls you hear out in California?"

"Not too many," Katie admitted.

"That's because they're all here, caring for their skin and their families. Speaking of families, Jem has been here to visit now and then since you left."

"Jem DeForges?"

"Well, how many Jems do you know, Katie?"

"Enough to know I don't want to get dumped by another one."

"Jem never would have done that. Three DeForges boys, and you have to pick the wrong one!"

"You're trying to set me up with Jem now? I'm going to Ryan's wedding, Mam, and that is the last I will see or hear from the DeForges family. This is my way of cleansing my soul of anything to do with them. But I look forward to seeing Jem. I hear from him once in a while through e-mail. I talked to him after Katrina and got the updates, but that, too, has to stop. I think he feels bad about what Luc did and wants to make it up to me by being my friend."

Her mother laughed. "Are you kidding me? Jem DeForges has loved you since he laid eyes on you when his brother brought you home from college."

"Mam, you always imagined that. Jem and I were friends, nothing more. He's like a brother to me. Besides, I'm done here. I'm done with New Orleans and anything with the name DeForges. I don't even shop in the store. I'm marrying Dexter Hastings, and I like California."

"We'll see about that. Not many a worthy Yankee out there. You've just left your roots for a time, that's all. Like the Bible says, raise them up in the way they should go, and they'll return to it. The South will rise up in you. You wait and see. I got us a forty-pound bag of mudbugs in an ice chest. We goin' to have us a crawfish boil tonight."

Mam said "crayfish beryle" in the Luziana accent that always came out when she cooked or when she was angry. Her IQ seemed to drop fifty points when talking food or making a point.

"Crawfish?" Katie clapped her hands together. "Really? I hope forty pounds is enough. It's been a long time."

"They's soaking now. Whoo-ee, you should have seen the mud in this batch. I think Rusty washed them out a good three times. You hungry? I'll get the water heating." She shouted into the house, "Rusty, fire up that propane torch. Katie's here!"

"Seriously, Mam, what are we going to do with forty pounds of crawfish?"

"Well, we're going to feed everyone coming to see my daughter, that's what we're going to do with it. Come on in the house here, you can help me shuck the corn."

"Mam, you invited people here tonight? I haven't even met my stepfather yet. I thought we'd have so much to catch up on."

"We ain't got no secrets. Just because you make me come

out to see you doesn't mean I don't bring the news back. I'm proud of my daughter."

Mam came to visit when Rusty was on extended fishing trips. And since Katie hadn't been back home, she had no idea what to expect in her mother's husband. She wondered if he'd be like Paddy. Or maybe his polar opposite.

"I'm just nervous, Mam. I haven't met Rusty yet."

"Crawfish boils aren't for a few, Katie Marie, they're for everyone within radius—and Rusty's everybody's friend. Food brings people together, or did you forget that out west? You're not eating your meals alone, are you? It's bad for the digestive system. It's bad enough Eileen is making you eat that watered-down food. You girls are too skinny."

"Eileen cooks good, Mam."

"Oh, Eileen. That girl doesn't cook. Is there even butter in your refrigerator?"

"I don't know."

"These mudbugs were fresh caught in the Gulf last night. You should have seen them squirm when we poured them out. Some of them look like the grandaddies of crawdads, so big it makes my mouth water just looking at them."

As if Mam would serve anything less. They may have been poor, but one would never have known it by the blessings on their table. Mam could buy any household staple with little more than a dollar and some skilled negotiating.

"Mam, what was that all about with Luc? You always loved him, I thought. I felt like a failure when he didn't marry me, like I'd let you down."

"Oh, I never expected him to marry you, Katie. Luc DeForges is about Luc DeForges. I never understood what you saw in him. There was a day when he wore that hat and could have been a homeless guy on Rampart. I told you a long time ago, there's men who are charming and then there's men you marry. Luc ain't the marrying kind, and I do think I told you that a long time ago too. You didn't want to hear it."

"No," Katie said in agreement.

"So tell me about this Dexter character. I nearly got on a plane to come meet him. Imagine my shock when you said you were coming home. With Luc," Mam added, as though she'd swallowed something bitter.

"It seems Luc is quickly running out of friends in my life."

"As well he should. So before you tell me about Dexter, I should tell you that Luc's little brother Ryan is marrying a lovely girl. It's been all the news, this wedding. I do wish I had been invited. The good Lord knows I've sold her daddy enough shrimp—well, her daddy's people." Mam laughed. "Imagine the invitation addressed to the lady who sells the freshest shrimp at the farmers market. Wouldn't that be a hoot?"

Mam opened the front door and gestured for Katie to enter.

"I see you painted another room salmon."

"And why wouldn't I? It's the color of freshly boiled shrimp, and fresh shrimping pays the mortgage. Well, your Paddy took care of that, I suppose. Shrimp pays the taxes and the insurance, that's more accurate."

"It's like living in the gut of a fish!" Katie complained. She looked around. Mam's new house defied her expectations. An Italianate Victorian, it had been split into two townhomes. On the outside the building fit perfectly into the large mansions that surrounded it; on the inside, however, it was comfortable and warm—except for the orangish-pink living room. "Couldn't you just do an accent wall, like they do on HGTV?"

"You move to California and suddenly you're an expert on decorating?"

"Well, not an expert, but—"

"Katie, don't be so negative. It's a color of life. The good life down here in N'awlins. I see no reason to ever leave, and I see no reason to ever leave a living room beige. Besides, it warded off Katrina. I think it's a lucky color."

Katie knew better than to argue with that. Like most N'awliners, Mam's faith was mixed with a large portion of superstition.

"The house is beautiful. I shouldn't have been so negative. Look at your lantern over the stairs. It's just like being in an outdoor courtyard."

"No, come see. I have a real courtyard!" Mam led her through the living room to an oversized beveled-glass door that led to the back gallery.

Stepping outside into the heat, Katie heard the roar of the propane torch under the boiling pot. She ran down the steps and sniffed deeply the spices added to the water to make a boil complete.

"This must be Katie Marie." Rusty Slater stood over two giant ice chests, filled to capacity with cleaned crawdads.

Katie felt a rush of emotion—first, that Rusty looked nothing like her father and second, that she'd forever associate him with one of her favorite things in life: a crawfish boil. Rusty was much younger than her father, even now, nearly ten years after Paddy's death. Mam had married her own age this time.

Rusty was a stocky, rugged-looking man with a mustache and clean-shaven head. He had a barrel chest and beefy arms, and as she reached to shake his hand, he pulled her into a bear hug.

"There's no excuse for my not seeing you before today," he said. He stepped backward. "You're as pretty as your mam. See them crawdads? Buddy of mine pulled them out himself last night. These are as fresh as you can get unless you live in Arabi and pull them out while the pot is berlin."

"I can't wait!"

"Your mother tells me you got a beau out there in California. How come he didn't come with you? You explained to him what family means?"

"He'll come before the wedding. He wants to meet everyone."

"What's he like to do for fun? Dexter, right? He fish? Play pool? Ping-Pong?"

"He has a Segway. He plays Segway polo with some of his friends and co-workers on Saturdays."

"He has a what, now?" Rusty cupped his ear.

"A Segway. It's a motorized mobility device. You stand up and lean into it with your hips to steer it."

"It's a what, now?"

"It's like a scooter that you stand up on."

Rusty nodded. "All right then. To each his own, I always say. Scooter polo."

"Segway polo."

"That right, now."

"Come on now, Katie," Mam called. "I want to show you the rest of the house."

Katie followed her mam reluctantly. So much change to take in, and she hated change. Maybe that's why she hadn't been home. Everything was different now.

Chapter 9

∾

Nevertheless

Katie's mother rambled on, shifting from house minutia to hometown gossip. "So as I was saying . . ." Mam was leading her back up the steps and halted on the landing. "It seems Ryan's bride is from Tyler Oil money."

"I heard that. Google."

"Google. When Google can keep up with the women at the farmers market, you call me. Ryan and Olivia met at Tulane. He went back to school, you know, to get a degree in something more practical. He hasn't done a thing with his Loyola theater degree, but then, we didn't have money to waste on a long shot like that. Talent will only take a person so far. Teaching pays the bills.

"The city is all aflutter because Miss Tyler is said to be wearing a local designer's gown, and everything is provided by local companies for the wedding. It's the way her father is playing the green card, but with the oil leak, he doesn't have a chance. This city is mad! They wouldn't even use Luc's bakery for the cake, can you imagine, because the business is nationwide now. That might be a way to make points with some folks, but it's no way to marry into a family."

"Can we talk about something else? Tell me about my stepdaddy. What's he like?"

"He's very forgiving, for one thing. He understands completely why you haven't been home in so long. I confess I'm not so understanding, but he says, 'Irene, honey, she's got her own life now. You did good, you sent her off to fly on her own. That's what you're supposed to do, raise them up to fly.'"

"I would have come home for the wedding if you'd told me there was one. Vegas, Mom? That's not like you."

"It was a quiet affair, and I was anxious to make it as low-key as possible. Rusty won a shrimping contest, and we used the trip to get hitched. You know how this town gossips. I told him, Rusty, if you take me to Sin City you're coming back with a wife, because I ain't that kind of lady."

Katie laughed.

"There's no sense in making such a big deal over a second marriage. It's better to do it quietly and let people find out you're married. You leave the gossipers to their own that way. It's too late for anyone to care much. You want some sweet tea, honey?"

"No thanks, Mam."

"Now that right there, that's your grammy's clock. I remember it from my childhood. Doesn't it look divine on that mantel?"

There were some heirlooms about that Katie had assumed left the family. The gilt bronze mantel clock was one of them. A gold cherub on a chariot of porcelain shells, it was rumored to be late eighteenth century but it appeared more early-American garage sale.

"That thing's still around, huh?"

"Wasn't it made for that mantel?"

"Mam, speaking of gossipers. Does anyone know I'm here for the wedding? Has it been mentioned?" She didn't ask her real question: *Do they remember me as the girl who pathetically proposed to New Orleans' proudest bachelor only to be turned down flat in front of loads of people?*

Her mother heard the real question anyway. "Oh, what's it matter what any of them say?"

"You just told me they're better informed than Google."

"But no one cares about it. It's just talk. Can't let a bunch of wagging tongues get to you." Mam lowered her voice as if they weren't alone. "There's speculation that you are Luc's local girl. You know, that he has many all over the world and he brings you home—"

"I get it, Mam. Thanks." Katie fluffed a tapestry pillow on the sofa out of habit. "After eight years, you'd think I'd at least qualify to be his Northern California girl."

"A girl may leave the South, but the South doesn't ever

leave her. Now this is the dining room. You see your grammy's Irish bone china in the built-in? Doesn't it look made for that spot?"

"It's beautiful." She loved how her mother used the good china every day of her life. Nothing was saved for special occasions, because to her mother, being alive was occasion enough. And after visiting the spot where her father died, Katie wondered if her own mourning hadn't been a prolonged and welcome excuse from living.

"Don't kid yourself, gossip doesn't have to make sense, Katie. It only has to sound good. Everyone still remembers the two of you on the covers of all those magazines when you were singing in that"—Mam stopped to shake her head—"in that barrelhouse." Her mother led her across the wide planked pine floors. "Now in here, we have the kitchen."

The Barrelhouse Club was the saloon Katie sang at during college, but barrelhouses were the types of clubs where early jazz and swing came to life—not the alcohol barrels depicted earlier. But Katie had left that battle long ago. Mam saw it one way, she another. She stepped into the kitchen.

"Mam!" Her mouth dropped. A chef's kitchen, with fire engine red, antique-looking appliances, white wood cabinets with French glass doors, and a large island with shiny granite countertops. "You're not in a shotgun house anymore. You might even fit the old house into this kitchen!"

"I miss that old house. That's why I painted the living room salmon. It's a little bit of home. That's how you know if you're marrying the right man, Katie. You can live anywhere.

I had a friend from high school. She kept moving from one parish to another until she finally figured out it wasn't the house!"

Mam's sage wisdom was peppered with Dear Abby common sense.

"I'm tired, Mam. Do you mind if I lie down?" Katie wanted to take a nap and forget the way Luc had stared at her on the street.

"I've got your room all set up. Come on upstairs."

"What am I doing here?"

"My point exactly. Word on the street is that Luc's engaged, and you're here to show the city that there are no hard feelings between you and the DeForges family."

"I thought you said they weren't talking."

"I said they weren't talking much, and they aren't."

"Luc's not engaged. He would have told me on the way out here."

Mam walked across the kitchen and picked up a copy of the *Picayune*. "It's all right here in black and white. Luc DeForges Sets Cap for Los Angeles Socialite Heather Wolf."

The paper whacked the table. Instead of a lovely posed shot of Luc and a socialite, there was Katie hoisted over his shoulder with her backside on the front of the *Picayune*!

"That's not—this could be anybody! Maybe somebody needed help to the car!"

"Let me tell you something about men, Katie Marie. They don't resort to cavemen unless they mean business."

"You say that like it's a good thing."

"I am only saying I remember a day when you wouldn't have minded Luc heaving you over his shoulder, but now that he's engaged and you're soon to be, I don't have to play nice with him anymore. I don't owe him anything. Just because he bought your daddy's business doesn't mean a thing."

"I never said it did! Fine. What's it to me if you don't want Luc in your house? Just keep Jem out too, or it's rude."

"Well, I like Jem."

"Remember how you made me invite everyone in my class to my birthday party? Even paste-eater Dannilyn? Not inviting Luc means not inviting Jem. It's the rule."

"It's my house, Katie."

Katie slipped the newspaper into her handbag and followed her mother up the stairs that still smelled of new carpet and floor finish.

Why did she want to believe in Luc so badly? With each new glimmer of truth, she dared to hope again. Like Charlie Brown trusting Lucy not to pull out the football, she'd run again with total faith. The separation between them, Uptown and Downtown, French New Orleans versus Irish, white collar versus blue collar—in spite of all that, she'd never believed in any separation. What was it going to take to sink into her thick skull that Luc DeForges was no more capable of being a husband to her than Eileen's dog Pokey? If she could only make her heart believe what her head knew for certain.

Mam stopped at the rail and pointed out all the black-and-white photos of dead relatives she'd never known.

"Now, I don't mind you mending fences with Luc," she

said, "but I think you should just play possum with him until this shindig is over. If this Dexter is all you say he is, the past is better left in the past."

"Yes."

"Here's your room. You lay down and I'll call ya before supper's ready." Mam pulled the paper out from Katie's bag. "Here's the part that pertains to you. 'Katie McKenna, daughter of the late greengrocer of the Irish Channel and the Lower Garden District Ian McKenna, is said to have forgiven Luc DeForges for publicly humiliating her at his graduation party from Tulane University by rejecting her public proposal of marriage. Miss McKenna will be attending Ryan McKenna's wedding as Mr. Luc McKenna's date to show their friendship has survived the breakup and his impending marriage.'"

Katie studied the headshot of the redhead said to be Luc's fiancée. "She's got red hair?" Clear, warm eyes stared back at her. Luc's expression, a separate photo, spoke to her. His business face. No smile to his eyes, no warmth or depth for the photographer. She handed the paper back to her mother. "That's just a business shot for Luc. He's not engaged."

"How can you be so sure?"

"I can't." Luc still had the ability to harm her, and that's what hurt most of all. She'd thought she was over him. "I just don't believe it, is all."

"It doesn't matter if you believe it or not—or even if it's true. Everyone who will be at that wedding believes it. Your hair is a wreck."

Katie patted her hair, which was ratty and thick from the moist air. "Thanks."

"Let's pin curl it after supper. We'll get it sleek and slick for your forties practice tomorrow, and it will be just like old times. The best revenge, Katie, is living well. Show him you're living well and done with his tricks forever."

Her cell phone rang. She stared at the number, even though she knew by "In the Mood" that it was Dexter again. She'd run out of energy and didn't have the strength to open the phone. "I don't deserve him." But it didn't explain why she didn't want to answer the phone.

"You're not going to answer?" Mam asked.

Mam would read too much into it if she didn't. "Yes, I am. I wanted privacy."

Mam took the hint and went out the door as Katie pressed her phone.

"Hi, Dex! Sorry I didn't call you back right away. Mam was giving me a tour of the house, and I met my stepfather."

"I just wanted you to know I was thinking of you. Did you get your flowers?"

"No, did you send me flowers?" She lay back on the white iron bed from her youth, glad her mother had kept it.

"Shoot. I wanted them to be a surprise."

"Dex, that is so sweet!"

Mam opened the door again carrying fresh towels, which she placed on the bed. Katie knew it was just an excuse to eavesdrop. She flopped over on the bed and faced the window.

"Mam, did Dexter's flowers arrive yet?"

"Oh, were those from him?" Mam asked. "There was no card, so I gave them to the neighbor lady."

She scowled at her mother. "They're here, Dex. They're beautiful! I'm going to lie down now before dinner. I'll call you tonight when you're home from work, all right?"

"We're having a Scrabble night at church, so I may not be home."

"All right, then. I'll talk to you in the morning."

"Get some rest, and don't overdo it."

"I promise."

"Bye."

Katie clicked the phone shut.

"He doesn't say he loves you when he hangs up?" Mam asked.

"He's at work!"

"I don't care if he's at work or not. You don't grow up around the water and not say you love somebody when they leave. Look what happened to your father. Imagine if he hadn't told us that morning."

"I'll change it, Mam. Why did you give my flowers away?"

"Poor Helena next door has nothing better to do than watch me leave and hire workmen so she has someone to talk to during the day. Her husband never pays her a moment's attention, so she's determined to get it anywhere she can. We have her over to dinner when Rusty has a big catch, and of course she's coming tonight. Big shot investor, her husband. He ought to be investing where it matters, before his wife takes her account somewhere else!"

"Mam!"

"We wouldn't think of having a party without Helena. She's a very particular eater though—reminds me of you when you were young. Takes the skin off everything, doesn't like anything fried. Imagine, in New Orleans, not wanting anything fried? Poor girl. I don't like that this Dexter character doesn't tell you he loves you when he says good-bye."

"You're just looking for an excuse not to like him."

"Maybe I am, and maybe I'm not, but it's a right good excuse just the same."

"So you know why I'm really home," she said, anxious to see the ring again.

Her mother sighed. "I know why you're really home. The question is, do you?"

"Huh?"

"Do me a favor, Katie. Don't talk about that ring just yet. We'll have dinner. We'll hear more about Dexter. You're in New Orleans now. Slow down."

Chapter 10

〜

THE MAN I LOVE

Katie stepped out of Rusty's truck. "Thank you, Rusty. You were right, it was too hot to walk." She smoothed her hair and straightened her tight-waisted red chiffon dress. It still fit. She'd tried it on in desperation to prove that she hadn't bloomed in size and that her magazine cover was merely a bad angle.

"You got California on the brain. Didn't want you to have sweat stains on that pretty red dress. I know your momma says ladies glow, but in this heat you'd be glowing like a nuclear power plant."

Rusty cackled at his own joke, and she slammed the door with a grin. How was it her mother had managed to pick two good men, and she still couldn't get one in the bag, as Mam would say?

Katie shaded her vision and drank in the memories. The Barrelhouse Club, with its inconspicuous front from its speakeasy days, looked tired, a shadow of its former self. She pulled open the door and waited a moment while her eyes adjusted from blinding morning light to black room. The atrocious smell hit her nostrils first, like a mingled mix of sins gone by: strong dark liquor, cigarette smoke, and grease.

She'd never been a drinker. Her father's warnings about the family history, combined with the reality of singing for drunks to earn money for college, had taught her never to touch the stuff.

Mam had pin-curled her hair and finger-waved the ends into sleek sexy waves with a peekaboo bang covering her left eye, then sprayed her to kingdom come so she'd stay sleek if Katrina's sister came through town. She felt as though her false eyelashes reached her heavily drawn eyebrows like a cocker spaniel's. When she blinked, her eyelids felt like they were doing heavy lifting.

As her eyes adjusted to the dim light, she could see that the navy-blue wallpaper had faded to a pale denim color, its gold-flaked sparkles now specks of snowflakes splattered across the walls. She might have known better than to be lulled by the romance of her former life. Standing in the dingy club for a mere rehearsal, she felt ridiculous in her scarlet chiffon swing dress. Here she had channeled her best

Veronica Lake for a band cast who probably had no more idea of the old film star than they did Ricki Lake.

She didn't recognize any of the musicians, so she stepped onto the stage, determined to get lost in the band's warm-up sounds. She figured when she was needed someone would let her know, but she wished she had Luc's company. A Bing Crosby tune crooned softly in the background, and she swallowed and grabbed the microphone in both hands. She'd been taught to tune everything out and focus on the performance, and she told herself that's exactly what she'd have to do until it was time to step off Luc's plane and back into her real world.

She'd been another person in this room: a star, the antithesis of her shy, schoolteacher self. For one night a week she became a torch singer bellowing to unrequited loves and a life she'd never lived. In this room, in those days, she played a part, and the old tourists who remembered the days of Doris Day and Ella Fitzgerald roared when she finished.

She didn't miss it: the crowds, the short-lived accolades. She received far more when an autistic child like Austin looked her in the eye . . . when he connected with the world because of all those days on her knees wearing oatmeal or yogurt. If Austin, or any of her kids at school, giggled, it was like God's heaven opened up to her for a moment, allowing her to reach for the light.

"I'm sorry I'm late." Luc's voice broke her thoughts, and she practically mauled him with a hug. "Well, you're friendly this morning."

"I thought I might be in the wrong place. I shouldn't have dressed."

"Of course you should have. What would the guys say if you showed up in your underthings?"

The sparkle behind his eyes made her smile.

Luc wore khaki pants and a camel-colored jacket with a light-blue collared shirt open at the neck. On his head was his trademark fedora, this one made of straw with a black band. He looked . . . in a word . . . heavenly. Not that she noticed.

"I didn't realize the club was in such bad shape. Maybe we should have used the conservatory at my mother's house."

She rolled her eyes. "Are we playing Clue? Maybe, like Miss Peacock, I should kill you with a lead pipe in the conservatory."

"Sorry. Did that sound pretentious?"

"You think?" She placed her thumb and forefinger together. "Just a little bit. To those of us who grew up without conservatories, anyway." She ran her hand along the dusty piano cover. "The glory has certainly faded. I remember thinking I was Doris Day or Ella Fitzgerald singing here, but now I see that maybe I was just a step above the star of a high school musical. Maybe less Billie Holiday, more Gwen Stefani. I'm beginning to wonder just how drunk the patrons were."

"Well, we'll just have to make sure the wedding guests are just as drunk, and there should be no problems."

"Are you trying to soothe my nerves?"

He grinned. "You should sing everywhere and anywhere." He surveyed the room. "It was a nice place back in the day . . . and it's only for practice." He moved in closer so that his words were accompanied by dream-inducing puffs of air. "You look absolutely beautiful in that dress. Reminds me all over again why I fell in love with you."

She cleared her throat and pulled at her white gloves. "I'm glad we're here. This will ease me into performing again."

He brushed her nose. "At the Café du Monde this morning, were you?"

"How did you know that?"

"You have powdered sugar on your nose."

"Oh, Luc, wipe it off! I knew trying to dress up like a siren was a long shot to get my confidence back."

"A siren's gotta eat, doesn't she?"

She rubbed her arms against the frigid air. "Do you want to tell me why I'm really here? Is it to sing or to offer you some sort of public redemption before you get married to Heather Wolf? Mam showed me the *Picayune*."

"Katie, I hate to point out the obvious, but that was *you* in the picture."

"I know that! But I read the article."

"So did I."

"Because, Luc, I have forgiven you, so there's really no need to pretend I'm here for another reason. If that's what you want, I'm happy to tell people aloud that I was as responsible for my bad decision as you were, but I can't take you lying to me. Not again."

Luc opened his mouth but said nothing, clearly dumb-struck. In the meantime, his cell phone chirped and chirped some more.

"You'd better get that. Don't want to lose a million or so over a simple conversation with the little harlot from your past."

"Katie! I've met Heather Wolf once, and that's the truth! But the woman slung over my shoulder?" He leaned in and whispered again. "I know her intimately, and if she's open to the idea of engagement, would you tell your client that I'm ready to enter negotiations?"

"Ugh! You are impossible. Everything's a joke to you."

His phone got louder. "Katie, that paper is ridiculous. I am not engaged."

"Then who is Heather?"

"I—"

"Just answer your phone, it's driving me nuts." She walked away, mumbling to herself. "He thinks I'm just a public relations ploy. How many women did he parade around with on the cover of those tabloids? 'Billionaire bachelor dates this starlet, billionaire bachelor dates that starlet, billionaire bachelor, is he capable of settling down?' Multimillionaire, ha. He's just avoiding the subject. The *Tattler* calls him a billionaire. How does he explain that?"

"Katie?" Ryan DeForges strode into the tarnished ballroom and stretched his arms toward her. He looked as if he'd spent the day, indeed his lifetime, on the polo field. Or, more likely, at a Ralph Lauren photo shoot. Ryan wore the youngest brother badge proudly without a hard day's work to show for himself.

The fact that the DeForges money came from bootlegging was an old New Orleans secret. The fact that the fortune was drying up from a lack of DeForges ingenuity or that the majestic house on Charles Street showed some wear and tear obviously had yet to touch Ryan. Rumor had it he was too proud to let Luc put any money into the house. The world would take care of Ryan somehow. It always had.

"Katie!" He skipped toward her and wrapped her in a hug. "Katie darling, oh my goodness, Katie." He pushed her away. "Let me look at you. Let me take a good look at you." Then he squeezed her tightly again. "You haven't changed a bit. Not one bit."

"It might be time for you to visit the eye doctor."

Ryan took his large hands and circled her waist with his thumbs meeting on her front and the fingers on the small of her back. "You still have that Katie Scarlett waist. Remember how we used to say that, Luc?"

"She won't for long if Poindexter has his way," Luc groused, one ear still to his phone.

"Who? What?" Ryan wrinkled his forehead.

"Ryan, Luc has yet to acknowledge that my pathetic marriage proposal eight long years ago is no longer valid or that I'm marrying another man. Who asked *me*, I might add. Maybe you could remind him that I'm only here to get my engagement ring, the family heirloom? And sing at your wedding, of course. Where is the bride? I can't wait to see who is marrying Ryan DeForges. What is she like?"

"You can't marry an outsider, regardless of what an imbecile my brother is. We always said he was slow with people and quick with money. He's come to his senses. Eight years, that's about right." Ryan grabbed her hand. "We don't mean to let you go."

As the rest of the members of the big band filed in, they stopped and focused their attention on her and Ryan.

"I'm going to warm up." The trumpet, oboe, and trombone players sat in their positions. She leaned over to the piano player. "'The Man I Love'?"

She cradled the old-fashioned silver mic. Not one of those modern emaciated contraptions, but a meaty chunk of metal she could wrap both hands around. "Someday, he'll come along . . ."

Luc slowly lowered the phone from his ear.

Katie searched for that ardent cavity in her soul where she connected with the deeper, mournful emotions and sang out strong. As the music faded into another song, she began an ode to unrequited love: "I'm Old Fashioned." She sang it directly to him, a song Rita Hayworth and Fred Astaire had sung to one another about their differences . . . and their similarities.

In that brief moment, eight years and a billion reasons faded in the darkness of the club. All the pain disappeared, and she loved Luc DeForges like no other man so why make apologies for it now? Sure, she'd decided to marry practically, but that didn't mean that their history wasn't rich and full of the bloom of love when they were younger. It was time to get over that romanticism, but she could still appreciate it for the beautiful gift it had been in her life. How would she have ever truly known what a torch song meant to the soul if Luc had never touched hers?

She stepped off the stage and heard the bandleader give directions to his musicians. She walked straight into Luc's arms, and he circled them around her. They clung to one another, swaying gently to the music in the background. If there was music . . . she couldn't be certain.

"Katie," he whispered in her ear. "Katie." His cheek pressed hard against her own. He kissed under her ear, tiny, gentle brushstrokes, and traced his lips down her jaw. His kisses grew more demanding. They stood in the dark of the club, completely surrounded and yet completely alone.

His name escaped her lips and he kissed her again. Words swirled in her head.

"Passion," Luc said.

"Dangerous," she answered between kisses.

"Heavenly." He pressed his lips against hers.

"Affected." She slowly regained her ground. "Hurt."

"No." He encircled her waist with his arms and kissed her urgently, his breath warm and rushed as he repeated her name. "I love you, Katie. No one else—"

The music stopped, and the house lights came up. A clearing of a throat interrupted them, and they looked around at all the eyes upon them. Strangers mostly, but Leon, Luc's driver, held a saxophone in his hand and started to blow to drown out the awkward silence and the stares.

"Luc, how could you? I'm going to be engaged!"

As the room grew louder, Luc's cell phone rang and they were alone in the chaos once again.

"How could I have let that happen? I should never have said yes to Dexter. I'm an adulteress, like in the Old Testament. My lips drip honey. I'm supposed to be engaged, just as soon as I could get my r—"

He kissed her again.

She stood silently, fiddling with the fabric rose corsage at her waist.

"You're shaking."

"This is so wrong," she said, but that wasn't why her whole body trembled. She'd forgotten the power he had over her. No, that wasn't true. She remembered it. She'd come precisely to inoculate the source, but to be caressed by his touch, to feel her body come alive, she realized she was no match for her emotions. Why did she have to be so weak? There was a good man back home. A good man who wouldn't make her feel any of these uncomfortable feelings. Dexter wouldn't make her question her faith or her force of will.

Luc did all of the above and more. Time had done nothing to relinquish his grip over her. When he looked at her, it was as though there wasn't another living being on the planet. The all-encompassment of it. In God's Word it said that women who marry didn't have the things of God on their minds, but the things of family. She couldn't imagine what a love like Luc's did to a woman. It couldn't be healthy. God was a God of order, not chaos. He preferred structure, reverence, thoughtfulness . . . traits she never embraced with Luc.

What kind of woman prepared for engagement to one man while trembling under the touch of another? Like the woman caught in her sins, she needed to go and sin no more. Katie clasped her eyes shut against the emotions that flooded her system. To give up Luc was to give up earthly love for something greater. She and Dexter would do God's work. They would build a family and a ministry together.

Go, she told herself. *Sin no more.*

Luc forced her eyes to his by tipping her chin. She felt like Ingrid Bergman in the arms of Cary Grant. The lovely blue with specks of gold sought something in her she couldn't name. Meanwhile, the brass section continued to warm up behind them, but to her it sounded like the strains of wounded fowl. In Luc's eyes, everything reflected more light, including the sounds around her. She drank in every detail.

"Do you love him?" Luc asked.

She resented the question. "I loved you, and a lot of good it did me." Her love with Dexter was manageable, a slow burn of respect and mutual desire that would increase with time and effort. "I want a balanced life. Whatever's between you and me—this doesn't last. It burns away with time. What I have with Dex will increase and burn steady."

"What you're telling me is that you want a can of Sterno rather than a bonfire."

"Do you think that a shared love of jazz standards and an era gone by is a better connection than what Dexter and I share? He and I want the same things, Luc. He wants a family, the white picket fence, a companion to share life with. Not a white picket fence around his private island or at the edge of his yacht. He wants a life with me."

Luc lifted a lock of her hair and twisted it around his fingers. "God didn't paint you with a brushstroke of safety, Katie. He brought out the fiery colors for you."

"I need to go." She straightened the sash about her waist. "I'm done defending Dex to you."

"Maybe you need to defend him to yourself."

"I'm going home to get my ring. I'll catch a commercial flight home."

"You're going to abandon my brother four days before his wedding?" Luc's phone trilled from his pocket. "Imagine what the papers will have to say about that."

"You're manipulating me!"

"I know where your nana's ring is, Katie-bug. If you can look me in the eye on Ryan's wedding day and tell me it's all right to marry without this"—he brushed his hand between them—"whatever this is, I'll get you the ring, and I won't bother you again."

She swallowed hard and felt the wind rush out of her lungs. Passion, like beauty, was fleeting. "Dex is a good man. I betrayed his trust. How much can one man be expected to hear his fiancée confess before the wedding?"

Luc pulled his hat over his eyes. "Maybe she's confessing

to the wrong man. It's better to marry than to burn with passion. Isn't that right, Katie-bug?"

She yanked herself away. Luc called her Katie-bug because she snuggled up to him like a roly-poly. Once it had been a term of endearment, now it sounded like a pathetic name for the desperate codependent she once was—so dependent on the opinion of the mighty Luc DeForges.

Chapter 11

~

Ain't That a Kick in the Head

"Are we gonna practice or not?" It was Scully, a tall, skinny black man who barely registered from behind his clarinet, which was the same shape as he was.

The band mumbled, but all of them moved toward the stage, and Katie instinctively joined them. Luc watched her go, his mind filled with plans.

Katie . . . her red dress swinging gently back and forth, embodied everything a man wanted in a wife: the girl next door, nurturing with just enough fight to keep it interesting, intellectual, generous to a fault, and of course . . . that heavenly figure. He'd made a tactical error. Revealed too much up front, lost himself in the emotion of his desire. *One has to be able to walk away from the table.* He laughed aloud. That might be an option in business mergers. In mergers of the heart, he wasn't so rational. Not when it came to Katie. He'd protected her from a truth she wasn't ready for, taken the high road, if you will—only to feel the full impact of his decision until this day. The question remained. Was Katie ready for the truth now?

He'd been so ignorant. Thought he'd make his money and come back and show her the security she craved. He'd missed that train. Security to Katie came in the form of a boring engineer who would be home for dinner when he said he would, who would protect her from the emotional pain she'd already endured—the pain Luc helped afflict in his youthful exuberance.

Katie glanced back at him from the stage, and he spoke to her heart. "What you don't realize," he murmured under his breath, "is that kind of life will ultimately kill who you are." A life without music, without her soul touched by the natural rhythm within her—was that a life at all? She was born for deeper things, the way music touched her. God had created the music within her.

Up on the stage, Katie embraced the microphone with all the ease and grace of the experienced musicians who surrounded her. In that moment, time disappeared. Not a moment had passed since he'd first laid eyes upon her. It still bothered him that Ryan knew her first. Ryan had brought him down to the club, where he'd gotten a job singing. His artsy flighty brother never did anything that was expected of him but somehow always managed to get away with being the chosen son.

The stage was filled to capacity that night with a full big band, backup singers, and a bandleader, but all eyes went directly to Katie. Including his own. She owned the stage and the audience. Ryan had met her in theater class, and her family had come upon hard times. Naturally, his bleeding-heart brother took it upon himself to get her work and recommended her for the Barrelhouse Club, an old drinking establishment meant to provide an alternative "safer" experience to the more wild Bourbon Street bars. The owner had founded it on his love of jazz standards and the way life used to be. Mr. Montrose and Katie found a mutual respect in each other. The rest was history.

Katie abandoned her shy background personality to bring home the bacon to her family. She'd loved to say that since her father owned a vegetable stand and daily grocery, someone had to provide the meat. Ian McKenna, God rest his soul, had always had more heart than business sense. The old man couldn't stand to see anyone go hungry and consequently gave away too many profits. Like Katie, her father failed to see the value in his gifts. Ian may not have been a rich man, but at his funeral, one saw how truly wealthy he'd been.

On stage, Ryan took Katie by the hand and called out to the band, "Singin' in the Rain!"

Luc's stomach tightened. The first moment he'd laid eyes on her she'd been dancing to that song with Ryan, and it was as though a fire had lit in him. Luc wasn't the sort to believe in love at first sight or soul mates, but he couldn't deny what happened to him in that moment—how she'd captured him in a place he didn't know existed.

As the music began, she and Ryan started to walk to the music and broke into their tribute to Gene Kelly's infamous tap dance, sans water, which they had learned for the stage at Loyola University. Ryan wasn't stupid. He knew that Katie at his side increased his value by large increments.

"I forgot how talented they both were," Luc whispered aloud.

"That's her? That's Katie?" asked a voice.

Olivia, Ryan's bride-to-be, appeared at Luc's side. Olivia was a beaky blonde with a short bob. Everything about her jutted outward in pointy ways: her knees, her nose, her chin . . . She was all angles, but inside she was as soft as butter. A smart practical girl with all the street smarts his brother lacked.

He nodded. "That's her."

"You stole her from your little brother and then didn't have the decency to marry her. Tsk-tsk."

"That's not what happened at all." He crossed his arms and faced her.

Olivia laughed. "Ryan said that's when you started wearing the fedora. After watching Katie dance."

"I did?" He hadn't remembered that fact. "I did?" he asked again.

"Love makes us do some crazy things, doesn't it?"

"Like marry my brother, you mean?"

"Like let eight years pass before realizing how deeply you care for the only woman you ever loved." She shrugged. "That's what I was thinking."

"It was complicated. Shouldn't you be at a fitting or some bride thing?"

"It's always complicated. Try explaining to my father why I'm marrying a singing, dancing DeForges without a real job. Two of you as rich as Moses, and I pick the poor one with the artistic nature. Do you think *that* was easy? Daddy, I've fallen in love. Imagine his excitement when I told him it was a DeForges. Yes, Daddy, the DeForges of Charles Street. No, Daddy, not the multimillionaire in natural foods. No, Daddy, not the jeweler from Royale either . . . yes, Daddy, the dancing one."

Luc broke into laughter as the tap dancing on stage grew more persistent. "Can you believe they're that close to the original after all these years?"

"I can. If there's any New Orleans voodoo your brother might believe in, I do think it's that he's the reincarnation of Gene Kelly. Good thing his faith tells him that's impossible, or I don't know if I could live with him. Ryan said you started wearing the fedora to hide your acne from Katie."

"Did he now?" He adjusted his hat. "I guess I'm lucky Katie was a Fred Astaire girl, not into Gene Kelly."

"Lucky for both of us, I suppose. Trust me, it was much easier to sell my father on the big band/swing wedding than the Gene Kelly idea. I mean, he could imagine the forties with Cary Grant and Humphrey Bogart, the romanticism of heroes after World War II. Can you imagine if I tried to get Daddy to pony up for a 'Singin' in the Rain' wedding, after Katrina? He would have disowned me."

"I doubt that."

"If it brought Katie back home, so much the better. For all of us. It's time you thought about your personal life, Luc. You're not getting any younger. Despite what the tabloids say."

He put his arm around Olivia and clutched her shoulder. "My brother doesn't deserve you."

"So will she sing if I wait around long enough?"

"Is your question, *can* she sing? She can."

"Your brother still thinks it was his idea to bring her here for the wedding."

"That was the plan," Luc said. "You won't rat me out, will you?"

"She's really beautiful, Luc. Just like you described her. There's something about her that makes me want to know her. I can't believe she's a special ed teacher. When you're plain like me, you think all women who look like that end up on Broadway or, at the very least, in the lingerie catalogs."

"Not my Katie." He paused. "And you are not plain, Olivia. Don't think I'll let that one slip by. In fact, I do think my brother got the prettiest girl in New Orleans."

He meant it. Olivia's nature made her beautiful to anyone who spent more than five minutes with her. And anyone who could put up with Ryan certainly took their sainthood seriously.

"Katie looks like Rita Hayworth. No wonder she's a Fred Astaire girl. Did you know they danced together? I do, because you see, Ryan thinks that watching old movies on the weekend is research." Olivia stared at the stage, knowing she was invisible to both Katie and Ryan in the dark recesses of the theater. "What will you do if she really has decided it's over? What if she gets married? She waited this long."

"Then I have to let her go. God's will and all that." Luc shook his head. "My real thoughts? I'll be hoping Dexter has a heart attack by the time he's fifty and she's free again. I know, I'm awful."

"But truthful. Better to get her back now before you wish some innocent dead."

"My thoughts exactly. Besides, have you ever seen me stop when I wanted something?"

"I don't think most wealthy men are good at hearing no, Luc."

"Uh-oh." He stared at the flash of sunlight as the side door opened. Standing in the doorframe was a very large road-block to his plan in a very tiny Pilates-shaped body. "Eileen's here. She certainly didn't waste any time."

"Eileen?"

"Katie's best friend and current roommate." Luc flicked his hat's brim with two fingers. "She's onto me."

"That ain't good." Olivia watched Eileen at the door with a sharp gaze. "Don't worry. I've got this."

Suddenly he understood how his passive brother ended up engaged. Olivia's take-no-prisoners attitude was his last chance to win back the woman of his dreams. No wonder he liked her. She was the female version of him.

"Don't underestimate Eileen. She's a Southerner too."

"Then she'll understand we simply don't have the room for another guest. My father is already having a gator over the body count."

"I don't think body count is the right name for wedding guests."

"If there are any extra guests at this point, it will be. And I may be on the first slab. You'll excuse me." Olivia sailed between the club chairs and tables on her way to the door.

Olivia's father was one of the wealthiest men in New Orleans. An oilman, he came to the financial aid of the city after Katrina and garnered a well-deserved reputation in town for his philanthropy. Until the oil spill, when all oil men were suspect again. No doubt he didn't want to throw a lavish affair that brought more attention back to the industry.

Luc called after her, "Don't tick her off, Olivia, that won't help."

"Please," Olivia said. "I'm Southern."

Luc's BlackBerry hadn't stopped buzzing since he'd entered the club, and now the familiar trill of constant text messages invaded. He looked at the face of it, only to discover his assistant's emergency text with only the current stock number. He groaned. This economy was killing him. People didn't care about organic vegetables when they just wanted food on the table, and Costco was starting to kill them in the organics by sheer volume. So far, though, his stock, a Wall

Street favorite, had escaped. Now his numbers would start to affect families and the working class with their money in natural food mutual funds.

Katie finished her dance, and the band started up her song. She took to the clunky, old-time microphone like Fred to Ginger. "There's a someone I'm longing to see . . . I hope that he . . ."

He closed his eyes and let the purity of her voice carry him away. Until, during a quiet interlude, his BlackBerry bleated again. He sighed and walked out the back door into the blinding sunlight and heavy gray air. "Yeah."

"You can't be out of contact right now. Do you have any idea how many board members have called me this morning? Yelled at me? Listen, I'm about ready to shove an organic leek where the sun—"

"Renee!"

"I'm sorry, but you forget I haven't even endured half of this day, and I'm ready to harm some of your stockholders, so you need to get busy and make an appearance. They think you're AWOL while stock dives."

"Maybe those things are connected, and I actually do something there," he said.

"That isn't it, and you know it. Just get yourself back here before I start taking out board members one by one. It would not be healthy to be a Forages stockholder if I hauled off on a spree. Just sayin.' "

"I wouldn't put it past you. You should really get more fiber, Renee."

"Listen, if my daddy heard the way these men talk to me, he'd come and take care of it for me. Fiber intake notwithstanding. Where are you?"

"It's only five days. My brother's getting married."

"Your *brother's* getting married, you aren't. Luc, this isn't the kind of job you can just abandon. I'm fielding calls from the press and—"

"Pass them on to PR. That's what they're there for."

"This is a big story. They don't want a talking head. They want Luc DeForges. They want to know where their leader is in a time of crisis."

"I'll call the chairman now and make a statement. In the meantime, tell them the truth. I had urgent family business."

"You have no family."

"I do have a family. I'm just not married. What do you think, I was raised by wolves?"

"Sometimes I've wondered."

He hung up and tried to open the back door, but it was locked. After fumbling with one door after another, he eventually found he'd walked around the entire building and twenty minutes had passed. When he finally got back in, it was to find the band members milling around looking at their song list for the wedding. Katie . . . and Eileen . . . were nowhere in sight.

Chapter 12

~

Swinging on a Star

Katie gave a thumbs-up to the band and stepped down from the stage. She'd been blinded by stage lights during Eileen's entrance, but she'd know that teenage frame anywhere. She grabbed on to her friend as if Eileen had been lost at sea. "How did you get here? You got your classes covered?"

"Not without some moaning, but I managed. My mom said Pokey's getting fluids this morning, and they have house-guests. So I'm staying at your place until tomorrow." Eileen led her around the velvet curtain and outside into the scalding sunlight. "You sounded great in there."

Katie blinked rapidly and her eyes watered as they tried

to adjust. The air loomed stiflingly hot, as if the entire city was situated inside a giant sauna bath. "Thanks."

"Olivia thought so too." Eileen stood back so that the two women could see each other.

"You're the bride!" Katie said.

"You're the singer! Let me hug you. You haven't been gone that long, to forget that we hug down here."

The blonde had a strong grip, and Katie felt a bit crushed. "You two have met?"

Eileen placed a foot on the wall of the building and stretched her hamstring. She bounced against the building, then switched feet. "Sure. Olivia was worried I might be an extra guest crashing her wedding. I assured her I wouldn't be there. If I want to hear you sing, I can just wait for your shower, right?"

Olivia looked mortified. "I didn't mean—"

Eileen waved her hand dismissively. "No harm done. I'm not really the cotillion type anyway, am I, Katie?"

"She doesn't even wear dresses," Katie said.

"I was telling Olivia," Eileen continued, "I came out early to beat Dex."

"Beat Dex where?" Katie asked.

"Actually, in the shins, but what I mean is he's flying here to New Orleans after work tonight."

Katie shook her head. "Dexter wouldn't do that. He hates surprises."

"Remember when he said that he'd meet your mother before the engagement? You know he's a very literal person, right?" Eileen stared at Olivia. "Dex is the one you have to worry about crashing your wedding. No offense, but I couldn't care less. I just had this sixth sense you'd need me to warn you."

Katie thought about the ramifications of Dex's coming to her home, how she hadn't prepared him for her mother's blunt ways and how he wasn't schooled in the fine art of subtle conversation with Southern women. Her nervousness about her singing dissipated amidst the reality that Dexter Hastings and Irene McKenna would be in the same proximity without a thorough briefing on one another. Mam spoke Southern Subtext and Dexter, Silicon Valley Literal. It would take a Geneva Convention for these two to come together.

"Dexter in New Orleans," she pondered. Her stomach jumbled at the thought that her boyfriend might have walked in on Luc kissing her. How would she explain that? How *could* she explain that? Her limbs began to shake as she absorbed what had happened.

"Don't take him to a restaurant. He doesn't eat spicy food, and there's nothing worse in this town than a man who can't down his Tabasco."

"Judging by your discussion with Luc this morning, he won't like sharing his date." Olivia's blue eyes ignited, and it was understood that the words were a veiled threat. Katie's escapade into history had not gone unnoticed by the bride.

"What discussion? Luc no longer has a say in anything Katie does," Eileen said.

"For someone with no say, his lips seemed to be doing a lot of speaking in the club."

"Luc's all bluster. Don't you know that by now?" Eileen asked, bending at the waist and dropping her arms to the banquette.

"Would you stop that?" Katie pounced. "You're making me as nervous as a cat!"

"It doesn't normally bother you." Eileen looked to Olivia. "I have a hard time sitting still. The body just wants to go." She rocked her fists like she was running. "So anyway, I think Dex is coming to meet your mam and propose, so he can get this wedding on. That boy is more anxious to get married than any woman I ever saw. You'd think he was the one people call an old maid."

Katie gave a nervous laugh. "So who are the guests your parents have in town for the wedding? Anybody I know?" She hoped to keep the two of them from saying any more about Luc.

"To tell you the truth, I didn't even ask. What's your momma cooking tonight?"

"Nothing good for us, if that's what you're worried about."

"I have absolution here," Eileen claimed. "The spices knock out the calories. Besides, I have to be sweating out about four times the calories in this heat."

"How'd you get a flight this late? Did your mother pay for the trip?"

"I already told you, I'm charging Luc."

"Considering you're here to make sure I never see him

again, I doubt he's going to be feeling generous toward you—although he'd probably give you return fare right now. But I can use you here, so let's wait on that. When do you think Dex will get here?"

"My guess is not until about seven or so. He was going to get off early from work."

"How'd you find all this out?"

"Well, when I saw that his status on Facebook said *Surprising the woman I love,* I did what any self-respecting best friend would do. I called his mother and asked what he was up to."

"You're wasting your time in a gym; you should be an undercover spy."

"I'll have to admit, I didn't think he had it in him to actually chase you. It shows drive and—dare I say it? Passion."

"Dexter has chased me before."

"When?" Eileen probed.

"He asked me to marry him, didn't he?"

Olivia grabbed them each by the crook of the arm. "I'm going to take you both out to coffee. We'll get to be friends, us Southern girls. I want to hear all about Ryan when he was in college!"

"Don't you have, I don't know, wedding stuff to do?" Eileen sounded annoyed.

"I'm Olivia Tyler." The young woman paused for recognition. "The bride. That means I can do as I like, and I'd like to take you both out for a café au lait."

Olivia possessed a Katharine Hepburn air about her; she

was a wistful, intellectual sort, slightly masculine in her features. Considering Ryan's artsy qualities, Katie supposed this was a good fit for each of them. Everyone needed balance in their lives.

"Eileen's probably tired after her trip," she said, while her roommate continued to stretch and twitch like a rabid ferret. "You know, emotionally tired," she added.

Olivia bristled. "Surely a café au lait won't take too long."

"I'm honored that you and Ryan asked me to sing at your wedding, Olivia. That song, 'Someone to Watch Over Me,' means a lot to me because it was one of the first I used to sing to the audiences here at the Barrelhouse Club."

"Luc told me. He has very fond memories of that song. I daresay I've never seen him quite so smitten when he talks about anyone."

"You should see him when he talks to the mirror," Eileen deadpanned.

Olivia ignored her. "Luc needs to settle down, Katie. He's losing himself in this job and he's ready. I don't know the full story about what happened, but I do know him well enough to know he's sincere in his feelings."

Eileen opened her mouth but shut it when Katie held up a finger.

"Olivia, there's romance in the air," she said by way of excuse. "But Luc and I . . . we're just working on closure."

"It's closed. Let's go eat," Eileen said.

"Is that what you call it? Closure?" Olivia fidgeted with an amethyst amulet around her neck, which hung on a raw black leather strap, giving her Bohemian classic look a permanency. "What I saw in there—"

"Closure!"

Eileen glared at her, and Katie felt color rush to her cheeks. "Maybe we might make those café au laits iced, you think, Olivia?"

Recognition dawned in Olivia's bright eyes. "Sure. Sure. My car is right this way. If you're hungry, we can grab a bite while we're out too."

"Oh." Katie held her hands up. "I don't have my purse. I must have left it in Rusty's truck this morning."

"It's my treat, I already told you. We can talk all about the DeForges family. I'm dying to know how you got along with Mrs. DeForges. Especially after that night. You have to tell me everything."

The words drifted off as Katie tuned out. She felt limp from the heat and the emotion of the day. This was exactly why she hadn't wanted to come home. "I'd really like to get home. I'm not used to this heat anymore, and my mother is expecting me."

"A coffee won't slow you down. People expect you to be late, you're in New Orleans."

"You're probably not eating well. Did your mother make you fried okra last night?" Eileen prodded. "I told you that you're allergic to okra."

"I did head to Central City for a beignet this morning."

"Of course you did." Eileen grasped her by the wrist and checked her pulse, as if she'd wilt right there.

Katie wriggled free. "I'm fine. Let's get that coffee." Her mind was full. She hadn't thought singing would bring memories to life, but dancing alongside Ryan was as though she was meeting Luc for the first time. It was as if she'd entered into a perfect moment, held still in time by a glass bubble. None of their history was there, none of the pain, only this man who stood out among many in the audience, a rogue beam of light concentrated upon him. His height and his distinctive, decisive good looks caught her attention like shiny objects to a catfish. She simply couldn't look away. She hadn't believed in love at first sight until that moment, because the way he looked at her, it was as though he saw inside her very soul. Now she wondered how she could have been so very wrong . . . how Luc's actions could be so incongruent with what she had thought him to be.

"My car's right here," Olivia said.

Katie looked at Eileen, then back at Olivia. "It's a Prius," she said. "I thought Luc said your father was in oil."

"He is." Olivia shrugged. "Get in."

Eileen opened the door. "We're going to do yoga with prayer when we get home, Katie. You need it. You look pale. Does your mother have carpet in her new house?" Eileen pulled a lever and opened the backseat, crawling in like a hermit crab into a new home. "Doesn't matter, we can use the grass out front. She has a garden in this new place, right?"

"Eileen, nothing says California weirdo like yoga on the front lawn. I just need a nap, is all."

She needed to let go of Luc DeForges and this fantasy

that he really loved her, that he would protect her from harm and not heap more on her. Isn't that how women got into abusive situations? They ignored the facts they didn't want to see? She wanted to have her eyes wide open. She sat in the passenger seat and exchanged looks with Eileen as they waited for Olivia to climb inside. It would all be over soon. Her feelings for Luc, and her ill-fated history, would all be forgotten. She just had to trudge forward and face her fears.

Olivia pulled out into oncoming traffic so quickly, Katie saw her life pass before her eyes.

"When Luc suggested we invite you to sing—"

"Luc? You mean Ryan."

"Right. Ryan. That's what I said, right?" Olivia said.

"You said Luc," Eileen said.

"Right. I meant Ryan. When Ryan asked you to sing—"

"Listen, I don't mean to be rude, Olivia. I'm really thrilled that you're having Katie remember just how talented she is at singing. If anything, maybe it will get her back into the church band that does concerts off campus and stuff, not the safe one that performs only for church on Sundays. But I really have to be straight with you: Katie is absolutely and diabolically opposed to any sort of future relationship with Luc DeForges."

"Is that so?" Olivia said, glowering at Eileen in the rearview mirror.

Katie swallowed hard.

"Sure," Eileen said. "If anything, she'd like to forget the past relationship she's had with him. In fact, if they ever allow that kind of technology where they burn memories out of your brain, I think Katie should totally sign up. It's *that* over."

"I think I'm going to be sick," Katie said. "Can you stop the car, please? Olivia?"

Olivia pulled out of traffic as quickly as she'd pulled in, and Katie nearly vomited as she stumbled out of the car. She stood on the banquette in her red dress and pumps and waited for the world to stop spinning.

"Do you need something to drink?" asked Olivia, who'd gotten out and hurried around to stand beside her.

"I think I just need air." She sucked in a deep breath but didn't catch nearly enough oxygen to satisfy her lungs. She tried again, nearly hyperventilating in the humidity. "I'm going to walk. I'll see you at home."

"We're in Central City," Olivia pointed out.

"She means you're dressed like a hooker!" Eileen shouted through the sunroof. Her best friend rose out of the hole at the top of the car and threw a garment at her.

Katie unraveled a wadded-up T-shirt and put it on over her dress. Next Eileen tossed a shoe at her. Then another. Katie stepped out of her pumps and sheepishly handed them to Olivia.

"You're not going to get a coffee with us?"

Katie clutched her stomach. "I don't think I could take it."

"Well, all right. If you're sure."

"I'll be all right. I grew up in the Channel," she said. "I want to walk by my daddy's store. Maybe my lungs will adjust after the walk."

"You can't walk to the Channel and then to Uptown in this heat. Are you insane?" Eileen shouted.

"I can take the streetcar if I need to or the public." The public was the bus system. For some reason, New Orleaners never added *bus* to the title.

Eileen was still yelling from inside the car. "No, wait. I'm coming with you."

"You have no shoes," Katie pointed out as she slipped them onto her own feet. "I'll see you soon. Tell Mam I'll be home for dinner."

Before Eileen could say another word, Olivia had climbed back inside, slammed the door, and squealed away from the curb.

Katie looked around. She was at the end of the Central, so she walked through the lovely Garden District dreamily . . . *it's de-lightful . . . it's de-lovely*. There was something magical about a canopy of trees that allowed her to escape whatever pain she might bear. The garden of green reminded her that she wasn't alone, that if God cared for the lilies of the field, how much more did he care for her? Marriage. Children. They were a woman's highest honor. Surely God would reward her. She was doing the right thing. She was walking away from temptation. Granted, one could argue she hadn't walked quickly enough that morning, but Dexter's presence would soothe her. He'd remind her how perfect everything would be, doing God's will for her life.

The Bible said to look at a man's fruit. Sure, Luc had a lot of fruit in the form of produce, but in actual good deeds? He didn't give anything away he couldn't afford to lose. Whereas Dexter . . . look at the time Dexter spent on church activities and committees. He was a man whose word meant something, a man of integrity.

Katie stopped before an ancient live oak with its magnificent low spread of branches and mossy boughs dripping, as though dressed in vibrant green scarves. Humbling oneself was a hard cross to bear with Luc in her midst. She felt like a fool falling for his beautiful words and deep, meaningful looks. A man's character was shown in his actions. Luc's actions were heart-wrenching and wounded her to the core. She wanted to rid herself of that weak part of her soul and skip down the aisle with Dexter.

She stared at her bare ring finger. If her mother didn't have the ring, she couldn't imagine where it might be. She removed the idea from her head that maybe she'd only come to New Orleans to be near Luc, to either offer him a final word of good-bye or let herself know that he meant nothing to her any longer. She wanted to start her life with Dexter fresh, and could she do that if she still held animosity for Luc and the humiliation he'd caused her and her family?

Luc's mentioning the ring to her forced her heart rate up. She couldn't bear to think that once again he had the upper hand, that she was nothing more than an idle bump in his road of life.

She walked south to Magazine Street but slowed her pace as she approached her father's old store. She clasped her eyes shut and sucked in a deep breath of languid air before taking the plunge to the next block. The store was gone, naturally, as were three or four of his previous neighbors. Luc's gleaming, shiny full-scale grocery appeared in neon: FORAGES—SERVING CONSCIOUS EATERS SINCE 2002. The sight of it overwhelmed her, and she felt her father's loss deeply as if it was as fresh as his produce.

On the banquette, her father used to pile old farming bins with the freshest local fruits and vegetables—and invite his friends to sell their fresh seafood catch when the season was right. Luc's store did the same, but in a glossy, overbearing way, almost making the fruit appear plastic. The wooden bins looked like something on Main Street in Disneyland.

"Help you, miss?" A young, skinny college-age student appeared, wearing a khaki apron with the conscious-eating slogan slashed across his chest. Conscious eating? She thought this kid made a better billboard for starving urchins in foreign countries. She was still on the banquette and was surprised to see him outside. She knew Luc specified service, but coming outside and questioning people at the bins, that felt extreme. Her father never would have pressured a customer. Of course, that's why she wore practical shoes and they lived in a shotgun house.

"What's the best kind of apple right now?" She pitched the question like a fastball.

"We've got these Jonagolds on special."

"Fuji," she corrected him. "In June, the Fujis and the Empires." She knew the Jonagolds were available, but it wasn't their peak. This fresh eating business was nothing more than a consumer ploy.

"Look at this one." He held up a large, round apple, perfectly unblemished.

"I'm the Empire of my daddy's eye, you know."

"Is that so?"

"See this?" She showed him the crown of a ripe Crispin apple and felt a bit like Snow White's wicked stepmother. "This brown at the crown is all the sugar. These pockmarks and lines mean this is the sweetest apple available right now. You don't want a perfect-looking apple."

"Let me know if you need any help," he said, as he backed away. Who could blame him?

She entered the store through the wide, open barn-like doors. Inside, the store expanded into a cavernous but warm warehouse. The exposed electrical system and greenery unfolded like a high-tech version of nature. Almost as though she'd walked into another world, not the normal sterile drudgery of a grocery store.

The LED lighting captured her attention and she twisted under the bulb, scrutinizing the way it imitated natural sunlight. She wanted to stamp her feet and scream that her father's food was a connection to the earth and its goodness, not a pale mockery of a farmers market with the illusion of conscious eating. But what did it matter? The illusion is what people wanted. Even her father would have admitted that much. The customer was always right. Even when they were wrong.

The stick-figure boy had followed her inside. He held the same apple, one slice protruding from the rest of the fruit, a paring knife in his other hand. "Customers want perfect apples, and that's what we strive to give them at Forages."

She took the proffered fruit and bit into it. "Good," she said. But not as good as Paddy's. It never would be.

Chapter 13

⌒

It's Delovely

Katie wandered deeper into the store and felt surrounded by lush greenery. Misters pumped fresh water onto the produce and floral arrangements. Copper-colored display counters were separated and marked by sections: Seafood, Fresh Soups, Garden Salads, Poultry, Meat. She wished life could be so easily labeled: *Feelings, Truth, God's Will, The Narrow Gate—Enter This Way.*

She sighed as she listened to the waterfall sounds trickle from a collection of tropical fruit under a man-made water fountain. Piled pineapples rose into a bark-sided pyramid and held a cup turned to its side, forcing the water to descend.

She wondered what her father would think of Luc's changes. Would he see them as a vast improvement or a crime against fruit and a terrible waste for people who simply wanted good food on their table?

Each circular aisle brought some new surprise, either a new way to display food or a different idea for cooking a rare food product, like couscous. Katie read labels, explored foreign recipes, and marveled at all the ways Luc created something special from the ordinary. He truly thought outside the box, and the world rewarded him for his creativity. Luc DeForges was extraordinary. The proof surrounded her.

She wandered the store, almost making a game of avoiding the overzealous and annoyingly helpful employees. At least an hour must have passed before she arrived in the colorful, fresh floral department, which dripped with blooms and aroused all of her senses.

She inhaled the fresh scent of roses and the heavy scent of gardenias, mingled in a perfect medley of sweet and indulgent. The roses aroused her memory of that awful night years ago in the DeForges mansion. Unwittingly, she drifted back in time . . .

YOU ARE CORDIALLY INVITED TO

A GRADUATION PARTY

TO CELEBRATE A

BACHELOR OF SCIENCE DEGREE IN APPLIED BUSINESS

Awarded to Luc DeForges

from

Tulane University

May 4th at seven thirty in the evening

At the DeForges Mansion

Charles Street, New Orleans

No gifts, please

"Mam! Mam!" She'd run the invitation to her mother, barely able to contain her squeals. "She's invited me. Mrs. DeForges invited me. I told you!"

Things would be different now. Luc's mother understood that she loved her son for who he was, not for his money.

Mam's brow darkened. "Sweetheart, that is wonderful, but I don't want you to read too much into this. It's only natural that she would invite Luc's friends to his graduation party."

"Are you saying I'm not *really* invited?"

"I'm only saying that I wouldn't read too much into it . . . the idea that it came from Mrs. DeForges. She's learned to do things a certain way. Properly. Inviting you to Luc's party is the proper thing to do."

"It did come from her, though!" She waved the invitation's vellum envelope in front of her mam. "Look, it has her seal on it and everything!"

"Katie, people—not just Mrs. DeForges, but most people—do things formally here. Mrs. DeForges is doing what all the other mothers are doing when their sons graduate from college."

"I'm graduating from college too, Mam. It's not like Loyola University is any less prestigious. I'm the first one in our family to graduate! Maybe we should invite Luc's family to my party. No one cooks better than you, Mam. We could use Grammy's china, and we'd have nothing to be ashamed of."

Mam brushed the bangs from Katie's forehead as if she was still a child. "We don't have anything to be ashamed of, sweetheart. If anyone looks down on another, it's their own lack of breeding."

"She doesn't, Mam. Paddy told me Mrs. DeForges would come around. He told me, Mam!" She paused. "No, don't make that face at me. He was right. He knew people."

"Your father, God rest his soul, your father only saw the best in people. I know Mrs. DeForges does a lot of good in this community, but that doesn't mean that she wants her son to marry you. You're both so young, and there's an entire world out there. I'm sure Mrs. DeForges has nothing against you personally—she just wants the best for her son."

"I am what's best for him."

"Then there will be time." Mam patted her cheek. "You have your daddy's ability to see the best in people, and that's a gift, Katie. But it can also be a curse if you don't protect yourself from the wrong sorts."

"How can you not see the good in her, Mam? She's invited me."

Katie clutched the invitation to her heart. It changed the game. Until that moment she'd been nothing more than a waif to Mrs. DeForges; an unclaimed friend of Ryan and Luc that she paid no mind. Nothing more than a ministry for her Junior League Friends, an Eliza Doolittle from the Channel.

Until she saw Luc and Katie under the magnolia tree. Mrs. DeForges' reaction sent birds flying off in several directions, but Katie forced that thought away. Paddy would want her to seek reconciliation. To see the best in others. And this seemed like the perfect opportunity to show how forgiving she could be—because Luc's love was worth the trouble.

"Katie, you're too young to be serious about any boy, much less Luc DeForges. There are two kinds of men, Katie. There are men who make you feel like Luc DeForges makes you feel with their skills and their charm, and then there are the men you marry . . ."

"Luc *is* the man I'm going to marry! He loves me, Mam! I know he does. I'll prove it to you. You just wait until after this party. You'll see."

Luc's graduation party wasn't the end, it was only the beginning, where they would announce their love publicly for the first time.

"Luc is the one and only man I'll ever love. Mrs. DeForges sees that now, and so will you."

Mam gave her a dismissive smile, which made her more determined than ever to prove her wrong.

"Gosh, what an idiot I was," Katie said aloud. She lifted a bouquet of red roses and sniffed them. Mam was right, of course. When had her momma ever been wrong when it came to the character of another person?

Katie searched the store for some reminder of her dad, some homage that paid tribute to the man who created Luc's spark for taking healthy eating global, while maintaining the idea of eating locally. Failing to find anything, her walk slowed and an employee managed to catch her.

The middle-aged woman, who did nothing to hide the Southern frizz in her hair and wore the same khaki apron as the kid out front, spoke to her. "Are you all right, miss? You having trouble finding something?"

"My dad owned this store," she said softly. "Before, when it was a real grocery and all. He just had fruit and vegetables and staples. You know, dairy, eggs, bread—oh, and peanut butter and jelly, because he always said inevitably some momma would forget about her child's lunch for school the following day."

"Bless yo heart, dahlin'. You come sit down right here." The woman patted a rattan chair she'd pulled next to the flowers. "Why are you dressed like that, sweetie? You been to a funeral or something?"

Katie looked down at her getup and shook her head. A red chiffon dress, tennis shoes, and an oversized T-shirt. The woman, whose name tag identified her as Pat, probably thought she was nuts. She knew her father would have treated a disoriented ragamuffin the same way had one wandered into his store, and it was as though his spirit was alive in the business.

"You've got a good heart, Pat. My dad would have appreciated that."

"Sit here for a minute, hon. I'm going to get you some water." Pat came back with a paper cup.

Katie drained the cold liquid and crumpled the cup in her hand. "It's nice here. Luc's done a good job."

"You know Mr. DeForges?"

"Well, I did." She shrugged. "Once."

"You must have never grieved his loss."

"Wh-what?"

"Your father. You must never have grieved his passing. You can't bypass that kind of grief. It only waits for you at the other side of whatever you've avoided it with. I've seen it time and time again." Pat's frizzled, weather-beaten look belied her warmth.

Katie wondered at how caring people could be. Had she avoided this kind of community since leaving home? If she was honest, even church didn't feel as warm as this solitary chair in Luc's store.

"Katie!"

She turned to see Luc rushing toward her, holding her handbag. "We've been worried sick."

"I just left the club."

He showed her his watch. "It's nearly eight o'clock. You left the club hours ago."

Katie searched for an acceptable excuse, but there was nothing more than she'd become consumed, spellbound by Luc's consideration of every detail. He'd created a world unto itself, one that made a customer forget the mundane task of marketing.

"Hello, Mr. DeForges." Pat held out her hand to her boss.

"Luc, this is Pat. She got me hydrated and stopped me from wandering your store aimlessly. It's incredible, Luc. I'm afraid I got rather lost in all the details."

"Actually, she wandered for quite a while before I finally got her a chair. I think she was avoiding me."

Luc put a hand on Pat's shoulder. "Thank you. Thanks for seeing to her." He knelt in front of Katie. "You ready to go?"

"I'm ready."

Luc stood and took her hand. "Come here. I want to show you something first."

She followed as Luc walked resolutely through the aisles and dodged carts until they passed the cash registers and came to a community bulletin board. It was next to the espresso café and over the condiment table, which was filled to the edges with Southern sauces and utensils for the myriad take-out items.

"Nice," she said. "It's making me hungry."

He seemed to want more from her. "No, look." He pointed to the wall.

A picture of Paddy stared back at her.

"My father!"

His smiling eyes and toothy grin met her, and she reached out for his sun-ravaged face. Underneath the photo, in gold, were etched the words IN MEMORIAM IAN "PADDY" McKENNA, FATHER OF FRESH EATING IN NEW ORLEANS 1954 – 2001.

She fingered the letters. Then Luc braced her elbows as she leaned into him, her back against his chest.

Katie beamed with pride. Maybe she'd been too hard on Luc. It wasn't his fault she'd made a fool of herself. Maybe she'd convinced herself by then that she was as good at reading people as her mother. Whatever it may have been, she needed to let it go. Luc had moved on; it was time for her to do the same.

"Luc." She turned her head so that her ear rested on his heart. His breathing sounded shallow. "I'm sorry. I blamed you because it was easier. I lost my way because I loved you and I wanted you to love me back." She felt lighter with the admission.

"Sh, sh. I did love you back. Do love you back."

She peered up under his strong jaw. From her angle, and in the store's light, Luc was all shadows and mystery, but his heart felt familiar. Like home.

"Men are different from women," she said. "It was my duty to stop—"

He kissed the crown of her head. "We need to go, Katie. Your mam's worried, I'm sure."

She twisted in his arms, and he surrounded her at the back of her waist. He made her feel so safe. How did he do that?

Chapter 14

In the Cool, Cool, Cool of the Evening

It was said by all who knew Irene McKenna Slater that she had a sophisticated understanding of proper society and how decorum operated. Irene knew her place in the world. While Papa told Katie that she could reach for the sky and pluck any star to her liking, Mam had a more practical theory on the futility of chasing rainbows. "People belong where they belong," Mam would say. "You can pluck an Irish Channel girl and put her somewhere else, but someone will remember her as the girl from the Irish Channel. There's nothing to be ashamed of in being who you are. If God created a person to sell vegetables, he should sell the best vegetables there are and do whatever he can to satisfy his customers."

Even as the Irish Channel's neighborhood grew in prestige, due mostly to its higher elevation and proximity to Uptown, Mam clung to the roots of the old neighborhood and what it meant to be a part of her Celtic heritage. Though most of the neighborhood was African American by the time Katie grew up, Mam never saw a bit of difference in a person's skin color. If they were in the Irish Channel, they were Irish to Mam.

So it just made no sense to Katie that Mam had moved to the Garden District. But seeing the gated Victorian, with its Celtic cross and statuary in the front garden, she supposed the Channel wasn't far behind.

"Mam's house looks a bit like a cemetery, wouldn't you say?"

Luc chuckled. "It's a nice house." He pulled to the curb in his brother's Prius. Apparently, Ryan and Olivia had been given matching cars for a wedding present.

Katie gasped. Her mother's covered gallery porch teemed with people under the light, but through them all she could make out Dexter's image.

"What? What's wrong?"

"Dexter's here."

"How do you know? The gallery's bursting at the seams with people."

Katie didn't answer.

Dexter stood against the front window, as though he

thought he couldn't be seen, but he actually made himself more obvious in his misty movements. His tall frame hardly lent itself to disappearing. Reaching for the car door handle, still with Luc at her side, she wondered how she'd explain their day together to Dex.

"What are they all doing here, anyway?"

"You know my mam. Every night's a party." She scrambled out of the car and ran up the steps. "Dexter!" she called over the hum of chatter. She ricocheted from guest to guest. Some she recognized; others were just random faces in all colors and sizes. So many chairs cluttered the shared townhouse gallery that the porch looked like a Mardi Gras float. The sky was just darkening, and she knew she'd created a stir being gone for so long.

"Where have you been?" Mam scolded. "We very nearly called the police! If it hadn't been for Luc saying he knew where you'd gone . . ."

"I'm sorry," she muttered. "The time got away from me. Have you met Dexter?"

"Yes, I've met him. I'm afraid he's not used to all of the noise in our house. We'll have to work him up to it."

"Dex is an only child," she said to her mother.

"So are you!" Mam answered.

"*Your* only child is a far different cry, Mam." Katie laughed but grew serious at the sight of Dex standing pressed against the wooden window frame.

He seemed agitated, but what right did he have to be angry? She hadn't asked him to come, and he certainly couldn't expect Mam to quiet things for him. At least not without warning.

She swallowed her guilt, remembering what it had felt like to be in Luc's arms again. What did that say about her? She knew what it said. It said she was as dumb as a box of rocks and not worthy of a man like Dexter, that's what it said.

"Hey, Dex, can I have a hug?"

He loosed himself from the wall and hugged her, then checked his watch. "I hadn't planned to be here this late."

"It's only eight thirty," she said.

"I brought work with me."

Eileen came up and wrapped an arm around her. "Dexter, Katie has a habit of disappearing, don't you know. Remember that time in high school when we snuck out for Mardi Gras? I thought your dad was going to kill us!"

"You snuck out in high school?" Dexter asked as if she'd committed murder one. Her beau was not a man to under stand misbehavior, not for any reason—but in New Orleans during Mardi Gras, it was practically cultural.

Eileen went on, oblivious to Dexter's shock. "When I saw the grill of his old Chevy truck coming around that corner, I knew we were toast. I couldn't think up a story that fast. Not one you'd go along with, anyway."

"We cleaned toilets at the store for two weeks after that," Katie said to Dexter, hoping he saw justice as served.

He pulled her into the doorway and spoke into her ear. "I'm here to ask your mother's hand, I mean, ask for *your* hand in marriage. I thought you'd want to start wearing your ring right away, and what kind of fiancé would I be if I didn't come down and ask properly?"

"That was sweet," she said truthfully.

"I wanted to meet your family first too."

"What do you think?"

"They're very . . . very *friendly.*"

Eileen, eavesdropping from the porch, laughed at his composure. "What's the matter, Dex? It's like you've got sand in your oysters. You're in New Orleans, loosen up!"

He stared at his watch again. "I'm sorry, Katie. I wasn't expecting all this ruckus. It threw me off my game. Then you drive up with Luc. Did you spend the entire day with him?" His jaw clenched. "When you weren't here, I got worried I'd made an error in judgment. I called Pastor earlier."

"You called Pastor?"

Dex paced the entryway. His expensive shoes clicked on Mam's hardwood floors as guests separated like the Red Sea. Dex turned back around and took her by the arm into the foyer. "I just got nervous. I'd expected to surprise you, and instead you surprised me. And what are you wearing, anyway?"

"You got nervous? About what? That your girlfriend was missing? Or that your schedule, which you didn't make me aware of, was rearranged?" She drew in a deep breath. If she was honest, it was her own guilt that forced her to snap at Dexter. He had every right to expect her to be at her mam's, not with Luc off on one of her jaunts. And it was sweet of him to go out of his comfort zone and surprise her.

"Katie, you're making a scene. I was worried about you." He gazed around him, as if he noticed the crowd for the first time.

She looked outside onto the gallery. If she'd made any sort of scene, no one but Dexter seemed to notice. "I'm sorry, Dexter. It's been a long day. Lot of emotion since yesterday. I need to tell you about something."

"I wanted to surprise you, Katie," he said warmly. "I'm doing my best to romance you. I'm clumsy at this sort of thing, but it doesn't mean I love you any less."

"Of course not. I know that, Dex."

"Your mom's having some kind of party. I think I should come back tomorrow when the house is quieter, so we can talk."

She nodded. She felt her heart thump in her throat, upset that they hadn't really solved anything. When Dexter didn't get his way, he generally threw a quiet, irritated tantrum or began negotiations to convince her of his side. His voice was always so measured, his demeanor so stoic—she'd never noticed until now, when they had an audience. She was Irish. When her family threw a tantrum, you good and well knew it.

He stepped into the hallway and withdrew a single black suitcase. "I need to get some sleep. Irene," he said to Mam, "may I borrow the phone to call a cab?"

"A cab? Where're you going? Don't we have the beer you like or something?"

"No," Dex said. "I'm tired. I wanted to head to the hotel."

"Hotel?" Mam squealed. "Listen, I've slept twenty in a shotgun row house. No guest of mine is staying in a hotel."

Dexter raised his suitcase. "I've got a load of work to do tonight. I want to have an important conversation with you in the morning." He slapped his suitcase. "Want to be in top form."

Mam grabbed at his suitcase, which Dexter wouldn't relinquish. The two of them stood there, locked in a battle of wills.

"Dexter, you may as well let go," Katie said. "My mother's not going to let you go to a hotel."

"I have a reservation," Dex said.

And Mam let go of the suitcase, just like that. Katie had never seen a guest win that particular battle with her mam, and she knew what it meant. Mam *wanted* him to go. The air rushed from her lungs. At home, Dexter fit so perfectly into her life. How could a change of locale make them so vastly different?

Her mother reached for the phone. "I'll call you a cab, Dexter."

"Very good." He glanced at his watch again. "Heavens, it's hot here." He tugged at his collar.

"Get that tie off, for one thing." Katie started to unfasten it, but he brushed her hands away.

"What time will you be free tomorrow for me to express my wishes to your mother and stepfather?"

"I don't know." She shrugged. "Mam, what's the schedule for tomorrow?"

"How would I know? It's still today. We'll figure out tomorrow when it happens. Rusty's going out shrimping tonight. He should be back home by about ten in the morning."

"Dexter wants a time."

"So give him one," Mam said. "We'll work it out."

"Why don't you come at eleven, Dex? I'll make brunch."

"On a weekday?"

"Yes," she answered firmly. "Dexter, I need to talk to you about something. Maybe we're rushing things a bit—"

Dexter pecked her on the cheek. "We'll talk tomorrow." He jogged to the street as the cab pulled up. The trunk opened, Dexter tossed his bag inside, and soon only red tail-lights marked his having been there at all.

Katie blinked slowly and wondered how to explain his strange behavior. At the same time, she wondered if maybe his social skills were skewed by the Bay Area's lack of connection skills. Perhaps she'd become immune, and he ceased to stand out there. What if she'd made a terrible mistake? Correction, what if she'd made *another* terrible mistake?

Mam grabbed her by the wrist, passed the settee in the living room, and walked up the stairs. She stared back with a look that said to follow her. Katie did.

When they reached the top of the stairs, Mam opened a door, led her into her grayish-green bedroom with the old cast-iron bed, and crossed her arms. Like a metronome, when Mam stopped walking, the silence clamored for attention.

"What was that?"

"I don't know, Mam. I've never seen him like that."

The questions came like bullets. "Why are you getting married to that man? Why are you home now? Why is Luc DeForges here in my house again? Why is your best friend on my gallery? What is going on? You come home for a visit and bring the entire state with you?"

Katie shrugged.

"I want an answer!"

"Sorry, I thought it was a rhetorical question. The house is full of people I've never met."

"I invited them. It's my house! Katie, that man is afraid of his own shadow. If someone breaks into your house, who's going to beat him off with a stick? You?"

"Well, I could."

"I know you could, but, Katie . . . I don't understand it. All these years you waited. I thought you were waiting for Luc, but then you announce you're marrying some stranger. I want to like him, sweetheart. But why now?"

"I'm getting married because it's time and I want to have a family."

"No, that's why men get married. Women get married because they're in love."

"I love Dexter but in a good, safe way. A healthy way, not where I'll lose my mind and make a complete fool of myself in front of everyone we know."

"Katie, listen. I may be old, but I have not lost all my faculties. Tell me what you love about that man, besides the fact that he isn't Luc DeForges. I will give him points for that much, but, Katie, tell me what I'm not seeing."

"You don't like him, then?" Katie wrung her hands. "What did he do?" She couldn't imagine what had Mam so agitated.

"Tell me what you love about him." Her mother sat on the bed and crossed her legs underneath her.

It brought her comfort to watch Mam do that. It was the pose she used to take every night before she read a bedtime story and prayed over her.

"Mam, he's very bright. He went to MIT, and he's—"

"He can be as bright as the North Star, but if he can't put two words of greeting together, he's no match for you. You're a social creature, Katie."

"Not nearly as social as I used to be." Her shoulders fell. "I can't defend him. I can't defend myself. Mam, I kissed Luc today." Without pausing she went back to describing Dex. "He'll be a good dad. He's very intellectual. He's punctual. He's had the same job since he got out of his PhD program, and that's not easy to do in the consumer electronics field. Technology changes daily. He picks up on the new stuff and leads the way. He writes iPhone Apps for a hobby, and he's made quite a lot doing that."

"What does he do with the extra money?"

"I don't know. It's not my business."

"Why isn't it your business? Your father didn't make a dime that I didn't know where it went. I didn't ask, but he told me because he said if anything happened, I'd need to know. And I did, so your father was right. Ignorance is not honoring a man, Katie. Does he try to keep it from you?"

"We just don't talk about money. It's not really an issue. We're not married yet."

"What's the last gift he gave you?"

"I don't know."

"You don't know?" Mam slid off the bed and went over to a wooden box on the antique dresser. She opened it, and "Some Enchanted Evening" began to play. Her mother dug both hands into the box and lifted out strings of glittering baubles.

Katie studied them closer and saw familiar things: strings of pearls, saltwater and fresh, a garnet pendant, her mother's birthstone, and lots of gold chains and ear bobs, as Mam called them.

"That's not fair. Dad's grandfather was a jeweler."

"Dexter is not . . . he's not *kind*, Katie."

Mam's words had merit, and it surprised Katie that she couldn't dispute them. Dexter did all the right things. He said all the right things, opened car doors for her, helped her on with her coat—but Mam was right, his actions weren't marked by a benevolent spirit.

"He brought me his extra suitcase to borrow," she said.

"Aha!" Mam said. "You saw the suitcase he had with him. Did he give you the good suitcase? Or take it for himself?"

Katie slid her hand down the long bedpost.

"That's what I thought. You know, Katie, you can plan so that nothing goes wrong in life. But something will, and it won't be what you expected to go wrong. So make sure you're with someone who will help you bail the water out of the boat, not someone who will blame you for the hole."

"Mam, what's going on down there?" She watched Olivia come up the walkway with Ryan on her arm. Ryan held a potted bromeliad that looked like a giant red pineapple, and two lawn chairs hung from his elbow. Several band members she recognized from the rehearsal also trotted up the walkway with cookies and various local treats in hand. It was then that she noted all the seating on the front porch and their sheer mass registered. Folding chairs, lawn chairs, deck chairs.

"Oh, they're here! I have to get down there. Katie, get some clothes on and come outside. Luc has a surprise for you!"

Katie turned off the light, so she couldn't be seen from outside, and tossed off her dress and pulled on a pair of jeans. She selected a lightweight cotton T with sleeves to fight off the mosquitoes. Then she went to the window and saw a large truck pull up into the street and two workmen get out and put orange cones around the truck's perimeter. They brought out white folding chairs and set them in rows on the front lawn. On every third chair they placed a can of Off. Next they rolled a giant red popcorn machine off the truck and donned white hats and aprons. Neighbors started coming down the stairs and filling the seats.

"They're here already," Mam shouted from the porch. "Katie, hurry up, child!"

Katie landed on the front gallery. "I'm here."

"Eileen, run in and get some sodas," her mother said.

"I took care of all the drinks. Sit down and enjoy yourself, Irene," Luc said. The workmen rolled off a wheeled refrigerator, the kind an ice cream man would push, and then hung electronic bug zappers on a nearby tree. Within a span of five minutes, the entire front lawn had been transformed into an outdoor movie theater. Judging by the wave of neighbors holding various snacks, Katie figured there must have been some kind of invitation.

Luc thrust a flyer into her hand.

You're invited to a

Classic Movie Night

Where: McKenna-Slater Garden

When: Approximately 9 p.m.

St. Charles Avenue

Bring food to share.

Within minutes the projector was set up, and the truck served as the movie screen. Katie marveled at how quickly Luc's money could make something happen. "You did all this?"

"I thought it would get us all in the mood for the wedding theme. Get it? *In the mood?*" He laughed.

People streamed in and filled the empty white chairs in the garden one by one. Luc patted the seat beside him.

"Dexter left before he got to see this," she said.

"I know. Bummer, huh?"

"I want to go down where the popcorn is." She skipped down the steps.

The film started to spin.

"Don't you love that old sound of the movie rolling? I'll go get us some sweet tea."

"It's *Casablanca*." She glanced at Luc. "Is this symbolic? Ilsa must choose between Rick, the dangerous love of her life, or Victor Laszlo, her husband and leader of the Resistance Movement. The past or the future. Desire or sacrifice. Casablanca or freedom. Love or honor."

"Love. Always love," Luc answered. "This isn't the French Resistance, and Dexter Hastings is no Victor Laszlo. Sometimes love and honor are the same thing. Forgiveness, the ultimate sacrifice."

He brought a chair beside her and sat down. As soon as the speaking parts began, Luc recited Rick's lines. "Who are you really, and what were you before?" He pulled his fedora down on his forehead.

As the Germans marched into Paris, Katie forced her eyes to the screen. "Maybe I'm not so noble."

Luc took her hand in his. "Maybe you are, but you're defining honor incorrectly."

She ventured a gaze into Luc's eyes. If it were only that easy. Love was more than a feeling, and wasn't it more honorable to honor her vow? Or was it more honorable to listen to her mam and abandon herself to the unknown? Luc may not have been the marrying kind, but did that make it honorable to vow herself to another man who didn't understand what Ilsa gave up? And never would?

Chapter 15

⌣

Moonlight Serenade

Katie lay still in the dark while Eileen fidgeted in the bed beside her.

Her friend exhaled. "You kissed him! When were you going to tell me?"

"I was praying," she said.

"For forgiveness, I hope." Eileen flicked on the light and threw something at Katie. "Here's your love scrapbook. You left it behind. I brought it so you could doodle little hearts for Dexter. Wait, I mean Luc."

"Why are you mad at me? Because I made the same mistake twice and made a complete fool of myself today? Or because I'm marrying Dexter anyway?"

"I'm mad because you don't know what you want! You'd rather live like a Stepford wife than really love and be hurt." Eileen picked up the book and slammed it down again. "I'm mad because you abandon that plan too, as soon as Luc gives you the time of day. And Luc can't stay in one place for long, so I'm worried you'll waste your life away waiting for someone else to make a move." Eileen was crying, and she leaned over and hugged Katie. "I want the world to exercise. What do you want, Katie?"

Katie thought for a long time. "I want to be unafraid."

God, please help me. I'm in love with the wrong man. Love is not a feeling. I can have power over my emotions, so, Lord, would you help me do that? Because if you wanted me to marry Luc, he would have said yes all those years ago. He would have come after me. He's had eight years! Why won't this go away? Luc only wants me now because Dexter has me. What am I doing wrong? I've prayed every day for this feeling to leave me. It's not right. I know I sinned, Lord. I got emotionally involved. I did things you said not to do outside of marriage. Lord, is this my punishment? To spend the rest of my days longing for something that I can't have, that I never should have tasted in the first place? I was young and stupid, but I'm not young anymore, so why do I still feel so stupid? I want to do the right thing. My memories of that night will never go away, but they haven't changed either. Does that mean that I haven't really repented?

Everything seemed brighter the next day. More sunlight that

morning, and with it came more clarity. She had to tell Dexter what happened the day before. Dexter, who seemed unchallenged by emotions such as passion, would never understand her impetuous behavior. There *wasn't* any acceptable explanation. But did she want to spend her life with someone whose love had to be earned? No boyfriend would put up with Katie's behavior, but Dex took it to a different level.

Katie was her father's daughter. She couldn't marry without love, and the realization settled as a knot in her stomach. Love, she reasoned, should feel like *love*, not a contract easily broken when the other failed you. She hadn't thought about the consequences of the contract being broken when love didn't exist. After all, how would she explain it to her daughter—and she knew that it would be a daughter.

—*Momma, when did you fall in love with Daddy?*

—*Ought to be pretty soon now, honey.*

She still believed in a practical partnership above a fiery yet waning passion, but she couldn't marry Dexter, because her mam was right. He wasn't kind. Every other annoyance about him was just a variation on that theme. He wanted her to behave a certain way, and when she didn't, tiny rejections were the result.

"Dexter's downstairs," Eileen moaned from the bed. "I can hear his monotone."

Katie didn't jump to attention at the sound of Dex's voice. She took the time to consider all that had changed. The fact that she might indeed be alone if she gave him up. Mam said it herself: Luc wasn't the marrying kind. Making this choice was making the decision she could maneuver life's uncharted waters alone, with only God as her guide.

"You know," Eileen went on, "if I had to wake up to that schedule . . . two poached eggs on Wednesday and Friday, fiber cereal the other days . . . oh, and oatmeal is in there somewhere."

"I don't know why Dexter's breakfast schedule bothers you so much. You're just as bad. Did it ever occur to you that he's the male version of my best friend?"

Eileen bolted upright. "You take that back! As a health instructor, fiber could not be more important to me. But I do think . . . I do think the homicide rate would be even higher if I had to dwell with Dexter Hastings. You're a better woman than I."

"Actually, I'm not," Katie said. "He came all the way to New Orleans to get the ring and ask me to marry him properly . . . and I'm going to send him home alone."

"Katie! What are you saying? Do you mean my prayer worked? That you're going to hold out for a guy with a whole name?"

"All I'm saying is I decided it's better to be alone than be married badly, and I think Dex and I aren't that great together."

"This is huge! Katie, I like Dexter, I do. I just don't like you with him. It's like you're this shell of yourself, and all the fun has been drained out."

"I feel bad for him. He came all the way here for me."

"He'll get over it. It's just like *The Bachelorette*! Remember the one where they stopped the train and dropped that guy in the middle of nowhere? That was cold. But in the end, isn't it better than marrying Dex when you don't love him the way you should? If you did, do you think Luc could have tempted you yesterday?"

"You came here to help. Bringing Luc's name into this isn't helping. It's got nothing to do with Dexter."

Eileen fluffed a pillow behind her and wrapped her arms around her knees. "I may not be helping, but I cannot say I am not going to enjoy this. Can I burn the faux romance scrapbook? Oh my gosh, when he was lecturing your mam on life insurance before you got here, I thought she was going to haul off and smack him."

The two of them giggled.

"Stop," Katie said. "We can't be mean. I'm a terrible person, Eileen. Why did I agree to marry him if I don't love him?"

"You're always on to the next goal. So now you have your next goal. Go break Dexter's heart. Trust me, it will be easier on him than it was on you all those years ago with Luc."

"What happened to him, Eileen? He was so sweet."

"That's why you have an engagement, Katie. To find out the truth. I mean, there are annoyances one can live with and then there's the crazy train—and any man who lets his fiancée to fly solo with Luc DeForges is on the crazy train."

Eileen leaped out of bed in her boy shorts and camisole and bent into the downward facing dog position, then rose into the cobra. "Come on down here. Nothing like a good stretch in the morning."

Katie closed her Bible. "I'll stretch after breakfast."

"I didn't press you last night, but I want to know what that kiss with Luc meant."

"How did you know about it anyway? Did Olivia tell you?"

"Olivia saw you?"

"Maybe."

"Well, she didn't tell me. I saw it written on your face. Katie, he intoxicates you."

"If you had your way, I'd never forgive Luc."

"Forgiveness is you saying 'Luc, it's okay that you dumped me in front of the entire town and anyone who mattered in my life and your own. I forgive you. Fool me once, shame on you, but fool me twice, shame on me, and I won't be fooled again, Luc. I loved you until you reached in, grabbed my beating heart, pulled it out of my chest, kicked it across the floor, and stomped on it like a used cigarette butt. But I totally forgive you.'

"Forgiving doesn't mean forgetting, and I've got a memory like an elephant." Eileen cinched her legs closer to her chest. "Do *you* have a memory? Do you remember what he did to you? It's not enough it was the humiliation of your life, but then you have to see him splattered over every tabloid with every two-bit Hollywood actress for the next eight years of your life? I mean, there's forgiveness and there's stupidity."

"Right. Stupidity. Kissing him yesterday was stupidity." Katie spoke without conviction.

"Like you believe that."

"I don't. You told me to stop letting men tell me what to think. Now I'm telling you. It was closure for Luc and me."

"The lipstick on your chin didn't look like closure."

"I loved Luc with all my heart. I never thought he was capable of what he did to me. Not in a million years. You could have more easily told me he would take a knife to me that night than what actually happened."

Eileen looked out toward the window. "If it makes you feel any better, I never could have imagined it either. I thought he loved you like your Paddy loved your mam. It rocked a lot of us to the foundations. The betrayal is that much worse when you think you know a person."

"I loved Dexter too, but it felt safer, less threatening."

"Not the right way, you didn't. You forget, I've known you since you were eight. I saw more spark with you in five minutes of you singing to Luc than in your entire relationship with Dexter. Do the right thing, Katie. Quit acting for God. And, though it kills me to say this . . ." She held her head in her hands. "If it's Luc you love . . . marry him, Katie."

———

"Mornin', Katie." Rusty met her at the bottom of the stairs with a cup of coffee. "Best way to wake up is to your momma's pretty face and a cup of her coffee."

"Thank you," she said. "How'd you know I was coming down?"

"This may be updated, but it's still an old house. You learn the sounds and know who's where. I think that's why everyone in New Orleans thinks their house is haunted."

Katie had wanted to dislike her stepfather, but she couldn't help taking to his warm, down-home ways. He was unlike her father in all ways but one: he loved her mam with a sacrificial spirit and acted as though the tide came and went with her. Once again she wondered, how was it her mother could locate good men with the striking aim of a laser, while she seemed to be flopping about like a catfish out of water?

"Pokey!" She looked down to see the little dog wagging at her feet. She lifted him up to stare into the animal's deep brown eyes, then let him snuggle into her neck.

"Eileen's mother dropped that mutt off," Rusty said. "I don't like dogs anyway, and that one's got two paws in the grave."

"Rusty!" She cuddled the dog. "Don't listen to him, Pokey. You're as fiery as when you shared pizza with us in the dorm."

"Rusty's full of garbage," Mam said. "He's been feeding that thing leftover steak all morning."

Katie looked up to see Mam standing in the arched doorway—and beside her, Dexter.

"Dex, you're early," Katie said as she nuzzled Pokey. "Look at my baby." She tried to give Dex a closer look, but he waved her off.

"Don't," he snapped.

"Dexter, what's the matter?"

"I came here for a purpose."

Mam gave Dexter a scowl. "He doesn't drink coffee or tea," she said, as if Dexter had announced that he didn't believe in crawfish, magnolias, or the South.

"Mam, are you cooking already? I was going to make brunch."

"Oh, I just threw in some leftovers for quiche. It will be ready soon."

"I'm going to have my coffee on the gallery. Let's go enjoy the morning, Dexter." Katie pulled him by the hand and led him to a pair of rocking chairs on the porch. Mam followed them out and stood in the doorway.

The morning was gorgeous, filled with the delights of the Garden District . . . ancient oaks, Spanish moss, and all the romanticism that made up the Old South.

"It was sweet of you to come and meet my mam," Katie said.

He grunted. "Katie, I talked to Pastor again last night when I got back to my hotel room. We discussed our differences at length, and they're extreme. Pastor says they can only get worse if the foundation isn't solid. What I'm trying to say, Katherine, is that I can't marry you in good conscience."

"You're breaking up with me?"

"You're breaking up with my daughter?"

"Mam, let me handle this, please."

Mam just gave her a look and went back inside.

"Katie." Dexter rubbed his lips. "You hurt me."

"I hurt you?" she pried, wondering if he'd found out about her illicit kiss.

"When we first started dating, you made me feel like such a big man. You complimented me on all the nice things I did for you. Every week you appreciated the flowers, and every Friday you'd thank me for the dinner. I could count on it."

He scratched at his collar. "But since coming out here, I see that you're used to chaos in your life. Plans get changed at a moment's notice. You're used to a loud household."

"Yeah, we're Irish. Music. Yelling. Food. Otherwise, it's not home."

"I know that if we had children and they were allowed to run wild, I wouldn't feel right at home. I wouldn't feel respected."

She nodded. "I understand. A man needs to be respected, especially in his own house."

"And a woman needs to be loved," he said.

"I did what I could to be lovable. I'm sorry, Dex. I wish I'd known before you made this trip out here."

"Katherine," he said, and leaned over to kiss her forehead. She averted her face, and his lips came to hers. He seemed annoyed. "Fairy tales end. There's no such thing as Prince Charming. I am solid husband material, but my suggestion is you take the time to grow up a bit and think about being a Proverbs 31 woman."

"Thank you, Dex." She kissed his cheek. "Since you aren't a big brunch fan, maybe you should clear out before Mam serves breakfast." The last thing she needed was Mam tearing into him and going on about promises made when the decision was as much hers as Dexter's. He just hadn't known it.

She could smell Mam's famous quiche cooking. If she didn't usher Dex out the door quickly, a long morning would ensue. "I'll walk you to your car."

Dexter stood and called through the open window. "Mrs. Slater, thank you for having me in your home. Katie, I'll see you at church when you come home. I'm sorry things turned out this way."

"Dexter, you're not leaving," Mam called back. "Breakfast is ready. We're eating! Get in here. You can't go on an empty stomach."

Katie knew there was no room for negotiation. No one left Mam's house hungry and lived to tell about it. She stood, and Dexter shuffled into the house behind her. She filled her lungs with the warm sent of Mam's kitchen as Dexter pulled her chair out.

Katie set her coffee cup next to her spot at the table and, like an attentive waitress, her mother filled the mug to the brim. There were so many delicious aromas: the chicory coffee, the sausage, the warmed breads. Katie's nose couldn't get enough. She wondered if Eileen would be able to resist the taste of home in favor of her macrobiotic diet or whatever health quest she was pursuing that week.

"Can I get you some juice, Dexter?" Mam asked.

"That would be nice."

"Orange, okay? I have grapefruit too."

"Orange is great." Dex pulled out his own chair and sat down.

Mam grimaced. "So, are we having a lovers' spat this morning? The heat can get to a person if you're not used to it, Dexter."

"Mam, what are we having for breakfast?"

Her mother may not have liked Dexter, but clearly she wanted to be sure before letting a potential suitor for Katie walk out the door.

"We're having quiche. I already told you."

"Katie's not herself, Mrs. Slater."

"Meaning?"

"It's not every day a man gets his heart broken. And your daughter is a very empathetic individual."

"Whose heart is broken?" Mam set down the glass of orange juice and sliced into the quiche. "How big?" she asked Dexter as she gauged the size by moving the pie knife.

"Just a small one."

Mam cut him a large piece anyway, added grits to his plate, and garnished it with a few strawberries and slices of banana.

"May I pray for the meal?" Dex bowed his head and started reciting. Everyone said "Amen" automatically before they realized there had been a prayer.

"Now," Mom said, "whose heart is broken?"

"I've come to the conclusion that Katie and I are probably not best suited to be romantic partners—you understand, married."

"I think that's very wise of you, Dexter," Mam said.

Dexter smiled proudly, and Mam and Katie exchanged a look. If Dexter was heartbroken, she failed to see the slightest crack.

"So what do you think of this forties fixation, Dexter?" Mam asked, as she served up the quiche for the rest of them.

"Leave it to someone who hasn't lived through the war to romanticize it."

Dex looked at her. "I don't really see the point. It's not the forties."

"The point, I guess, is that it's what Katie enjoys. She and her nana shared a love of old movies and swing music. Nana would tell stories about the USO and all the soldiers coming home on furlough. Katie romanticized the era, I suppose, but she always did have an active imagination. Failing to see her passions might be one good reason you two aren't suited for one another."

"I think you're right. Yes, ma'am," Dexter said, as he shoved a forkful of fruit into his mouth.

"Well, Mam, Dexter, it was romantic," Katie protested. "I mean, the music carried so much emotion, the dresses were so feminine . . . and men in uniform fighting for their coun- try . . . What can I say to that? I mean, even you can see the romance in that, Dexter. Right?"

"That depends . . . would you want me to wear my Boy Scout uniform when we got married?" he asked.

"I suppose it doesn't matter now."

"I wasn't expecting breakfast, coming over so early, Mrs. Slater. Thank you kindly for having it ready."

"We're morning people down here," Mam told Dexter. "Except for Katie, who never did care much for mornings. Sometimes when Rusty shrimps at night he'll sleep in but never past eight. I don't know what you young people do to tire yourselves out so."

Dexter took his first bite of quiche and washed it down with his entire glass of juice.

"Too hot for you?" Mam laughed.

"What's in that?"

"Nothing but a little cayenne and Tabasco," Mam said innocently.

Dexter's eyes watered, and he held his cup out to Katie. She filled the glass to the brim with more orange juice. "Have some grits," she said. "They'll clear your palate."

He lifted a forkful to his mouth, then opened his mouth like one of Katie's kids at school. "Ugh, what is that?"

"It's grits!" she said as he spit into his napkin.

"I'm sorry, Mrs. Slater. It's just the texture . . . I'm not used to the texture."

Mam patted Dexter's hand sweetly, as if she hadn't added extra cayenne and Tabasco to her recipe. "I'll get you some more fruit," she said. "Would you like me to make you some toast?"

"I'll just eat my bread, thanks," he answered sheepishly.

"So, Dexter, what kind of work do you do?" Mam asked him. "Will they give you time off for a broken heart?"

Katie wished they'd just put an end to this charade. Southern manners!

"I design optical equipment for medical machinery. Katie wouldn't have had to work when we were married."

"Then I suppose it's all for the best. Katie loves her work. Always had such a heart for the downtrodden. Just like her father that way. Why carry the weight of a quarta when your brother needs it?"

Dexter punched a fist to the middle of his chest. *Indigestion*, Katie thought. *Irene McKenna's way.* The kind that would burn for a good, long time. Katie knew her mam—if a man was going to run about saying he was heartbroken, he should feel something.

"I wanted to marry a teacher," Dexter went on. "Good with kids, summers off until we have children, so we could travel."

"You had it all planned," Mam said, patting his hand again. "Such a pity this didn't work out."

"Our pastor says one shouldn't force things before the wedding."

"Absolutely," Mam agreed. "It's hard enough after the wedding. Did you need a ride to the airport, Dexter? I think I just heard Rusty pull up outside."

Dexter stared at her and choked down some more water. "That would be great." He pressed his open palm to Katie's cheek. "Are you going to be all right, darling?"

Katie urged a tortured expression from within. "I think so, Dexter. I'm so sorry you came all the way out here."

"I had to be certain I wasn't getting cold feet. I thought I came for your ring, but subconsciously, I must have been coming for answers."

She nodded. He patted her face again. It took everything she had not to grab his hand and twist it behind his back.

"Very heroic of you, Dexter," said Mam. "It's good when a man is able to stand up for what he knows is right, even when it hurts."

Dexter walked out the door as though he was Superman himself.

"All that's missing is the cape," Katie said aloud as he climbed into Rusty's truck. She'd gathered a new appreciation for her mam.

Chapter 16

⌢

MAKE SOMEONE HAPPY

Katie relaxed immediately as she walked into the darkness of the familiar Barrelhouse Club for another practice session. She set down the wrapped package for Olivia's shower later in the day. Billie Holiday's emotive voice played and led her in with a soft hand. The smooth, sultry song lulled her into a sense of peacefulness where the struggles of life were easily forgotten. Though she knew Luc had no reason to attend practice, she had a feeling he'd show up any moment.

Stepping across the stage, she leaned against the wall and allowed the music to calm her senses. It was a good thing he wasn't there. The last thing he needed to know was that another man, a far less interesting man, had dumped her as well. Several musicians were warming up around the room and acknowledged her with a nod, but she felt alone. Alone and blissfully happy.

The lights clicked on, and she closed her eyes. In that moment, she knew what she wanted. She understood why her life felt so unbalanced, as if she was waiting for the world to start spinning again. How much of her life had she handed over to other people without considering what she liked? It had been easier to acquiesce, to wait for instructions rather than decide for herself. Now she stood at a crossroads, where if she allowed someone else to decide she'd live a life of constant sacrifice with nothing to show for it. What point was there in giving Dexter the life he imagined? His children wouldn't complete her, nor would they take her memories away. The only way to move forward was to admit what she wanted and feel the pain of its loss.

She wanted to be loved with abandon. She wanted to love with abandon. She wanted too much. That was what she wanted.

Suddenly Luc hopped up on the stage and leaned into her. "Good morning, beautiful."

"I—I didn't expect to see you again today."

"Would I miss seeing the great Katie McKenna sing? If the great Katie McKenna is planning to retire, I'd have to be nuts to miss one of her last times on the stage."

She rolled her eyes. "What do you want in life, Luc?"

"That's a random question. Everything?"

"You've got all the money you might have imagined, the success that the world pines for. What's left for you?"

"The woman I love."

"A convenient answer. Like King Solomon's seven hundred wives?"

"I only want one. I can only handle one. With the Irish temper, I think it's more like one and a half anyway."

"Be serious."

"I am being serious. You look incredible, by the way. I love that dress." He held out a hand and led her down from the stage and around the room, their bodies naturally waltzing as they spoke.

She loved how easy it was to be with him, how he stimulated her mind and soothed her soul at the same time. She could live on the memories of these moments forever. Maybe that's why God ordained this trip? To show her she could be alone and still have her memories.

"Why the sudden interest in my aspirations? I want what I've always wanted."

"And what's that?"

"A life like your father's."

"My father's?"

"Because your father was the only man I ever knew who I thought was truly happy in this world. Maybe I hoped it would rub off on me."

"He wasn't happy at the end of his life."

"No," Luc agreed. "He had worries. That keeps a man down. But he would have been happy again if given the opportunity, and he still could have told you a hundred things he was grateful for on his worst day. Nobody's life is perfect. We all have valleys."

"You, the great Luc DeForges, billionaire at large . . . . what do your valleys look like? The price of asparagus is high?"

"You say billionaire on purpose, don't you? You like to make me correct myself and humble me at the same time."

"Maybe."

"If I become a billionaire, what then?"

"I'll have to go with gazillionaire, I suppose. So what do your valleys look like, Luc? Do you run out of Perrier on your private jet?"

"My valleys are the same as yours, Katie-bug. I believe my work can fulfill me and I run full-speed ahead, until I remember what I had here once. Home, family, a woman I loved with all my heart."

"Luc, cut it out."

"I made a mistake eight years ago that I can't seem to recover from. Will you ever risk your heart again? Or will you settle for a reliable life, free from danger and all this—" He spread his hand out toward the stage. "Did you ever think that might be the most dangerous route of all?"

"Paddy never had all this, and you seem to think he was the happiest person you knew. You don't think it was his business and customers that made him so happy?"

"I did then, but I know better now. He worried that he wouldn't be able to provide for you and your mam, but things would have turned around. I admired the way he took immediate action and sold the business, but I don't think he knew what to do after that. It sucked some purpose from his days." He paused. "I think you blame me for that."

Maybe she did.

"Katie, your father asked me to buy the business. I bought it because he asked me to and for no other reason. I borrowed the money from my dad, knowing my inheritance and graduation was coming."

She took time to process his words. "What could have changed? People still needed vegetables. And why would he ask you, of all people?"

"Thanks."

"Because it wasn't making it, and he thought you with your business degree could turn it around?" she asked, hoping to solve the mystery.

"The business was fine. In the black." Luc rubbed the back of his neck, a sign that he felt uncomfortable. "I suppose he trusted me and I told him he could buy it back if he changed his mind, but he assured me he wouldn't."

She wished Luc would come out and tell her all he knew. All the prancing around the facts. Why? Why did her dad sell his beloved business to Luc? To anyone for that matter?

"I don't know why he asked me to, but he came to me in need. And he was a proud man, Katie. I knew he wouldn't have come if he didn't need to sell. I had too much respect for him to ask him why."

Nothing made sense to her. "But surely he might have sold it another way. Publicly."

Luc shrugged. "Maybe he knew I wouldn't ask questions."

His BlackBerry trilled, and he stepped away from her. "I just need to take this."

She grabbed the phone from his hand and threw it to the back of the room.

"Katie!"

"If you're serious, you have to know that I don't like to be ignored for long periods of time. And if you want to be happy like my Paddy, well, he would have never brought his work home to interrupt family time. Can you handle the constancy of Paddy's life? The slowness of it?"

The phone buzzed again from the back of the room.

"It still works. You can get it later." She placed her hands in his again for the dance.

"So I guess this means *you're* serious? You're ready for the truth?"

"You forget, I have nothing to lose now. I already look like an idiot, and here I am again at a DeForges family function playing the lost little puppy dog. My bum is on the cover of the *Tattler*, and they said your so-called fiancée has put on a few pounds and is pregnant, hence the wedding. So you need my wild Irish blood. Who else could put up with that kind of stuff?"

"There was something more going on with your father, Katie. I didn't know what it was, and I worried if I said yes to you, the insurance people would start investigating and you and your mam would be left with nothing."

She steeled herself. "Why is my mam mad at you? When

my mother makes up her mind about someone she never changes her mind, and she is not nice to you right now. Why not?"

"That part of the story I'm not sure about. I didn't ask why your dad had to sell me the business, and he never told me. He was very adamant that no one find out it was in fine shape." Luc's cell started up again. "Katie, I just felt God saying, *No, not yet* when you asked me. I wanted to ask *you*, but then—there were all these questions. You still didn't have your insurance settlement."

"Eight years and two hundred blondes or so just sort of slipped by." Her voice took on a hard edge.

"Look me in the eyes and tell me what you believe to be true about me, Katie."

She stared into his eyes, and her stomach filled with butterflies, her throat became parched, her defenses weakened. She felt her chest pounding. She'd read that men's cortisol levels rose when they met a beautiful woman they considered out of their league—it was bad for their hearts. She wondered if being with Luc DeForges was bad for hers.

"Your eyes tell me what your lips won't. I know what you think of me, Katie. Even if you fight it with everything in you." Luc reached into his pocket and pulled out a small gray box. He opened the lid, and she gasped.

"My ring! You had it all along?"

He knelt in front of her. "Katie McKenna, marry me."

She covered the bottom half of her face with her hands. "Where did you get that?"

"Your father gave it to me." His gaze didn't waver. "Answer the question."

She shook her head. "He didn't. You had a copy made."

He stood up and took the ring out of its box. He brought the ring to her face and showed her the engraving on the inside: *My Everlasting Love.* "It's yours. Your father gave it to me on the day he died. I knew he wouldn't have killed himself, but I didn't want the insurance agent to have any reason to assume he had. So I kept it all these years. He asked me to give it to you on your wedding day. I almost told you so many times that I had it, that it was time, but you were so angry with me. And then the years passed and I didn't know how to go back. Then you went and got engaged to someone else, and it was fish or cut bait."

"I came home for that ring. All this way, and all this trouble, and you had it in California?"

He swallowed visibly. "I needed time to show you I'm not all about the money. That you can trust me."

"By lying to me?"

"I fudged the truth a bit. I said no that night to protect you and your mother, but you never let me explain. You were grieving. You didn't have the insurance settlement, and I didn't have my own inheritance yet. There were a billion reasons why I said no that night."

"My father loved that store. He would have never sold it if he could have made it work. Why couldn't you have lent him the money to fix the business?"

"Katie, listen to me. There was nothing wrong with the

business. It was in the black when I bought it. I told you, I don't know why he had to sell it, but he came to me saying he had to."

"If you wanted to marry me, you had eight years to make it happen. Why would you wait until I was engaged to another man? You just want to win!"

"What have I won? If anything, it looks from my point of view that I've lost what matters most to me. I've lost your faith in me."

"No, you still have all that money, your private jet—" She didn't have the strength to say any more.

"Money won't ruin us, Katie. I promise you. There's no reason to fear it. You can start your own foundation, give it away any way you see fit."

"It's not the money I fear."

"You can't marry Dexter. If you found out that Dexter kissed a woman as passionately as you kissed me yesterday, would you marry him?"

She went numb. Of all the things he might have said . . . "Just because I made an error in judgment doesn't mean I should relinquish my whole future. A kiss isn't that powerful. You're only trying to confuse me."

"Am I?"

His cell phone kept ringing. He closed in on her again. She smelled his delicious light cologne and she felt his warmth and was suddenly transported to eight years prior. *I love you, Luc. I always have. Always will.*

"Here's lookin' at you, kid." He touched her chin. "When

Bogie says that line, he's telling Ilsa, *I see you. I know who you are and why you have to go.* I know who *you* are, Katie. Inside. I know what makes you the most beautiful woman on earth. I know you can't live a passionless life. If I'd said yes all those years ago, this anger over your father would be in our marriage. Solve this with me. We've got our whole lives ahead of us. You need to forgive me and understand I only had your best interests at heart. I still do."

"You're not going to try and tell me you did me a favor?"

"You wanted to escape the pain of your father's death, Katie. Admit it. You used me as a salve, and I let you that one night and then you questioned my motives from then on. When I said no to you, you would cry, but you still cried over the wrong thing." He stepped back, and she looked at her feet rather than admit any of his words were true. "I see you, Katie, and I will always love you. But you've told yourself you were being loyal to your father all these years, didn't you?"

"Did it bother you when you learned I was engaged? Did you care that I dated? Where were you, Luc?" She pounded on his chest. "You come into my life every year or so to update me with a bullet point memo on your life, like I'm some Christmas card recipient? And I should have felt I was one of the special ones because I got a phone call and a real signed card, not a printed one?"

"I see the woman I love, the only woman I've loved, making a mistake. I'm trying to stop you from doing it. You don't love Dexter Hastings, and you never will. Don't bother lying to me. I can see it in your eyes."

"It never occurs to you that you might be wrong, does it, Luc? Does that confidence come with being a billionaire?"

"No, it comes at the multimillionaire stage, apparently. What's it going to take to prove it to you?" Luc looked at her with those deep blue eyes, and her stomach fluttered.

She held out her hand. "I'll take my ring now."

Luc snapped the hinge closed, and the ring disappeared. "Poindexter can come and get it from me."

"You can't do that. It belongs to me."

"It belongs to you when you get married, and you told me yourself you're not engaged yet. Let Poindexter come ask me for it. If he's man enough."

"He's not going to do that! He shouldn't have to do that!"

"Your father gave the ring to me. I'd say Poindexter does have to do it."

She should tell him the marriage was off, but her blasted pride kept rearing its ugly head. "Stop calling him that! You're behaving like a child." She straightened her spine. "All right, we're going to play like this, are we? Give me the ring or I'm not singing at your brother's wedding." She placed her flattened palm in his face.

"I'll hire Harry Connick, Jr. He's in town this weekend."

"You do that." Katie smoothed her skirt and picked up the gift Mam had wrapped so carefully for Olivia. Gift-wrapping was a Southern skill she never could seem to master. She turned to Luc, who followed closely behind. "You can make this as difficult on me as you please, Luc DeForges, but you won't break me. My fiancé can buy me another ring if you choose to keep mine. Maybe I'll make a visit to your brother Jem's store tomorrow."

"Katie, battle me all you want, I can take it, but don't dig yourself into a hole to fight me."

"Wish me luck. I'm off to see your mother."

"What about practice?"

"Maybe you should ask Harry Connick, Jr. to practice with the band today."

She stepped out into the excruciating heat and leaned against the building's wall, letting her pulse slow. She wanted to just swallow her pride, jump off the cliff, and go back and shout *yes!* Yes, she would marry him. Instead, she did what the new, reserved Katie McKenna always did. She went where she was supposed to be, on time, gift in hand.

Chapter 17

ALL OF ME

You Are Cordially Invited to

A Luncheon Bridal Shower

To Honor

Miss Olivia Tyler,

The Future Mrs. Ryan DeForges

Wednesday, June 9th at Twelve O'clock in the Afternoon

Given by Stacy Gibbons,

Maid of Honor

At the Home of Mrs. Aimée DeForges

R.S.V.P. 555.4232

At one time a luncheon at the DeForges mansion would have sent Katie into a panic, but she took it in stride as part and parcel on the road to closure. She was living fearlessly, no worries about what some man expected of her. Mrs. DeForges garnered no power over her anymore, and the house never had. She hated its cavernous rooms and stark beige interior—there wasn't a hint of warmth in the place to make it a home. She wondered if a coat of salmon paint wouldn't do the DeForges family some good.

She took the streetcar to the infamous estate, dressed in the most inconspicuous dress she'd brought with her: a gray boat-neck, shantung silk with a tight bodice and full A-line skirt. With the shoes, she'd only paid fifteen dollars for the outfit at a secondhand store, and she felt compelled to tell Mrs. DeForges about her bargain. It wasn't difficult to see where Luc had gotten his negotiating skills; for all her wealth, Aimée DeForges loved a good bargain. If you complimented her on a piece of furniture, she'd tell you the price and bartering skills she used to buy it. Luc used to say she'd find a way to tell the deal she'd gotten on her casket when the day came.

"Luc tells me you live in a shotgun house down in the Channel. When did your parents buy that house?"

"I don't know. Before I was born."

"And how old are you now?" Mrs. DeForges asked.

"Eighteen," she'd said.

"Eighteen!" Mrs. DeForges looked to Ryan. "Is this girl old enough to be in the college Bible study?"

"I started college at seventeen," she'd explained.

"Very well. So your parents probably paid about . . ." The *older woman drummed her fingers on her chin. "About twenty-five thousand dollars for that house, and now, if it's in good shape, they probably . . . Do you know what their mortgage is?"*

"Ma!" Luc had snapped.

"I don't know," Katie said again, sheepishly.

"All in all, an excellent bargain. There is no better money-maker than staying in your home. You tell your parents for me they've made wonderful choices."

"I will, ma'am."

Aimée DeForges kept a dark, dirty little secret behind the walls of her great mansion. There were very few people in town who knew that Aimée, with a French pronunciation, had grown up near the Warehouse District as plain old Amy Aucoin. Mam said the wealthy socialite would never go back to that life again, and putting a price on everything was Mrs. DeForges' way of finding her value in life.

Katie approached the arched sandstone exterior, which looked more like a city museum than a home, and shifted her gift from one hip to the other. "Here goes nothing." She pressed the doorbell, which chimed for an eternity until a Creole woman answered the door dressed in a frilly white uniform that not only looked ridiculous but harkened back to another era. She wondered if Mrs. DeForges wasn't taking the forties theme a little far.

"Mornin', miss. May I take the gift?"

Katie passed off the box, which was a collection of 1940s big band and swing CDs and some candles Mam had lying around the house. She'd wrapped them all in pink cellophane, so it appeared more celebratory than her teacher's salary could afford.

"The ladies are all in the salon. Come this way."

Katie passed the ornate dining room with its carved mahogany ceiling and seating for too many to count. It was a pity someone had to dust that thing continually. Her mam would *use* a table like that. Luc told her Mrs. DeForges hadn't entertained since that horrible night Katie caused the family "great embarrassment," as his mother had put it. *Great embarrassment for whom?* she'd thought at the time, but she was so traumatized by the experience she'd just nodded and apologized.

She'd prayed up a storm that morning for the stamina to keep a smile plastered on her face and reminded herself that she needed to face her fears. Otherwise she'd be forever defined as the girl who'd ruined Luc's graduation party and announced her loss of innocence to New Orleans society at large. She steeled herself as she stood beneath the great arched entryway to the salon. No music played in the background, and the room appeared as cavernous and stark as ever. Not so much as a streamer hung from the ceiling, and not one of the maybe twenty people in the room had a drink or an hors d'oeuvre in hand.

Olivia saw her coming and hurried over. "Katie, you made it!" She took the gift from the maid. "You didn't have to bring anything. I just wanted you to come."

Two steps below, several faces gazed up at her. She

recognized Mrs. DeForges, of course, with her dark, penetrating eyes that didn't miss a trick and the wispy, silver-blond expensive haircut.

"Mrs. DeForges," Katie said in her best drawl. "It's been so many years since I've seen you, and you look wonderful. You haven't aged a day. Thank you so much for inviting me."

"Thank you, dear." Mrs. DeForges addressed the other guests. "Katie here was once in the college Bible study I taught. Look what a lovely young lady she's grown into."

"Is that so? I never knew you taught a class, Mrs. DeForges," someone said above the murmurs.

"I wasn't always this old." Mrs. DeForges laughed. "No, I used to have a lot more life in me, and teaching the Lord's Word gave me such pleasure."

"No doubt. It's the small contributions in life we remember," an older woman, with a name tag that read *Mrs. Fredrickson*, said. "Katie, you are such a beautiful girl. That red hair. You can't buy that in a bottle."

Katie smiled politely.

Mrs. DeForges spoke again. "I do believe all of my sons were in love with Katie at one time or another."

"Oh, I think that's an exaggeration."

"It most certainly isn't," Mrs. DeForges said. "That's why Katie will be singing in Ryan and Olivia's wedding. She and Ryan used to perform together at college and then at that horrible bar. Won't that be lovely for Ryan? She knew him when he first toyed with the idea of show business."

Katie stepped into the living room and looked about for a

seat. She was making her way to a solitary French chair when Mrs. DeForges stopped her.

"Not that one!" The older woman dropped her painfully thin arms, marbled by blue veins, and regained her composure as the rest of the women stared at her. "It's an antique."

"Sit here," Olivia said, offering her seat. "I'll sit next to my mam."

"Not everyone will be able to see you open the gifts from the sofa," Mrs. DeForges said. "Katie, why don't you sit on the sofa where Olivia is, and she can come over here to this chair."

Mrs. DeForges pointed out a French tapestry chair similar to the one Katie tried to sit in, but apparently it wasn't as valuable. Either that, or Olivia would inflict less damage upon it.

"Jennifer," Mrs. DeForges said to one of the bridesmaids, "you sit at the end of the sofa there so you can see the gifts well to make a list for thank you notes. Stacy, you're in the middle where you can monitor the games. There, that's better." Having arranged the guests to her satisfaction, Mrs. DeForges finally sat herself.

The shower consisted of a majority of older women and a few younger ones, obviously friends of the bride. Katie felt as much out of her element as a po' boy amidst Oysters Rockefeller, but she took Olivia's seat, if for no other reason than it was the farthest away from Mrs. DeForges.

"Is that her?" An old lady, well into her eighties or beyond, screamed at Mrs. Tyler, Olivia's mom.

Mrs. Tyler patted the old woman's leg and spoke loudly.

"That's Katie McKenna, Mother. She's going to sing at the wedding."

"I mean is that the one Ryan's brother is going to marry?" the old woman shouted.

"No," a younger attendee said. "She's engaged to someone in California."

Mrs. DeForges' stick-straight back seemed to curve a bit. "Engaged, are you?"

Katie paused, unsure how to announce her single nature without arousing the mother bear in Mrs. DeForges. "I came home to get my engagement ring," she said.

"What do you do out there in California?" Mrs. Tyler asked.

"I'm a special needs teacher. I specialize in autism spectrum disorders."

"And how is your momma?"

"She's great. She got married to a fisherman and she sells his catch at the farmers market. She lives in the Upper Garden District now."

"Yes, well, Katrina enabled a lot of people to move around."

"It left a lot of people worse off too." She tried to keep the snap from her tone.

"That's true," Mrs. Tyler said. "We have twice as many homeless as we did before the storm. Homelessness kills people. It's a vicious blight on our city."

"Yes, well, this is a happy occasion. Stacy, why don't you begin the games?" Mrs. DeForges spoke to a young blonde who hardly looked old enough to drive, much less be a maid of honor in a wedding.

Californians didn't seem to get married as young. Katie felt aged and defective among the group of old Southern married ladies and young women on the verge of their entire futures.

Stacy looked like your typical sorority sister in her tea-length dress—she appeared nervous as she stood in front of the group, and the tablet in her hand trembled. "So this game is how well the bride knows the groom. We're going to ask questions about Ryan, and Olivia has to answer them, and so do all of you!"

Stacy was an optimist, full of Southern charm and cheer-leader enthusiasm. She reached into the bag of goodies below them on the sofa. Katie could see streamers and party favors that probably didn't go with Mrs. DeForges' décor, so they stayed in the bag. Stacy pulled out a Ziploc bag of golf pencils. "Katie, will you pass these around?"

She stood, grateful for something to keep her hands busy. She rounded the room slowly so as to make the task last. She hurried back to get the papers and passed those around as well. When she finished, she sat gingerly on the sofa and read over the paper.

1. What was the name of Ryan's first pet?

Since most of the topics were familiar to her, if not from Ryan, then from Luc, Katie scribbled the answers quickly like it might win her freedom from the party. Gazing about the room, she noticed everyone was still entranced by the questions. She sat patiently until Stacy read off the answers. To her horror, she hadn't missed a single one. She slid the paper into her bag, but Olivia saw her do it.

"Katie, what are you doing?" Olivia snatched the paper out of the handbag pocket. "Momma, she got them all right. You got them all right, Katie."

"I don't believe it. Let me see," Mrs. DeForges said.

"She did!" Olivia exclaimed. "She got more than I did! I didn't know Ryan had a pet when he was young, and I didn't know his first kiss was with a girl called Janice. Hmm." Olivia playfully put a fist to her hip. "We'll have to have a conversation about that one. How did you know that, Katie?"

"I was there. It was in theater group. Janice played Juliet, Ryan was Romeo."

"His first kiss was in college?" Olivia asked.

"That's what he said then."

"That can't be true," Mrs. DeForges snapped. "Let's go on to the next game."

"Wait a minute—Katie won a prize." Stacy reached into her bag of tricks and pulled out a small box wrapped in metallic silver paper.

Once again Katie felt all eyes on her and wished she could crawl out the large stained-glass window. "It's all right, I didn't win. I just knew Ryan at a crucial time, that's all."

"You won, Katie, enjoy it!" Olivia took the gift from Stacy and handed it to her.

Katie felt Mrs. DeForges' scowl, though she couldn't have

proven it was actually there. She took the gift from Olivia and sat down slowly. The next game she'd throw.

The Creole maid brought in glasses and a pitcher of sweet tea and set them on a table covered by a white linen cloth. Katie marveled at how a woman like Mrs. DeForges could let her guests sit around without so much as a pretzel to nibble on. Mam would have already served three courses by now. But she was thankful for the tea. Her mouth was dry as a bone.

"Ah, the tea is here. Ladies, help yourself to a glass. There are stem bracelets in different colors so that you can tell your glass from someone else's. Take note of your color," Mrs. DeForges said, "so we won't need to use more glasses than necessary."

"Aimée, I never realized you were so earth conscious," Mrs. Tyler said. "That's wonderful."

"We've all got to do our part, especially after that terrible oil spill." Mrs. DeForges brought her fingers to her mouth. "Oh dear, I'm sorry."

"It's all right," Mrs. Tyler answered. "We do all need to do our part, those of us in oil as well."

"The next game is to design a wedding dress for the bride!" Stacy pulled out rolls of toilet paper and started handing them to every fourth guest. "Break up into groups of four, and pick your model. Three of you will make her a wedding dress of toilet paper."

Katie flinched, but she crossed the room to Olivia's friends, who had already made up their foursome. As she went from group to group, watching as the others formed groups, she and Mrs. DeForges fell into an uneasy standoff.

"Katie, you needn't be afraid of me."

Mrs. DeForges carried herself with an air of importance, like a family heirloom kept locked behind the glass. Katie understood why her three sons used to prefer cramming themselves into her shotgun living room rather than hanging around this cold place. All at once, her history with this woman made sense. Mrs. DeForges was jealous of her. Not hateful. Not bitter. *Jealous.* Katie had come into her life at the exact time Mrs. DeForges' children were lifting anchor and setting sail.

While the rest of the group made their teams and chattered excitedly, Olivia sat beside Ms. DeForges on the French sofa.

"I know," Katie said to her. "Let's make Momma DeForges' gown. What kind of neckline did it have?"

"Mine?" Mrs. DeForges looked startled, then pleased. She stood up and pulled Olivia to her feet too. "Well, it had a sweetheart neckline, with lace wrapped up high around my neck like this." She grasped the roll of paper and began to unwind it around Olivia's torso. "Then it had a very tight bodice. I was cinched in like an oyster . . ."

Katie fumbled her way through another hour until tea sandwiches were served, followed by a too-sweet King Cake with coffee, then watched while Olivia opened and admired her gifts. As soon as she felt she could make a gracious getaway, she crossed the room to Olivia, bent to kiss her cheek, and said, "I'll see you at the rehearsal dinner."

Olivia stood and gave her a hug. "Thank you for coming, Katie."

"I'll walk you out," Mrs. DeForges said.

Katie's heart throbbed in her throat. Her last private conversation with Mrs. DeForges had not gone well . . . The memory of it still haunted her, and the words were as fresh, as raw as they'd been the last time she'd stood on DeForges property.

She'd worn Mam's best gold earrings and Eileen's yellow chiffon to Luc's graduation party, and though everybody had something more posh from the Bon Marche, she'd felt like the belle of the ball. She was, after all, dating the man of honor.

Luc looked magnificent. When she saw him across the ballroom in his sharp tuxedo with his hair styled and short, she couldn't believe she was standing in his home. That someday, it might be their home together.

She'd walked confidently across the room, letting every boy take a good gander while Luc waited. Mam had taught her to let a man appreciate her. "Nothing wrong with a little healthy jealousy," Mam always said, "as long as you don't take it too far. Let a man know what you're worth, so he understands the value."

"Hi, Luc," she purred. His friends cleared away.

"Hi, Katie. You look incredible. Do you want to dance?"

Luc's dad had hired the big band orchestra from the Barrelhouse where Ryan and she worked. She'd begged for the night off, and they found another singer, but they weren't happy about it. She remembered thinking Mam was right—maybe now they'd understand her value and pay her a little more. But it didn't happen.

She didn't think Luc's mother cared for her much. She'd always felt as though Mrs. DeForges kept a watchful eye on her in Bible study—like she might run off with the silver if left alone. But that magical night, nothing could go wrong. She imagined Mrs. DeForges being transformed by the knowledge that her son was in love. Or perhaps Mrs. DeForges thought Katie, like a bad penny, was going to keep popping up, and getting used to her would be the simplest route. Surely Mrs. DeForges would see by Katie's continual presence and the way Luc obviously felt about her that love conquered all. As a mother, she'd want what was best for her son.

"Just one song," Luc said as he lifted her from the waist onto the stage and put the microphone in her hand.

She felt so happy, she worried she'd split her dress from breathing in the sheer euphoria. She and Luc had sealed their love. He belonged to her now.

"Luc?" She pulled him into a corner.

"Yes, sweetheart."

"Luc, will you marry me? We can be married now that school is behind us and we'll both be working." Hadn't he implied that very thing the night passion overruled wisdom . . . faith . . . innocence?

Luc wasn't answering. Why wasn't he answering?

"Did you hear me?"

"Katie, I don't think we should have this conversation here."

He didn't sound like himself. His voice had hardened into a business tone that created a measurable distance between them. She'd felt herself diminishing, waning from his world.

She remembered that sickening feeling as euphoria turned into dread. What was that expression on Luc's face? He looked as if he didn't even know her. "Luc," she said, "I thought we were going to be married. I gave my innocence to you. I love you, Luc!"

In her desperation, she hadn't noticed the growing silence around them . . . or contemplated the ramifications of the mic she held in her hand. There was a gasp throughout the room then, and she stared out into a sea of stony cold faces. But the face she remembered most was Luc's. She'd become invisible . . . void . . . worthless. She felt naked and alone. Betrayed by the man she loved. At the time, she didn't care about making a fool of herself or what the gossip would do to her life. She had stumbled outside, Mrs. DeForges raging after her like a violent southern storm.

"Do you know what I spent on this party?" Mrs. DeForges screamed. "I trusted you with my son. With my sons! You bring your alley cat ways into my house? I invited you into my home. Taught you the Word of God. And this is how you repay me!"

Katie had sobbed some sort of answer.

"You've ruined everything. My boy's reputation, his party, maybe even his future. What do you have to say for yourself?"

"I love him." The truth washed over her like a heavy rain. "He doesn't love me."

"Men are different, Katie. You should have known better. We talked about this in Bible study. You can't say you didn't know any better!" Mrs. DeForges continued to rage. "Your mother is going to be mortified. I am mortified!"

"I thought he loved me," Katie had cried. She walked home in the rain, thankfully letting it wash away the sights and sounds of her humiliation.

"Katie!"

Once again Mrs. DeForges had followed her out onto the front gallery.

Katie felt torn. Forgiveness, absolution . . . that's why she'd come, for closure. Only now that Luc's mother stood in front of her, she didn't feel any forgiveness. She felt her own shame bubbling, gathering into a churning tight ball in her gut.

Help me, Lord. "Yes, Mrs. DeForges."

"I didn't think you'd come to the wedding. When Ryan and Luc told me their plans, I thought—quite frankly, I thought you very brave, Katie. It's not everyone who can face their mistakes head-on. You do realize so many of the same people who were there the night of Luc's graduation will be at Ryan's wedding."

"Ryan asked me to come. I didn't want to let my humiliation stop me from being here for a friend. I've moved past it, and I hoped your family had too."

"Not everyone in town feels that way. You understand? I think it's the reason my boys haven't married yet. Their reputations in town were soiled a bit. I believe they were all gun-shy."

Katie's stomach roiled. "I understand. It takes a long time to overcome a darkened reputation, but God is good. I have overcome it."

"That's good. You can't let the mistakes of youth stop you from living your life. I do hope my behavior that night didn't keep you from returning home all these years."

"There are lots of reasons I've avoided New Orleans, Mrs. DeForges. Now that I'm here, it's hard to believe I stayed away so long. It seems selfish to me now."

"You're a bold girl. Luc tells me you use that spirit to fight for your special needs children now in school. Not a lot of funding out there, I guess."

"It's expensive to educate these kids, but it's worth it. It is worth every penny." Katie remembered who she was talking to.

"You're so much like your mam. Do you know, she was the most popular girl in school back in the day."

"My mam?"

"All the boys wanted to date her. Even boys from outside the district. My own husband had a crush on her at one time. The Uptown boys would steal into our dances at the high school. I saw that as my ticket out of the Channel—those Uptown boys."

Katie glanced over Mrs. DeForges' shoulder at the mansion. "I guess it was."

"I admired your mam, Katie. And I admire you. You live your life honestly and state what you want. When I was your age, I didn't know what I wanted. I just thought money would bring it. God was kind enough to honor my marriage any-way. The more years that pass between Luc's graduation and today, the more I realize how brave you were. I had high hopes for Luc back then. He always had such a busi-ness mind, and I didn't want to see him throw it away on an impetuous college romance. But . . . this isn't easy for me to say . . . I believe I was wrong to judge you and Luc by your age."

"Really?"

"Truly," Mrs. DeForges said.

Katie's heart lightened. "But I'm not so honest anymore, Mrs. DeForges. I'm not engaged any longer, for one thing."

"You're not?" Mrs. DeForges brushed her silvery-blond hair behind an ear. "Does Luc know this?"

"Does it matter?" Katie asked. "Luc lives in a differ-ent world from me. I think, like my mam, I'd rather be in shotgun row." Katie smiled and took Mrs. DeForges' hand warmly. "Thank you for the invitation to the shower. I'll see you at the rehearsal dinner."

"Katie?"

"Yes."

"Sometimes we suffer when we go against God's will."

"Don't I know it."

"Sometimes we suffer when we *do* God's will."

Katie didn't understand, but it hardly mattered now. As Eileen said, it was time to figure out what she wanted. To live her life void of fear.

"You and Luc made a mistake," Mrs. DeForges continued.

"But coming back to this house, being willing to sing at the wedding, you've proven to me that you're bigger than the passion of your youth."

Katie walked to the gate with her head high.

╭─

Chapter 18

You Do Something to Me

Luc DeForges uttered a prayer before ringing Irene's door-bell. Katie would be at the bridal shower, so this was his opportunity to set the record straight.

Irene answered the door and wiped her hands on a tat-tered apron with a hand-painted crawfish on it. "Luc, I've been expecting you."

He coughed. "You have?"

"I assume you have Katie's engagement ring," she said.

Luc swallowed his surprise. "I do."

She nodded. "Come on in. I'll put some coffee on."

He followed her to the kitchen and sat at the table.

"There're lace cookies in the Tupperware. Help yourself."

"Don't mind if I do. Being welcomed with cookies beats getting shooed off your property with a broom."

"I let you stay for your makeshift movie theater, didn't I?" Irene asked as she heaped ground coffee into a countertop machine. "So is your plan working?"

"My plan?"

"Your plan to get my daughter back into your good graces. I assume that's why you brought her here for Ryan's wedding."

"No," he said. "It isn't working. I suppose that makes you happy."

"Katie being happy makes me happy. And right now, she's not happy." Irene poured water into the machine and flicked the switch. "Heaven help her, she loves you. But she's got this harebrained idea that if she'd marry practically, without love, she'd be safe."

"How do you know all that?"

"A mother knows. She should run for the hills. I've told her that for years. You're trouble, Luc DeForges. You and your billions."

"Millions."

"Are you correcting me? Because I could give her a billion reasons why you're a terrible choice of husband for her. My mother told me the same thing about Paddy, but there was one good reason *to* marry him, and it outweighed all the rest. I loved him."

Katie's mam kept her cards close, so Luc didn't venture to believe she was on his side. Not yet. "You don't think Dexter is the right choice for her, then?"

She ignored his question but smiled slyly. "So you've had Katie's ring all these years. I wondered. I knew Paddy gave it to someone for safekeeping."

He didn't know what to say.

"Don't you want to know why you've had it? Why Paddy gave it to you and not to me or to Katie herself?"

"Do you know why, Mrs. Slater?"

"There was no else he trusted with it. You proved your worth to Paddy. I love you for that, if nothing else. But what you did to my daughter . . . letting her take that scoffing all by herself when you ruined her in this town. Sure, it's a lot less scandalous now, but it's not remembered that way by the townfolk."

"Fair enough. But I don't want my life defined by one mistake any more than Katie does."

"Two mistakes."

"Two. I should have married her. I should have asked her to marry me."

Irene stood and pulled two coffee cups from the cabinet. "You should have." She filled the cups and set one in front of him. "Cream or sugar?"

"Black, thank you."

"I worry Katie is going to define herself by that mistake— to the extent of marrying the wrong man to prove she's a good girl. Maybe not Dexter, but maybe someone else who doesn't render her weakened. It's like she wants to punish herself. Have you seen him with her? He tells her to jump and sets his watch to time the action."

"I've noticed." His jaw set, and he ground his molars.

"Love is a weakened state by its very nature, because the other person matters so much. Paddy gave you the ring for the same reason he sold you the business. He gave it to you so that I wouldn't hock it."

"Hock it?" Luc laughed.

Irene sat at the table. "Can I see it? The ring. Do you have it?"

He stood and pulled the gray velvet box from his pocket, setting it on the table. "Your new house is great," he said, looking around.

"It's not new anymore," she said, as she closed her hand around the box. She picked up the box and flipped the lid. "I don't see what all the ruckus is about. This is barely a chip of a diamond, and the emeralds are faint."

"They match Katie's eyes."

She slid the box back toward him. "Even if I had sold it, I couldn't have gotten more than an afternoon out of it. Katie's eyes. Nana's eyes. He couldn't afford good emeralds, that's the real tale." She topped off Luc's coffee. "But I admit to liking the romanticized version better myself."

"You've lost me."

"Paddy thought you'd marry our Katie, but that's not why he gave you the ring." Irene drummed her fingers on the table. "Why did you buy the business, Luc?"

"Because Paddy asked me to. He wasn't a man I'd ever seen ask for help, and I knew if he asked, he needed it. But when I got the books for the business, everything was in the black. No debt, steady income, loyal customers . . . I didn't understand."

"I don't know how to tell you this. Mostly, I hate to say it because it makes what your mother has said about us true. In a sense—."

The front door opened, and a moment later Katie entered the kitchen with her shoes in her hand and a run the size of the Louisiana boot in her stockings. She looked worn out, physically and emotionally, and he wondered how much he'd contributed to that. More to the point, how much his mother had contributed to that.

"I'm back." She dropped her bag and shoes at the kitchen entrance. "Luc!"

"What on earth happened to you?" Mam asked. "You look like you've been dragged through the bayou. Katie, I don't know what it is about you, but you always manage to come in looking like you got into a fight with something."

"She was with my mother," Luc said.

"Sit down, I'll pour you some coffee."

"What are you doing here?" Katie asked, taking a chair.

Luc took her feet from the floor and placed them in his lap. He began rubbing them, and though she struggled at first, she finally relaxed.

"I was—"

"He was just leaving," Mam said. "Weren't you?"

"I thought—" One look at Irene, and he gently put Katie's feet back down on the hardwood floor. "I was just leaving."

He slid the box into his jacket pocket just as his Black-Berry trilled. To his good fortune, Katie didn't seem to notice. But he wasn't going to step foot out of the house until she looked at him. He couldn't let her deny her feelings in order to do the "right" thing and end up suffering for it, living out of moral obligation rather than what she felt. How she could think God would want her to live a life of loneliness and sacrifice to be considered worthy, he never would understand.

"Where's Eileen?" Katie asked.

"She went shopping on Magazine Street with her mother. She took Pokey in an old purse of mine." Irene laughed. "You two and that dog. You treat it better than we mommas treated our babies, and we were good to you. That dog is old."

Katie laughed. "We feel guilty for abandoning him." Her smile disappeared as she focused on Luc. "I thought you were leaving."

"I'm sorry about my mother," he said, finally getting her attention.

"She was very kind to me, actually. She told me she appreciated my authenticity. I think that was her kind way of saying she excuses me for my emotional public outbursts."

"I thought Dexter would be here," he said, hoping for an explanation.

"Your phone's ringing. Again."

"The stock is down. Nothing awaits me but bad news."

"You can answer it."

"I can't fix it here. I have to go back to Los Angeles."

"Now?" She sounded worried.

"Don't worry, I'll be back before the rehearsal dinner. By the time you finish your rehearsals, I'll be there."

He saw that his sudden absence worried her. He took her hand, which trembled at his touch. If he walked out now, she'd make her decision for "safety" and the man she could count on to be at her side. He reached into his pocket and shut off his phone. The beeping stopped.

"I'll stay."

"No, no. I'm not going to be responsible for the downfall of your business. You go ahead; I'll steel myself to handle your mother until you get back."

He knelt down beside her. "You're so quick to give yourself up for others, Katie. What is it *you* need?" In her eyes he saw the vulnerability she tried so hard to mask.

She whispered in his ear, "I want to come with you."

He rubbed the back of his neck and tried to make sense of her plea.

Irene looked at the two of them. "Luc, I think you should go. Katie, I want to speak with you alone about Dexter."

At the sound of Dexter's name, Luc rose and let go of Katie's hand reluctantly. He stared at her, hoping to convey his meaning. *I'll be there for you.* "Thanks for the coffee and cookies, Mrs. Slater. Fabulous as usual."

He strode out the door without looking back. Katie had to make her own decision. He couldn't make it for her.

———

Katie brushed the wayward tendrils from her updo off her face. Mam had seen what passed between her and Luc. Her face flushed with guilt. "I know, Mam. I know."

244

"Katie, what am I going to do with you? The two of you are so stubborn, you deserve each other! You don't just dance on the dance floor. He comes forward, you step back. You step forward, he retreats. It's enough to drive a woman who wants grandchildren nuts."

"It will be over in three days, Mam. I won't ever have to see Luc again."

"Katie, all he has to do is snap his fingers. Be honest with yourself."

"I pledged myself to Dexter, and look how that ended up. Luc does just have to snap his fingers and I run, and that's the problem."

Mam rolled her eyes. "You couldn't have married Dexter, and it has nothing to do with Luc DeForges or the way you look at him."

"It doesn't?" She brightened. The very idea of marrying Dexter seemed abhorrent to her now, but she'd felt bound by her promise, tethered by her integrity and what it meant to be a Christian. *Let your yes be yes, and your no be no.* She feared if she didn't live as she said she believed, she'd be no better than Mrs. DeForges, who admitted she had married for security. Was there any real faith in Katie if she married either Dexter or Luc out of fear? Yet there she was, asking to go with Luc on a business trip, the epitome of pathetic.

"Luc has your ring," Mam said.

"I know."

"I want you to know why he has your ring."

"He said Paddy gave it to him."

Mam nodded. "He doesn't know why Paddy gave it to him and not to me, but I do. I know why Paddy sold him the business too, and if you knew it might change the way you see Luc. It might change the way you see his answer to you that night at his graduation party."

Katie swigged her coffee in preparation for whatever her mam might say. "I don't know if I'm ready to hear it."

"I gambled, Katie. It started out innocently enough. I'd make my few dollars from selling produce on the carts, and I'd rush over to Canal Street and spend my meager earnings. Sometimes I'd win, but most of the time I'd go home empty-handed. Then it became more of a compulsion, and my meager earnings weren't enough. I started selling a few things around the house: jewelry, Irish china Grammy had given me. Eventually, I took out a loan here and there. To make a long story short, we were about to lose the house when your father found out. He asked Luc to buy the business, and he bought this house with the money. It's in your name, this house."

"What happened to the old house?"

"We lost it, of course. It went into foreclosure. The bank sold it, and they asked me to move out. Three months after you left."

Her mother may as well have told her she was adopted.

"I don't understand. What does any of this have to do with Luc? Or with Dexter, for that matter?"

"Your dad never told Luc why he needed the money, or what he did with it. He was so big on life insurance, everyone just assumed that's how I purchased this house. That's what you thought, right?"

Some men put their trust in money and others in good friends, but her father had sworn by the value of life insurance, drilling the message into her head with the consistency of an oil rig. *There's no reason in this day and age for a man not to have life insurance, Katie. Life insurance used to be just the good luck of God's will. If my papa was out of work, my family scraped and did what they had to do until more work came by. If you were lucky enough to find a man to hire you, you'd work your fingers raw if necessary. Not like that today . . . Insurance is the friend of the workingman.*

Katie nodded. "I was sure the entire town bought life insurance after the accident."

"Paddy did that to protect me. When he died, I knew it was my fault. If his mind hadn't been on other things, like how he could rescue his family from my addiction, he would have never been sidetracked and walked in front of that streetcar. Your Paddy knew their schedules better than anyone. When he stepped into that neutral ground, the median, I know his mind was wandering, and I know why. He wanted to know if he'd done enough. If anything happened to him, were you protected? Was I? Had he done enough?"

"I never knew any of this was happening. Wouldn't there have been signs?"

"Oh, I was careful. You were off at school, and rather than face the empty house every day, I went to the casino and I felt surrounded by friends."

"I would have come home. I didn't need to live at school, it was less than a mile away!"

Mam waved off her concern. "It was time for you to go. That's what I raised you for, to be a strong, independent young woman. You're missing the point."

"I guess I am."

"Your dad protected me even when I didn't deserve to be protected, even when he was protecting me from myself. He made sure we were provided for, even if he wouldn't be there."

"You stopped gambling?"

"The second Paddy died. I understood then what my selfishness had caused. The house was nothing compared to Paddy. Once he was gone, I understood the repercussions. I quit cold turkey."

"He never told Luc why he was selling the business?"

"He just asked Luc for the favor. I think the boy was surprised when he saw the business wasn't in trouble, but your dad always said Luc had incredible ideas for the business, and if he were a younger man, he might have taken him up on them."

"How come you didn't like Dexter right off the bat, Mam? I mean, I know you've always been good about reading people, but Dexter. He was always so nice to everyone at church. In love with God and always trying to do the right thing. What did you see in him?"

Mam groaned. "I saw in him what I always saw in Mrs. DeForges—even when she was a little girl. She could adhere to all of the rules and come off as the belle of the ball or even, as you once saw for yourself, as a great spiritual leader. She can do everything that is required of her and look gracious doing it, but she is not kind, dear. And neither is Dexter. I saw no humility in his nature."

"Mrs. DeForges was very nice to me at the shower today. I think she's just scared of people judging her."

"I'm sure she is, Katie, but that doesn't make for strong character. Look at Luc. He's got you slung over his shoulder in that picture in the paper, and he never bothers to answer such an insulting implication. That's character."

"You knew that was me?"

"A mother who doesn't recognize her own child's bum isn't fit to be called a mother."

Katie giggled. "Why didn't you say anything?"

"I was worried you'd leave before the wedding, and I wanted you to face everyone from that night. The reality that you aren't your mistakes—I thought it was an important quest for you."

"I don't know how it is you can seem so ridiculous and so brilliant all at once."

"One day your child will think the same thing of you."

"So back to Dexter. You didn't think he was kind."

"Did he ever enter into your world, Katie?"

She thought about the question for a long time. "I guess he didn't. He just invited me into his."

The doorbell rang, and they overheard Rusty speaking to someone, but Mam was intensely focused on the conversation and ignored the interruption.

"Ask yourself this, Katie. If you gambled your life away, his life away . . . would Dexter offer you grace or condemnation? Protection or anger? The truth is, we see people's real character when we blow it."

"Dexter!" Katie jumped up. "I thought you left town!"

Mam busied herself at the countertop, scrubbing the granite with a kitchen towel.

"I had to get something off my mind before I left. Rusty let me in."

"Come in and sit down."

He sat at the table, and Mam poured him a cup of coffee. Even though he didn't drink the stuff, he sipped from the mug before he spoke. "I think I've made a mistake. I do want to marry you. I mean, I don't get all this dancing/singing business, and I don't understand why you want to dress like you've been in a time machine, but I'm sure there are things you don't understand about me as well. Maybe I wasn't being fair."

Katie blinked rapidly and searched for the right words.

"I'll admit I had trouble with the fact that you'd given yourself to that character. It bothered me that you hadn't been smarter as a young woman, but then I thought, I'm not perfect either, and if Katie loves me, what does it matter if she loved someone else once?"

"The thing is, Dexter. All those things you don't understand about me? They *are* me. If you were intrigued by those things it might work, but it sounds as though you see them as character flaws."

"If we're committed to the sanctity of the institution of marriage, then I fail to see how it could be a problem."

She put her hand on his and held it tightly. "I think I want more than that, Dexter."

"Meaning?"

"We're forcing something together that maybe doesn't fit."

"Katie, you're not that young anymore."

Mam coughed.

"I'm only twenty-nine. I'm not ready for the pasture just yet, thanks."

"I'm willing to make this right. I'm willing to marry you. I don't want to treat you like something to be discarded. Do you want to be put out with yesterday's news?"

"The thing is, Dexter, I'm not afraid to be single. So that's not a reason to get married. Once I made a mistake that cost me my reputation and a lot of years to overcome. Big decisions scare me, and you can see why, but I don't think we can compromise in ways that matter. I believe by not being able to decide for certain, that leads us to our decision."

"I'm not going to offer again," he said.

"I understand."

He slammed the mug on the table. "I need to catch my flight. The cab is waiting." He swept out of the room so quickly, she felt his wake.

"He'll be engaged by the end of the year," Mam predicted. "Men like him just get married when they feel ready. Kick off the dust, Katie. He isn't worth your tears."

"That's the thing. I don't really have any."

Mam stroked the back of her head. "When the storms of life push against you, our real temperaments come out to dance. We're all entitled to a tantrum now and then, Katie. No one is perfect, but the man who would take your darkest secret and use it against you for power? It's the ultimate betrayal. You told him the truth about your past with Luc, and he used it to make you feel undeserving of real love. That's criminal."

"I had to. I couldn't marry him and not tell him that."

"No one who truly understands grace will tell a person their sin is beyond it." Mam lifted Dex's coffee cup and wiped away any trace of him.

Chapter 19

⌒

Que Sera, Sera

"Katie, you'll never guess who I found! Katie!" Eileen shouted through the house.

Katie wiped the tears from her cheeks with the back of her hand. Her face felt pudgy and swollen from crying, and judging by the hair in her face, there was nothing left of her updo. As she walked into the living room, Jem DeForges stood in the entryway, his imposing frame overwhelming the small room. Pokey jumped at Katie's feet.

"Katie!" Jem extended his arms to her and pulled her into a tight Southern hug—the kind she'd received more of in the last few days than in her entire eight years in California.

Jem's clothes looked as though he lived an island life—

khaki pants, a camp shirt finished off to look professional, with a cotton blazer. He was a walking Jimmy Buffet song.

She pulled away and patted at her hair. "Jem, I look terrible. Why is it gorgeous men never walk into my life when I look my best? You're here looking like Ernest Hemingway in the middle of the day, and I'm a wreck."

"Katie-bug, I consider it a favor. I can't handle you all dressed to the nines. It's too much for my fragile heart."

She playfully hit him. "I forgot how charming you could be."

"Jem has something for you, Katie," Eileen said from over Jem's shoulder. "I was shopping at his Canal Street store—"

"I thought you went to Magazine Street."

"I got lost," Eileen said with narrowed eyes. "Jem asked if I saw you anymore because he had something for you."

"Didn't you know I was here for the wedding?" she asked Jem.

"I did, but I didn't want to give you this in front of everyone. I've been saving these for years, and I didn't want the family flapping their gums about it."

Her interest piqued, Katie said, "I've forgotten my manners. Come in and have a seat. Can I get you some coffee? Tea?" All she had to add was "me" to her offer, and she'd be as cheesy as Luc's air hostess.

Jem, the oldest brother in the DeForges trio, didn't seem like a jeweler. He wore no jewelry for one thing, and he possessed no salesmanlike qualities. The jewelry shop had been the last business, besides the real estate holdings, left in the family's economy, and like a dutiful son, Jem had taken it over when his father retired. Where once the DeForges boys had seemed like one entity, surviving their mother separated them into three different worlds. Ryan took on the typical youngest brother role, playing the role of Momma's boy and not entering the competition between his older brothers. Luc survived by besting his mother's expectations and then escaping Louisiana altogether. Jem, Katie thought, had survived by sheer force of will and determination.

He stretched out his long legs on the settee and reached into his jacket pocket.

"So what is it with you and your brothers wearing suit coats in the middle of a New Orleans summer?"

"It's what we do here." He snapped his lapels.

"The Deforges are Renaissance men in the truest sense of the word."

Jem held up a black velvet jewelry box. "These came into the shop a few years ago. Believe it or not, I saw them and thought only of you." He placed the box on the settee, and she sat next to it.

"For me?" she asked stupidly. Pokey tried to jump between them, but his small legs wouldn't reach. Katie bent down and pulled the dog onto the sofa with one hand. "Now we have an official chaperone. Just like the old days when this settee was made."

He laughed. "And this one bites, so I will keep my hands to myself."

"Just open the box. I'm dying here!" Eileen said. "I had to wait through the whole car ride."

Katie lifted the lid. Two green gems in the shape of cat eyes met her.

"They're earrings," Jem said. "When I saw them I thought, *Where have I seen that color?* I tried to place it but couldn't. So I put them aside. And then it dawned on me. Katie's eyes. They look exactly like Katie-bug's eyes. I always planned to send them to you, but good intentions only go so far. I didn't have your address, didn't want to ask my brother for it. You know the drill."

"They're beautiful, Jem. But I can't keep them."

"Why on earth not? You think I let them gather dust all those years to have you hand them back to me in a split second?"

"Jem, you just don't give earrings to someone you haven't seen in eight years."

"Is that how long it's been?" He shook his head. "It feels like yesterday you left. You're not someone who just left town, Katie. I associate you with most of the good times my family had."

"Surely they started before college," she said.

"Coming-of-age good times, then, if you will."

"They look like my ring. Well, the ring I hope to have again at some point."

"Green. They're fair emeralds. Not worth as much on the open market, but they're priceless when you put that color on a pair of eyes."

"They're emeralds too?" she asked.

"Yes, but you know, the color of an emerald is what

determines its value. Even with inclusions, a darker emerald with brilliant color will be worth more."

"Stop," Eileen protested. "You sound like Dexter!"

"Dexter?" Jem asked.

"My ex-almost-fiancé."

He thought about that for a second. "So you're not engaged?"

"Not engaged. Your brother apparently has my engagement ring, and I don't think he was keen on giving it to my ex-almost-fiancé."

"Why would he be? Luc's going to marry you."

She chose to ignore his comment. "So you're telling me this emerald that I love, which matches my eyes, isn't valuable?"

"I didn't mean it that way. Beauty is in the eye of the beholder, and I think the fact that these emeralds remind me of your beautiful eyes is enough reason to make them valuable. Valuable enough for me to hold on to them all these years."

"Wasn't that thoughtful, Katie?" Eileen asked. "Jem always was so thoughtful."

Pokey wandered into her lap, and she held the earring box in one hand and petted the dog with the other. "Yes, he was. He is." She looked at Jem. "I didn't mean to talk about you in the past tense."

"I suppose I am in the past tense for you. Tell me about this wonderful life you lead in California. I hear you're a full-fledged teacher lady now."

"Well," she said, seeing Eileen jitter out of the corner of her eye. "Eileen, would you sit down, you're making me nervous. Even Pokey is worn out. Look at him!"

The dog looked upward with mournful eyes that all but shouted, *Help me.*

Eileen sank onto a nearby chair, her hands placed gently on her knees, her legs poised together at a perfect sixty-degree angle. "Go ahead."

Katie looked at Jem. "I'm teaching. I have a classroom full of special needs kids, and I specialize in autism spectrum disorders. Most of my kids are fully autistic, with other added diagnoses and physical handicaps. I also do tutoring on the side, and I teach other schools how to handle their students with concrete concepts and pragmatic language."

She could tell she'd lost him. "Higher-functioning Asperger's kids, they get anything concrete, like math—but throw in the concept of money and it's too abstract, so I teach teachers how to get them to understand it. It saves a lot of frustration on both sides, student and teacher."

"Now who sounds like Dexter!" Eileen rolled her eyes. "Jem brought you earrings, Katie!"

Katie grinned. "I think I'm boring my roommate."

"You're not boring me," Jem said. "I think it's the perfect job for you. I'm just not sure how you got there from singing torch songs in a barrelhouse."

"I only did that to earn my teaching credential. I was never very good."

"I beg to differ," Jem said. "You always held the room captivated. You certainly captivated the DeForges brothers, anyway. I always thought one of us would marry you."

"Which one?" Eileen asked.

Jem laughed. "I thought it would be Luc. How long did you two date?"

"Too long," Eileen said. "I never thought Luc was right for her. He was all into money and stuff, and Katie never cared about any of that."

"No," Jem said. "She didn't. You're right, but Katie and Luc . . . there's something special in the two of them. I can't imagine either one of them with anyone else."

"I can," Eileen said. "Besides, she has a theory that money gets in the way of relationships. Don't you, Katie? That's why she's determined to stay poor by teaching."

"I'm not opposed to money, Eileen. Just to the love of it."

"Right. Totally," Eileen said. "Like, I love my mansions all over the world, and my private plane? That kind of love."

"In my brother's defense, money was his escape. The more he made, the less he had to listen to my mother's fears he'd run out of it. She and Luc never did see eye to eye. And some of the things money can buy are pretty nice," Jem said. "I know I'd like to have that private jet of Luc's. And a nice frock from Ginger Rogers' closet wasn't so bad, huh?"

Katie felt guilty. Had she dissed Luc?

"Well." Jem slapped his legs and stood. "I should get going." He bent over and kissed her on the cheek. "Katie, it was lovely to see you again. You look as beautiful as ever. I'll see you Friday night at the rehearsal dinner."

"Do you have a date?" Eileen asked him. "I mean, are you seeing someone special now?"

It didn't sound remotely natural, but coming from Eileen's cute self, it didn't have to.

"As a matter of fact, Eileen Ripley, I do not have a date for the rehearsal dinner." He walked across the room and took her by the hand. "But I would be honored if you would attend with me. What do you say? Are you busy Friday night?"

"Um, no, I don't think so," she stammered.

"And maybe, if you have fun Friday night, you'll have mercy on me and go to the wedding with me Saturday."

Eileen gasped. "I—me?"

"Are you busy? It's only two nights away, and I understand a pretty girl like you doesn't sit home too often."

Katie grinned. If he only knew how often she and Eileen had discussed the benefits of Netflix on dateless weekend nights.

"She's not busy," she answered for her friend.

"But—"

"We'll see you then," Katie said, walking Jem to the door.

"I'll pick you up at six. Dress nice. My mother will be there, and you'll want to escape the radar. Oh, and, Katie, I don't know if you've seen it yet, but my mother had a story planted in the paper that Luc was engaged. He's not, but you can expect a few uncomfortable questions on Friday night."

"This so-called fiancée is blond, and everyone will know I'm nothing more than a stand-in," Katie finished for him. She stretched her arms across the room. "Luc DeForges Brings Rejected Suitor to Wedding!"

Eileen, having changed into lavender yoga shorts and a fuchsia tank top, walked to the wall fountain on the side of the stairwell and flipped the switch. The soothing sounds of trickling water took their effect, and both women sank to the floor with their backs against the settee. Pokey snuggled between them.

"This is how life should be. Uncomplicated, slow-moving, filled with good food and good friends." Eileen laid her head back on the settee. "Men complicate life. We should get us a dog."

"We have us a dog."

"Let's take him back with us!"

"I thought he was on his last legs." Katie looked down at the wide-eyed mutt, who looked no worse for the wear than any of them.

"Momma said he'd been fighting pneumonia, and the vet said his lungs were filled with fluid, but he seems fine now. He wasn't supposed to live this long from the start, but you're a strong one, aren't you, Pokey baby? How's Momma's baby?" Eileen swung the dog in the air and kissed his snout.

Katie rested her head on Pokey's back. "He sounds fine to me."

"So . . . Dexter?" Eileen asked her. "You seem fine."

"I guess that's the benefit of a practical engagement. The breakup is practical too."

"For that I can be thankful. Because I sure can't take another real breakup. Speaking of which, where is Luc?"

"He had to go home on business. He'll be back by the rehearsal dinner."

"If there's one thing you can count on with Luc, it's that something will come up. That's why I think Jem is the man for you."

"Too bad he thinks otherwise." Katie looked at the doorway. "Or are you still under the impression this date is about getting close to me?"

"I don't understand it. Jem was always crazy about you. He saved those earrings all those years? I thought for sure he was coming here to put the moves on you."

"Men don't go after women their brother has dated. It's too weird. But their best friend . . . now there is a match made in heaven."

Pokey barked in agreement.

Chapter 20

⌐~⌐

I Got Rhythm

Luc rang the bell at precisely 6:45 p.m. Katie noticed because it was the first time she remembered his being on time for anything. Before she opened the door, she gave Mam a stern look. "Remember, nothing to him about Dexter."

Mam pretended to lock her lips.

Katie opened the door and caught her breath. Luc wore a three-piece gray suit with a gray flannel fedora. "You look like Cary Grant."

"I feel like Cary Grant. You look more beautiful than I've ever seen you, Katie." He handed her a single red rose, then lifted her hands. "Turn around."

It had been a long time since a man complimented her

and it felt authentic. For all his niceties, she realized, Dexter had done a number on her self-esteem. Maybe even more than getting dumped publicly in New Orleans' society.

Luc whistled. "It's not polite to show up the bride. She'll be nervous enough, marrying my brother tomorrow."

Katie wore a vintage-inspired green silk taffeta cocktail dress with a sweetheart neckline, gathered bodice, and cinched waistline, with a graduated veil of green crinoline over the backside, like a fitted bustle. She'd paired her new earrings with a green rhinestone necklace of Mam's. No one would ever be the wiser, with Luc on her arm. They'd think she could afford whatever baubles Jem carried in his shop.

"Stand there for a picture," Mam directed them.

Now that Mam knew where the ring had been all this time, and why Luc possessed it, her countenance had changed. Luc was apparently restored to her good graces. Katie only hoped Luc proved worthy of Mam's trust, now that Dexter had bailed from the race.

"We're off. I'll have her home by midnight," Luc called out to Mam. "Don't want her shoes to turn into a pumpkin or— what is it?" His gaze fell on her feet, and he whistled again. "Those are hot. Not the ones you're getting married in."

"No, these are my swing shoes."

They were nude in color, so they made her legs go on forever, with a small champagne-colored ruffle around the back of the heel and a Mary Jane strap so they didn't fly off when she danced.

"I thought Dexter didn't dance."

"He doesn't," she said. She tapped her way down the steps and crossed the brick path to Luc's waiting limousine. Leon was out of his band uniform and in his driving suit. "What will you wear tomorrow?" she asked him.

"Whatever Mr. DeForges tells me to. You look fine tonight, Miss Katie. Mighty fine."

"I'll take it from here," Luc said, grabbing the doorframe. He climbed in beside her and slammed the door shut. Then he pressed the button, and Leon's compartment magically disappeared.

"That was rude."

"Boundaries, Katie. You don't check out your boss's date."

"Are you jealous?" she asked, feeling uncharacteristically flirtatious. She leaned toward him, and he refused to look at her.

"I'm not sure I like this dame. She's got attitude. Loads of it. What's different about you?"

She giggled and brushed a kiss across his cheek. "Luc, I'm—the thing is—Dexter—"

"Is on a plane headed home, and you dumped his smarmy self. I know. I wondered how long it would take you to come clean."

"How did you know?" She sat upright and leaned against her door.

"Katie, I don't miss a lot."

She pouted.

"Especially when it pertains to the woman I love."

"Don't." She placed a hand on his arm. "No pressure tonight, all right? Let's simply have fun."

"Done."

The rehearsal dinner was held at the Commander's Palace, a five-star restaurant for old money on Washington Avenue near the streetcar. The restaurant endured, a staple of New Orleans cuisine since shortly after the Civil War. Katie had never before entered its hallowed halls. Though she might have afforded such a dinner for a special occasion, that occasion had never presented itself. And if it had, most likely Mam would have cooked something special at home instead.

The limo pulled up into a line of fancy cars under the striped awning that surrounded the deep aqua Victorian with the bird's-nest spire at its corner. Her nerves returned at the thought of getting out of the limo. She prayed she'd know which fork to use and the proper way to lay her linen napkin across her lap. Mrs. DeForges probably expected her to fail—the worst she could do was live up to the expectation.

The door opened, and Leon helped her out of the car. Luc stayed alongside her as they followed a steady stream of guests into the building.

"What's the matter, Katie?" he asked.

"Nothing, why?" Her voice shook.

"You're squeezing my hand to the point of cutting off my circulation."

She dropped his hand. "I'm sorry. I'm just nervous, I guess. I suddenly realized we never practiced in front of an audience."

"Just imagine them in their underwear. Isn't that what they say?" Luc grasped her hand again. "You ever been here?"

Amidst all the beaded gowns and tight, dewy skin, Katie felt like a lone orange in the apple cart. "No."

"Don't worry. Once this crowd is plowed with wine, they'll seem no different from the drunks in the Barrelhouse. Besides, that's tomorrow. Tonight we dance, right? God has made everything beautiful in his time, no?"

"Yes."

As they entered she nearly expected to be announced, like they did with all the princesses in the movies. Luc raised her wrap from her shoulders and handed it to a coat girl in exchange for a ticket.

Katie wondered if her Paddy could see her now, acting every bit the lady at Commander's. What a laugh he'd have over her singing at a DeForges wedding.

"What are you smiling about?"

"I'm happy," she answered.

"Good. You should be."

Stepping inside the richly decorated private room, Katie gasped. "It's amazing!"

Crystal drop chandeliers with candles hung from the ceiling, vintage silver "walls" were created from Victorian ceiling panels, black tablecloths and tiny white lights were draped everywhere, like magical stars from the night's sky. The room had a long head table on a pedestal and several round tables below. Katie walked closer to the first table, anxious to see each tiny detail that Olivia and her mother had created for the silver screen look. She lifted a place card and read the name, then bent to smell the fresh rose scent of the white centerpiece.

"Luc, can you imagine? All of this for a rehearsal dinner!"

He flashed a condescending smile, and she stood upright.

"I wasn't implying—"

"No, I understand," he said, yanking his cuffs from underneath his suit. "Tonight. Remember?"

She felt her bottom lip tremble.

"Now, Katie, you're the one who said this. We're luggage-free tonight. No history. No baggage."

She nodded. "I know. You're right. But I really didn't mean—"

"And whatever you imagined my face to say, it really didn't mean—"

"Katie, Luc, you both look stunning!" Mrs. Tyler rubbed Katie's back gently with the kind of warmth that only mothers seemed to possess. "Luc, you and Katie are up at the head table next to your mother. Katie and your mother were getting reacquainted at the shower. I thought it would be nice for them to have more time."

Luc and Katie looked at one another and grinned.

"No, wait, I forgot. We moved you to make room for Olivia's maid of honor. We didn't figure you'd care. You're down here at the round table with us."

Katie breathed a sigh of relief. Although it seemed strange that the mother of the bride was on ground level, she wasn't about to ask questions or stir up trouble where she didn't need any. Mrs. DeForges was probably where she might do the least amount of damage and still feel the most important.

Katie mingled with the crowd, her dress making her feel as though she belonged. She chatted up strangers as if she was Ingrid Bergman on a binge in *Notorious* or Katharine Hepburn working the press in *The Philadelphia Story*.

Finally, worn out from her one-act play, she sat before the place card where her name was printed in careful script.

"I can't wait to dance with you," Luc growled into her ear. She turned her head as if his voice did nothing to her, when really she felt it to her toes.

"Relax. We still have dinner, speeches, and bread pudding to muddle through, and the dance floor hardly looks inhabitable."

"Not here."

She raised her brows. "Luc DeForges, if I've learned anything in my lifetime, it's not to go anywhere unattended with you."

"Jem and Eileen are coming too. I asked them."

Dinner plodded along. Dishonest speeches were given. Warm family toasts were read from 3 x 5 cards. Luc's dad was the last to speak, and he sat alongside Mrs. DeForges in a chillingly vertical stance, the life force seemingly drained from his body. Luc recognized it too, and he stood, apparently to make amends for his father's lackluster speech. He tapped on his champagne flute with a fork.

"Excuse me, everyone. I'd like to make a toast."

Katie loved that he spoke from a place of strength and

virility, as if to say that the DeForges family line was solid and their commitment to New Orleans, and now to the Tylers, was everlasting.

"But before I do, I'd just like to clear up some confusion. I'm here with my beautiful date for the evening, Katie McKenna."

There was a light round of applause.

"I'd like to congratulate my brother Ryan on selecting such a wonderful addition to our family. You're not worthy of her, bro, but we're thrilled to have you, Olivia. When you first knocked my brother over on roller skates, I never imagined I'd be standing here today. The emergency room, yes, but not here. You two bring out the best in each other. You have more fun than any couple I've ever seen, and I plan to be standing here toasting your fiftieth anniversary."

Applause filled the room again.

"And if you'll permit me one more thing. With the gracious permission of my brother and his beautiful bride, I'd also like to take this opportunity to announce my own engagement."

Katie's eyes went wide. She scanned the room for some blonde worthy of being Luc's trophy wife, but she knew exactly what he was doing.

"That is, if she'll have me." He bent on one knee and opened her ring box.

"Luc, no. Not here," she said through clenched teeth. "Fun, remember?"

"Katie McKenna, would you do me the honor of becoming

my wife? You've always been the only one for me, and it's time you made an honest man out of me."

She felt the heavy stares all around her and the heat flame in her face as cameras flashed. She stood and pushed the microphone down and whispered in his ear, "We said tonight. It was just going to be tonight, no history, no future."

"*You* said tonight." He nodded. "I'm asking for forever. I'm greedy that way. Check my bank account."

The walls felt tight. The colors and faces swam together. She had decided to live her life without fear, but that didn't mean she was ready for this. Where would they live? Would she lose her school? Would she just trade being Mrs. Hastings for being Mrs. DeForges and lose all her independence again? Her faith? She had a terrible habit of waiting for men to rescue her rather than relying on her own faith in God.

Luc blinked. His confident air seemed to falter.

"Excuse me," she said, before she ran from the room. She didn't even realize she'd offered him no answer until she was outside under the streetlight wondering which way to go. She heard voices—Leon's, Eileen's, Luc's—calling her name.

"Katie!"

"Katie!"

"Katie!"

She whirled around and felt her heel drop into a crack on the sidewalk.

She heard Fred Astaire singing "Cheek to Cheek," and she began to sway to the music. She wrapped her arms around him and recalled what it felt like to hear the music for the first time, to watch Fred Astaire dance on air and take Ginger in his arms with nary an effort, as if they'd both sprouted wings. The music soothed her, and her feet took small steps to the dance floor that appeared, white and empty, with only a single spotlight shining like an invitation. It was her moment, her chance to shine. She felt the luxurious ostrich feathers of Ginger Rogers' gown, the smooth satin against her waist, and hummed along with Astaire. Out of the surrounding darkness Luc appeared, wearing a topcoat and tails and a smile. His magnificent, warm smile. His long, lean legs stepped toward her, and he whirled her into his arms. The warmth of his hand on her back caressed her and she inhaled the thick, clean scent of him, tasted the resonance in his voice as he sang, "Heaven . . . I'm in heaven . . ."

She rested her head on his shoulder and let him lead with all the grace of Fred Astaire and the strength of Burt Lancaster. He twirled her about the room, and she dared to look into his eyes. His ardent, deep blue eyes, which held years of memories and the spark of hope to a magical future.

God had created Luc DeForges just for her. His body next to hers—the perfect fit—the last piece of the puzzle that connected their lives, their families. Love appeared and filled in the space between the DeForgeses and the McKennas, Uptown and the Channel, Northern California and the South, 1945 to now . . .

"Kiss me, Luc. Kiss me like you've never kissed another soul." But as she reached for the key that unlocked the secret, her vision became misty until it evaporated into thin air.

"Katie!"

She groaned. "My head." Her forehead throbbed and her vision blurred. "I can't see."

Someone pulled her lace hat away. Her vision cleared. Feet surrounded her, and she recognized her peep-toe heels on Eileen.

"I'm on the ground," she said—half statement, half question.

"You ran into that post." Eileen banged on the solid block of wood. "You were like a chicken with its head cut off. You kept running, and we were all shouting your name. What were you thinking? Didn't you hear everyone calling you?"

"Oh my goodness, what did I do?" She sat up, embarrassed, while Uptown guests waiting for their cars stared down at her. "Olivia! Did I ruin her night?"

"Olivia's still inside dancing, having the time of her life," Eileen reassured her. "She has no idea you're out here splayed on the banquette. And your mam's on her way. You were out cold, but I told them you'd done this before. Remember the time you walked into the post at Nordstrom?" Eileen giggled. "Girl, it's like you got a magnet in your head sometimes. I know, it's totally not funny, but one minute you're up and the next . . . splat!"

"Ugh. Why didn't you just kill me and put me out of my misery?"

"Because then I wouldn't get to be maid of honor at your wedding."

"Dexter went home, Eileen. It's off."

"You did hit your head. Your wedding to Luc, silly."

"I'm not marrying Luc. He just did that so I could turn him down in front of everyone."

"Katie, I don't think he asked you for that reason."

"I know he didn't." Jem reached down and helped her off the ground. "Katie, lean against the post." He righted her and helped her straighten herself. "Luc asking you to marry him in front of everyone? That was real. He asked for permission from Ryan first, so as not to upstage the happy couple. He thought it was important to propose publicly, since he"—Jem cleared his throat—"well, since he rejected you publicly. But it turns out, now you've rejected him publicly. So you're either terminally incompatible, or you're even."

"Where is he? Where is Luc?"

"He had an emergency."

She rubbed her forehead and captured a small dab of blood on her palm.

"Mrs. DeForges will never forgive me. I've ruined another one of her parties."

"Wait until she sees the paper with your unconscious self sprawled against a lamppost and the announcement that her son asked for your hand in marriage. That's not going to be a fun breakfast table," Eileen said.

"Oh, my head aches." But Katie didn't care about any of that. She wanted to know where Luc had gone. "Jem, if you see Luc, would you tell him I don't hold him to anything. I've made a fool out of him again tonight. I know he needs a wife who can talk politics or the stock exchange, all while walking in heels. Tell him I'm sorry."

"Unfortunately for Luc, he's in love with you," Jem said, rubbing her back.

"You are engaged," Eileen said. "You have been engaged since the moment you laid eyes on Luc DeForges, and you can't tell me otherwise. If you had ever talked to me about another living soul the way you do Luc, I could grant you some leeway, but the fact is, your heart has been engaged since the moment he walked into that bar."

"Of all the gin joints . . ." Jem began, in his best Bogart voice.

"Even if Luc broke your heart a thousand times, another man didn't stand a chance. He's waited long enough, and so have we. Put us out of our misery already."

If only she could.

Chapter 21

⁓

In the Mood

"Mam!" Katie emerged from her room in her nightgown. She struggled to breathe. "Mam!" she called over the staircase landing.

Her mother appeared at the bottom of the stairs. "Katie, what on earth? Are you all right?"

"Mam, my gown is missing! I opened the zippered bag—" She stopped to catch her breath. "I opened it, and the dress is gone. The pink one with feathers—it's gone. There's a white one in the bag. It's not my dress at all." She rubbed her forehead. "Could I have left it in the limo? Maybe the plane! Oh, Mam, I think Luc was mad enough when he left me last night, or he would have said goodbye, at least found out if I was all right. What if he doesn't want me to come?"

"Relax. Luc was here this morning, and he switched them out himself. Didn't you hear the doorbell?"

"No."

"He said the band is going to be in tuxedos, so he thought white was better." Mam tapped a finger on her chin. "I'm supposed to tell you something else."

"The orchestra was always going to be wearing tuxedos. I can't wear white to someone else's wedding. It's the—Mam, are you wearing makeup?" She could count on one hand the times she'd seen her mother made-up.

Mam patted her coiffed hair. "I am. I'm trying something new."

By trying something new, she assumed her mother meant in this decade. But judging by the 1978 frosted pink lipstick, it appeared everything old was new again.

"Luc was here this morning? In my room?"

"Yes. He's got Harry Connick, Jr.'s big band now, so they'll be your backup."

"Harry Connick is nobody's backup. Least of all mine. Where is Eileen?"

"She took Pokey home. Luc's invited her too. Actually Jem did the inviting. They're getting along like two frogs on a lily pad. Eileen likes Harry Connick, Jr. too. You know, that puts it into perspective for me, Katie. I get it, the fascination with the smooth standards, when you say 'Harry Connick.' What a talent that boy is. And so handsome."

"I'm glad."

"I saw him on Canal Street once. Did I ever tell you that?"

"Yes, Mam." Only about a hundred times. "You let Luc into my room?"

"Well, I told him where the dress was. He knocked. I heard him knock. You must have been exhausted after your adventure last night."

"Where is Eileen?"

"You already asked me that. She went to take Pokey home. She'll be back. You're so high-strung this morning."

"Mam." Katie tried to calm her voice. "Why would you let a strange man into my room by himself?"

"Luc isn't a strange man. And you were asleep."

"What if I was sleeping naked?"

"Well, that would be strange. I never taught you that it was all right to sleep naked." Mam paused. "Were you naked?"

"No! But look at me! My hair's a mess. I have no makeup on. What if I was drooling on the pillow?"

"Ick. I'd have to get a new pillow. Did you do that? Because they're having a sale on pillows right now at Target. Maybe I should pick up a few."

"Mam! Help me here. This gown is an antique white. It definitely looks like a wedding dress. I'm a good Southern girl. I can't wear white to another woman's wedding."

Mam shook her head. "*That's* what Luc told me to tell you. It's the dress from *Swing Time*. I will never understand your fascination with that era. There was a war on. What's romantic about that? Nana said it was miserable. Harry Connick I can understand, but the forties?"

"The other dress was from *Top Hat*. The feathered one. Luc had it copied."

"Right. This one is an original. It's the one Ginger wore when she kissed Fred Astaire in *Swing Time*. *That's* what I was supposed to tell you." Mam patted the banister. "You're supposed to be very careful with the gown because it's from a private collector. It hasn't been seen in public since a museum gala in New York City. Oh, and the cape isn't with it because it's apparently too fragile to travel." Mam smiled, apparently well pleased with her memory skills. "There's a cape."

"You mean there's *not* a cape."

"Right. But originally there was a cape."

"It doesn't matter, because I'm not going." Katie started to walk back to her room. "This is nothing like what I promised. I'll buy my own ticket back to California if I need to."

"Sure you will. Luc's invited us so that we can see Harry Connick. He's from New Orleans, you know."

"I'm going to sing at a wedding with Harry Connick, Jr. with no practice whatsoever? In a white wedding dress? I'm thinking not. This is just a bad *American Idol* episode waiting to happen, and I'm not starring in it."

"You have a lovely voice, Katie. It was good enough to put yourself through college. Don't sell yourself short. Besides, I'm sure it's all right, if Luc has it set up this way. And you already embarrassed yourself twice in front of all these people—they'll be expecting it. Anything above total humiliation is a win."

"Thanks, Mam. That's comforting." Katie narrowed her gaze. "Since when is Luc DeForges your best friend?"

"Are you hungry? I've got some—"

"I'm not hungry. That gown isn't very forgiving. What do you have for Spanx in the house?"

Mam looked confused.

"A girdle. Do you have a girdle?"

"What would I have a girdle for? When you have fish guts on the front of your shirt, you tend not to suck your fat in."

"Pretty."

Mam giggled.

"Did you just giggle?"

Mam covered her mouth with her hands, which were manicured, of all things, and flapped them as she tried to conceal laughter.

"What is so funny?" Katie pulled her hair back into a loose ponytail and tied it into a knot. "I'm glad you have a reason to laugh, Mam. Maybe if you share it I won't remember how much my life stinks."

"Honestly . . ." Mam's laughter stilled. "What do you have to complain about? You come here on a luxury private jet, you're wearing Ginger Rogers' original gown, and you have a multimillionaire in love with you. I fail to see which part of your life stinks."

"The part where I wasted eight years of my life and now it may be too late for Luc and me to ever get it right. He looked really angry with me when he walked away last night, Mam. Almost disgusted."

Mam giggled again.

"Stop that! Why are you like the cat who ate the canary?"

"I'm happy. I'm free. Katie, when I told you about my gambling problem, I had no idea how uplifted I'd feel. Almost like I was flying. I've kept that a secret for so long, so that you wouldn't think badly of me. Today I feel a hundred pounds lighter. And I've harbored this grudge against Luc for so long, and he never knew why. I should have known Paddy would always protect me. It's not fair, really. I didn't deserve it."

"That's what grace is, Mam. What better expression is there of love?"

"I never dreamed it would cost *you*, Katie. I would have said something years ago. I never knew Paddy didn't tell Luc the truth."

Katie waved her hand. "It just wasn't meant to be."

"You're wrong, Katie. Luc protected you too. Maybe not in the best way, but he did what he thought was right. Just like I did what I thought was right by keeping my secret—never knowing it was causing you to think ill of Luc. Though what did I expect, when I thought ill of him myself?"

"I could have told you that Paddy would have done anything to protect you. And he certainly wouldn't have shared a secret like that with Aimée DeForges, your archenemy."

"It all seems obvious now, doesn't it?" Mam started climbing the stairs. "Let me come see this dress." She stopped midway. "I think you should go today. You should do what you promised and stop worrying about the consequences."

Katie nodded. Everything sounded so simple when her mother said it.

"Leon's picking us all up at five. Eileen will be here by then, and we'll all go together in the limousine."

Katie hung the garment bag on Mam's antique mahogany armoire. She unzipped the bag again, cautiously this time. She touched the gown lightly. "Mam, I can't wear this. It's got to be worth more than my annual salary."

"What isn't worth more than that? You're a teacher."

She pulled the gown out of the bag. The dress was structured underneath with a 1920s-style bathing suit and short tap pants attached. "Mam, look. It's got the girdle already in it!"

The gown was the palest of pinks, not white as she'd first thought. The skirt was long and flowing and weighted down at the bottom by something sewn into its hem. She imagined it helped the gown move correctly as Ginger danced.

In the front of the Grecian-style gown was an X of hand-sewn sequins. Another sequined X made up the backless dress and attached to the skirt at her lower back. She held it up. "It looks long enough."

"Ginger was five foot four and a half, just like you. Luc said so. He said if it didn't quite fit not to pin or anything."

"Duh."

"I'm just passing on the message."

"Are you going to try it on? Or just stare at it?" Eileen walked into the room holding her own garment bag. She threw it onto the mangled bed, causing Mam to start tugging at the sheets immediately.

"What if it doesn't fit? What am I supposed to do then? Why would Luc take the other dress?"

"You're afraid of your own shadow," Mam said. "Enough already. Try it on, for crying out loud."

"Why do you think he did this? What was wrong with the first gown?" Katie asked.

"Maybe he was trying to get this dress all along and hadn't gotten it yet, so he had a backup made. Maybe he wanted you to wear the real thing so that you felt like Ginger herself. Maybe, just maybe, you should stop overanalyzing everything poor Luc does and say thank you for a change."

"Did that just come out of your mouth, Eileen, or am I in the Twilight Zone?"

"New Orleans, same difference," Mam said.

"Jem told me I had misjudged Luc," Eileen said, "but I didn't believe him either. Luc has that cocky swagger that drives me insane! My mind was made up after years of listening to your crying, but now I think Jem is right. I think you'd told yourself that story so many times about being rejected by Luc, you weren't able to hear an alternative—and neither was I. I get it now; you were afraid. It makes sense that you tried to marry a man you didn't love. So that everything would be safe. But love isn't safe."

"What is this, Dr. Phil? Listen, here's the truth: Luc dumped me eight years ago. And last night he left me splayed out on the banquette, and now he's got me dressing like a bride at someone else's wedding. You all can wax poetic all you want, but Luc puts on a good show. When the rubber meets the road you'll find out how serious he is about commitment. Mark my words."

"No, Eileen's right," Mam said. "Love isn't safe. And whoever you love will hurt you. It's part of the human experience. No one is perfect, not even your Paddy, Katie. People make mistakes. The secret is to focus on what they do right and decide what quirks you can live with."

"I know," Eileen said. "Can you live with the quirks of a rich man? Because I don't know . . . I think I might be able to get past the European vacations, personal stylists, and the private jet-setting, but no way could I live with the shopping sprees. No doubt about it."

"Eileen, this is Luc. He only has the plane for convenience. He doesn't live like that."

"Why don't you tell him you know that? That you know him?"

She shook her head. "It's too late. I have ruined my last DeForges shindig."

"It's too late if you're afraid of getting rejected again," Mam said. "But sometimes love is dangerous. Are you willing to take the risk?"

Katie looked at the gown once again. The first thought that came streaming into her head was that Harry Connick, Jr. would laugh her off the stage, but then, would that really be worse than Luc rejecting her again? All she had to do was don the gown and tell him she loved him. That was it. Simple. *Luc, I love you. I've never stopped loving you, and I've been waiting for you to come get me for eight years, and if you don't act now I am going to throw a major hissy fit at this party!*

The rest was up to Luc.

284

"I'll never know if I don't try."

"That's my girl!"

Katie sucked in a deep breath and approached the gown. "I'm not going to chase him. If he wants me, he has to make his move. I have to leave with some kind of dignity."

Mam shook her head. "Oh, then you're not ready after all."

Eileen rolled her eyes. "Because flying you out on his private jet and renting Ginger Rogers' gown and proposing to you in front of all his brother's wedding guests, those weren't moves at all. You're right, Katie. I really think you should wait until pigs fly. Then you'll know for certain."

Maybe she *had* put too many constraints on love. Jesus loved unconditionally. Wasn't that the example? She prayed for the strength to dance like no one was watching, sing like no one was listening, and love like she'd never felt pain.

Chapter 22

From This Moment On

Katie felt amazing in Ginger's gown. The shoulder straps glistened in the evening light, and as the crickets and frogs started their beautiful night song, she felt infused with confidence. She looked ahead at the road, anxious and filled with the good kind of adrenaline. If there'd been a benefit to ruining the rehearsal dinner, it was that she'd completely lowered expectations for the reception.

Neither Ryan nor Olivia wanted a church wedding, which seemed strange to Katie, with their mothers both being doyennes in their church. Then again, that's probably why they chose a different locale. The wedding was to be held on a rooftop terrace at the historical Hotel Monteleone. It overlooked the French Quarter and bustled with old-fashioned romantic ambiance—the closest she'd ever come to Paris. The French Quarter came alive at night with an energy all its own. Jazz echoed off its classic architecture and wrought iron galleries.

The Monteleone itself stood at the edge of the Quarter, and its locale on Royal Street freed it from some of the darker aspects of the city. It always bugged her that New Orleans took the rap for so many drunks in the streets, when most of them were tourists from other places who descended on the city for their dark reveries. Although only a block from the infamous Bourbon Street, the hotel embodied the sophistication worthy of its nickname, the Grand Dame of the French Quarter. It was a natural locale for a DeForges wedding. The reception, where she would sing after the rooftop ceremony, would be inside the Queen's Ballroom.

The golden glow from the hotel lights shimmered off her gown as if she wore her own spotlight. She felt like a star in the Mardi Gras parade, compelled to do the princess wave as people passed her and commented on her gown.

"Beautiful dress."

"Thank you, it was Ginger Rogers'!"

"I knew it looked familiar."

She fell into character, just as she'd done all those nights at the Barrelhouse.

The magnificent lobby opened before her like a sparkling secret world that the gown had given her access to. A lobby of enormous proportions with towering ceilings, marble floors, and climbing columns in differing shades of gold and crème gave her the oddest thought. "I'll bet there are absolutely no salmon walls in this hotel," she said.

"Don't be so sure," Mam said. "My, my. Imagine what it must cost to have a wedding here. We were just going to boil some crawfish in the backyard when you married Dexter."

"We were not," Rusty said. "Don't tease her, Irene. She's nervous as it is."

Her gaze focused on a lone figure in the middle of the lobby's vast floor. Luc stood in a tuxedo, his hands crossed in front of him. His expression told her nothing, and under the light, his small, cross-shaped scar beneath his eye became more evident as she walked to the center of the room.

"What's with Luc?" Eileen asked. "He looks like the bachelor at the end of the show, when you don't know if he's going to dump the girl or propose to her."

Katie wheeled around. "Thank you, Eileen."

"He does," Eileen said.

"So you've watched that show enough, which is it? Is he proposing or dumping me?"

"I don't know. I didn't see if you were first to get out of the car or not. Plus, they edit, you know."

"I'll meet you guys upstairs. The elevators are that way." She dismissed her group and they tottered off, unfazed.

Katie pranced toward Luc and twirled about in her dress, letting the weighted hem take flight. She lifted her skirt and curtseyed. "Your Majesty. Is this what you had in mind?"

He raised one brow but said nothing. She turned again

and gave him the view of her exposed back embraced by the glittering straps.

"Luc? Will you rob me of my compliment?"

He didn't move. Instead he crossed his arms in front of him.

She stepped closer to him. "Is this a wax figure? Or is the magnificent Luc DeForges present?" She got close enough to snap her fingers in his face.

He twitched, but like an English Royal Guard, he didn't move.

"You're not going to ruin my evening, Luc DeForges."

"I should hope not. By the way, you throwing my Black-Berry at the Barrelclub? Cost me a pretty penny."

Her eyes narrowed. "Was I worth it?"

Despite himself, he grinned. "You were. That's my problem."

"There are easy couples out there. They meet. They fall in love. They get married and have 2.5 children." She spun around just to feel her dress take flight. "We, Luc DeForges, are not those people."

"No, we aren't, but I am in desperate need of your help this evening."

"My help?"

"To redeem the DeForges family name and rescue it from the public humiliation hall of fame."

She put a hand to her chest. "But that's my specialty. Not the redemption part. The dragging your name through the mud part."

He grinned. "After you."

Her heels tapped along the marble floor when the dress

overtook her. She stuck out her arms like an airplane and lifted them up to the sky as she spun away again and smiled. "Well, if it's of any interest to you, I love you, Luc DeForges."

She looked back to see Luc sprinting toward her. He swooped her up into his arms, and she squealed like a child. He headed toward the elevator, and she traced her finger along his scar as they bounced.

"Have you told anyone else how you really got that scar?"

He grinned. "It's so unmanly to say my little brother wielding a switch gave it to me. I prefer the mystery. It makes me more Bond-like. Have you told anyone else how you got the nickname Katie-bug?"

"No reason to tell anyone. I'm not the snuggly type any longer."

"We should fix that."

The elevator doors opened and swallowed them into its gold entrance.

Luc put her down and gazed at her menacingly. She stepped back until she felt the wall at her back. Luc leaned over her, his forehead on hers. "Listen to me, Katie McKenna. This mission is very important, should you choose to accept it. You have been asked to redeem the DeForges family name. Should you undertake this mission, you will receive my family's undying love and me as a consolation prize."

"I don't think so."

"Don't think you'll accept the mission?"

"That you're a consolation prize."

"Not if you believe the tabloids." He chuckled.

"Good thing I don't. Do I make a good Ginger?"

He shrugged. "You know I never cared for blondes. I was more of a Rita Hayworth man myself. Maureen O'Hara. Let's see, who is another redhead? Wait a minute, wait a minute. I got this . . . Oh yeah, you!" He pressed the button.

"This is the wrong floor," she said when the doors opened.

"Already correcting me. We're like an old married couple."

"You did that on purpose."

He shrugged. "Maybe." He led her down a hallway until they came to a set of double doors, where he slid a card key and opened the door to a luxury suite.

"What is going on?"

"Wait here." He left her in the foyer and walked to an elegant French chair covered in gold tapestry. He lifted a shirt box from a marble-topped table and handed it to her. "Open it."

She pulled the lid and saw the cape to her gown. "You had it all along!"

"Actually, it's a new one I had made. The dress is original, but I wanted to make some changes to the cape, so I had it fashioned."

"You're turning into quite the designer. It's kind of creeping me out, actually."

He shook out the cape. It reached to the floor and had French seams like a bat wing, encrusted with hand-sewn sequins that matched the dress.

"That's not a cape."

He shook his head. "It's a veil. See?" He showed her the crystallized combs that would attach to the crown of her head.

"Luc."

He placed it on her head, then knelt before her. "Katie McKenna, before you send me to an early grave, would you marry me already?"

"That's not romantic!"

"I beg your pardon? You are in a luxury suite, wearing Ginger Rogers' gown and a handmade veil. What is it you want from me, Katie? I'm a guy, for crying out loud. Give me a break, will ya?"

She felt her eyes tearing and wanted to strike herself for ruining the moment. "That was it. That's all I wanted. A proposal. A proposal from you, Luc, the man I love. The only man I've ever loved."

His eyes met the floor. "Should I mention that this is actually your third proposal? Or that you are wearing on my nerves?"

"No, that definitely takes the romance down a notch." She snuggled into the crook of his neck, then stepped back to see his reaction. "You're pouting. I said yes! Let's forget I said anything else, okay? Do you have my ring? You have my ring, right?"

"Katie, if this is going to work, you have to trust me and give me the benefit of the doubt that I only want the best for you. Do you believe that? If I don't do what's best for you, you can tell me afterward, all right?"

"Absolutely!" She nodded. "But I still want a ring. I mean you say you asked three times, but there's something missing."

"Naturally, you noticed. In return for you giving me the benefit of the doubt, I will understand that my life will never be absent of drama. Agreed?"

"Would you want it to be? I mean, really? If you did, wouldn't you have just married one of the Barbies in LA?"

Luc laughed. "The thought never crossed my mind. And how about you give me a break on the Barbies? The press loves a good story, but you know my heart and my fondness for a certain redhead."

She nodded. "I do know your heart, Luc, and it's the most beautiful heart I've ever seen."

Luc held her barren hand, and she felt the need to fill the silence.

"The stock price go back up? I never asked you after your trip. Because you know, realistically, you could eventually be a billionaire."

He shook his head. "Does that matter to you?"

"No, it was simply quiet, and I thought I needed to fill the air. Sorry. You were saying?"

He lifted a brow in that lovely cocky way she relished. "Our honeymoon."

"Honeymoon? Aren't you forgetting something? The stock price? I mean, do you really expect me to settle for a multi-millionaire when the potential for billionaire is there?"

He chuckled. "You may just have to set that dream aside. I imagine my marriage is going to require some time off. Jem's going to take over the company for a while."

"Jem?"

"He's on my board of directors."

"Jem is? Your brother Jem?"

"He doesn't want anyone knowing he's wealthy, but Forages has made a bundle for him. Jem says it attracts the wrong sort of people, so he's a silent member."

She pondered that chewy piece of gossip and wondered if she could keep it from Eileen, who'd taken quite an interest in Jem the jeweler.

"No, you can't tell her," Luc said.

"How did you know what I was thinking?"

"You wear your heart on your sleeve, Katie. All anyone has to do is look. How do you think I knew there was nothing between you and Poindexter?"

"I just assumed you thought no one would like Poin—I mean Dexter. And you do think very highly of yourself. I'm sure you thought he was no competition."

"There is that. I'm getting up now, my legs are cramping." He stood to his full six foot three.

Her heart raced. "Gosh, I love your height. I mean, I know you are way too tall for the likes of an average girl like me, but I love your height and you rock that tuxedo and I cannot believe that this ring makes you mine, and it's going to be legal and then, there will be nothing you can do about it. You will be stuck with me for life."

He grinned. "I already was."

"Luc," she purred and rested her head against the crook of his neck.

"Now for the particulars. Your mission." He reached into

his pocket and pulled out a gray velvet box. "Katie McKenna, will you do me the honor of becoming my wife, officially?"

"Yes, yes, a thousand times, yes!"

He placed a strange ring on her ring finger.

"What's this?"

"It's your engagement ring. Jem made it for you so that it goes with your nana's wedding ring."

"It's incredible! But where is my nana's ring?"

"I'm holding it hostage until I know for sure you'll go through with this." The ring, made of antiqued gold and an emerald-cut diamond turned on its side, seemed almost transparent in its perfection. "There is a catch."

"I knew it. A prenup? I figured."

He laughed. "Not a prenup. If you want half my money, all you ever have to do is ask, Katie McKenna. If you ever need anything, I'll find a way to get it for you."

She let her head fall against him again.

"No," he said into her ear. "The condition is that you marry me tonight and rescue the DeForges family from another bomb of a social function."

"What?" She pulled away. "Tonight? You mean after Ryan and Olivia's wedding? Like go to Vegas or something?" She tried to veil her disappointment.

"Katie, we're in our hometown. Do you really think I'd drag you to Vegas to get married when everyone we love is here?"

She shrugged. "I really have no idea what you'd do, and that is one of the many things I love about you."

"We're getting married here, at the hotel. Tonight. Olivia

295

and Ryan have run off and eloped. But rather than let my mother suffer yet another humiliation at the hands of her impetuous sons, I say we stand in and let the tabloids believe it was our ruse all along to keep the paparazzi away."

"What, you've arranged for the pastor to stay? What about my singing? Do you still want me to sing? Or is that why you hired Harry Connick?"

He put his forefinger in front of his mouth. "I should have told you the truth that I knew years ago. No vow is more important than the one I made to you—that I'd love you forever. Than the one I'll make to you in front of God and his witnesses tonight." He straightened the veil and brought it around her shoulders. "I promised to love you all those years ago, and it hasn't waned. Not one bit. Let's do this. We're not getting any younger."

"Did Olivia and Ryan really elope?"

"Olivia had enough. She wanted to marry Ryan in a small ceremony in a roller rink. Between me pulling this forties bit and the two mothers-in-law bickering, they decided they'd have their own wedding and do it their way. If you didn't notice, Olivia calls the shots in that pair, and she called this one last night after the rehearsal dinner. That's where I ran off to. To get the marriage license."

"For us? You did paperwork for us?" She didn't know why she found that so endearing, but she did. "But where could you do that at night?"

"I went to a friend's house. A judge who had this prepared for me." He pulled out a marriage certificate. "All I needed was your social security number and the judge's signature to bypass the three-day waiting period, and it was mine. Your mother was gracious enough to give me your social security number."

"Mam? Mam knew about this?"

"She had an idea, but I didn't confirm anything. I didn't know what you'd say."

Katie grinned. "Did you know Ryan and Olivia would run like this?"

"No, that was icing on the proverbial wedding cake."

"I thought we'd have a church wedding. Isn't it bad luck to get married in a hotel, rather than a church?"

"That's the beauty. It's Olivia and Ryan's names on the invitations. We'll have confused fate. We can get married in the church later, but for now, my mother's pastor is waiting upstairs to marry someone. Might as well be us." He led her through the doors into the hallway. "Everyone we love, and a few we don't, are upstairs waiting for a wedding. Shall we give them one?"

Katie laughed. "Are you kidding? I'm not letting you get away this time." Sprinkles of elation shot through her body, and she looked deeply into Luc's eyes. "Although I could just stay here and look into those eyes."

"You could, but we already know where that leads, so let's go make it legal." He pressed the button for the elevator. "I bought your old house in the Channel. It's our vacation home now. I assume you'll want to come see your mam, and she'll want to see any grandchildren we might bring into the world."

"Doesn't a millionaire want a vacation home in the French Riviera or the Bahamas? Not a shotgun house in the Irish Channel."

"Not this millionaire. This one wants to make his wife happy. Do you want a vacation home in the Bahamas?" he asked as the elevator doors opened.

"I burn easily," she said. "It's that Irish skin, pasty as a ghost. Then, there's the whole Bermuda Triangle thing going on down there. And us? In a private plane? It's asking for trouble."

"I agree. Besides, with a vacation home here, I won't have to hire a cook. We'll just go to your mam's."

"I beg your pardon. I can cook."

"Really?"

"Don't act so shocked. Irene raised me. Where will we live?" she asked as they stepped into the elevator.

"I thought we'd divide our time between San Francisco, Los Angeles, and New Orleans, but it's all negotiable. You have summers off, isn't that right?"

She smiled. He'd thought of everything. He always did. As they stepped off the elevator onto the rooftop deck, the night air felt magical. A jazz quartet played "Moon River" softly in the corner, and excited guests murmured into the violet sky.

Luc cleared his throat loudly. "If I can have your attention, please!" he yelled to silence the gathering crowd.

Mrs. DeForges gazed their direction, and her eyes landed on the sparkler on Katie's left hand. Instinctively, Katie covered it with her right.

"I know you've all come here for a wedding tonight . . . and Miss Katie McKenna and I are planning to give you one."

She looked up at his strong jaw, the way he tied her stomach in knots every time he gazed at her with those stunning blue eyes. She reminded herself that there were a billion reasons why she and Luc DeForges did not belong together, and only one that bound them together.

Love. The kind of love worth having required surrender. Would she vow before God that which cost her nothing? Love endured forever and no fortress built around her heart was strong enough to withstand its mighty power.

She looked up to the starry night and whispered, "I surrender."

Acknowledgments

I am so grateful to the Thomas Nelson team for a safe place to create. When a brain is filled with imaginary characters, often it's lacking in linear cognitive skills. Thank you to Ami McConnell, whose editing skills are unmatched. She can so easily tell me what's missing in a way I completely understand how to fix the issues. Finding a partner like that is incredible. But to find two? Unheard of! Thank you to LB Norton, who will no doubt have to fix my grammar in this very acknowledgment. You were amazing to work with, and I do hope it happens again soon. Thank you to the whole team at Nelson, who will put this book in a package that rocks the house and see my love of the forties through to fruition. To my team: Colleen Coble, Diann Hunt, Denise Hunter, and Cheryl Hodde—thanks as always.

Reading Group Guide

1. Do you ever find yourself fantasizing that money could solve all your problems? Katie thinks money is the source of her problems; what kind of power do you place on money?

2. After enduring a particularly humiliating situation back home in New Orleans, Katie has "moved on" with her life. What do you think about the way she chose to move on— what might you do differently?

3. The Bible says love is patient and love is kind. Would you have trouble believing a passionate connection like the one Katie shared with Luc was really love? Why or why not?

4. Katie has chosen to live a life with the predictable Dexter so that she might maintain control over her emotions. Have you ever risked truly being hurt to follow your conscience and forgive someone?

5. Dexter represents what a lot of churches have come to represent: predictable, organized and rule-based. Did you see anything missing in his character? Or did you prefer his order and lack of chaos?

6. Katie's best friend Eileen has seen her through all of her life, the pain of losing Luc and her current life as a successful teacher. Has there been a time in life when a friend saw you more clearly than you saw yourself?

7. Which character in the book did you identify with the most? Why?

8. When Katie tries to clean up her image, she only ends up humiliating herself further. Have you ever tried to make a situation better only to make it worse?

9. Katie felt her faith was strongest when her emotions were not involved. Have you ever had to relinquish control to God only to find the answer in your own weakness? When?

10. Do you think Katie made the right choice at the end of the story?

TEN RANDOM QUESTIONS WITH KRISTIN BILLERBECK

You've just read her novel, but how well do you really know Kristin Billerbeck? Come on—admit it. You have at least ten questions you've always wanted her to answer, right? Well here they are. Ten Random Questions answered by one of your favorite authors.

THOMAS NELSON FICTION: What is your all-time favorite novel? What is your all-time favorite Christian novel?

KRISTIN BILLERBECK: Favorite all-time novel would be *Far from the Madding Crowd* by Thomas Hardy or *The Thorn Birds* by Colleen McCullough. As for favorite Christian novel? I'd have to say *This Present Darkness* by Frank Peretti because it changed how I looked at prayer, and I loved being reminded of the war going on in invisible realms.

TNF: What is your favorite movie?

KB: *Notorious* with Ingrid Bergman and Cary Grant

TNF: If you could only eat one flavor of ice cream for the rest of your life, what would it be?

KB: Easy, Chocolate-Mint

TNF: What is your favorite Scripture verse?

KB: Proverbs 16:2—it reminds me that even though someone did something I view as ugly, God may have a different view based on that person's motive, which may have been from their heart. It reminds me not to judge other peoples' actions with a broad stroke.

TNF: Is your closet filled with more vintage or contemporary clothing?

KB: So I have sort of an OCD-thing going on with regards to vintage clothing. Same goes for the library. I like things to come to me fresh. LOL My wardrobe is very contemporary, probably too much so for my age range.

TNF: What is your dream vacation?

KB: Part one would be a spa where there was only me, the sound of trickling water, and a pile of books. Part two would be a literary tour of Jane Austen's England, Thomas Hardy's England, and finally, Dickens' England. I guess that means, England, no?

TNF: If you could have any superpower, what would it be and why?

KB: Easy again: I'd be invisible, so I could listen in on great conversations and get new plot developments. Though I will say, my bff and I are pretty stealth at eavesdropping.

TNF: What do you always overspend on and then have buyer's remorse?

KB: Whole Foods is my danger zone. I love the organic lotions and soaps, candles and scents, ooh, ooh and of course, the fabulous food that's healthy and already made for you. (I hate to cook!)

TNF: Who is your all-time favorite musician or band?

KB: David Crowder Band. I love the purity in his voice and the passion for Jesus that oozes from his soul.

TNF: What was your first job?

KB: I worked under the table at Round Table Pizza making pizzas and my life's goal was to get a job where I didn't smell like it when I left.

All she wants is a cute Christian guy who doesn't live with his mother . . . and maybe a Prada handbag.

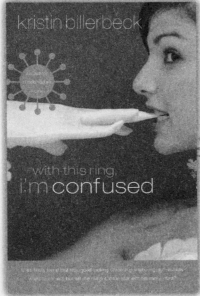

The Ashley Stockingdale Series

The pursuit of life, love, and the perfect pedicure

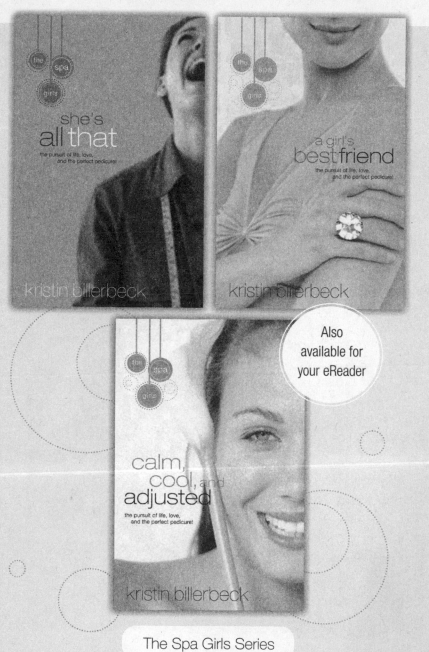

She's **armed**—with hot irons, sharp shears, and a flair for color. She's **dangerous**—truly bad news for bad hair. And she's going to do whatever it takes to make a place for herself in the exclusive Beverly Hills salon.

splitends

sometimes the end is really the beginning

A NOVEL

kristin billerbeck

ABOUT THE AUTHOR

Michael Hawk Photography

Christy Award finalist and two-time winner of the ACFW Book of the Year award, Kristin Billerbeck has appeared on *The Today Show* and has been featured in the *New York Times*. She lives with her family in northern California.